THE
FIRST LAW
OF
NATURE

BY
PAPA SAK

1

Self preservation is the first law of nature!!!

That Twenty-Two is Caught!!!

My words are slurred through slang and metaphor
My life is a maze as I graze the concrete floor
The woes that's buried in between cracks
Draining someone's blood cause mercy is what the street lacks
Predator or prey the jungle's my domain
Every angle there's a curb waiting for me to get slain
Calling my name scapegoated for my hustle
Cause a 9 to 5 plantation...
Ain't my home
Systematically beaten but don't settle for defeat
Woven into injustice so poverty is what I reap
But tears won't fall even though my back's against the wall
Reagan and Noriega was the ones that made the call
Through government scheming I stretched raw like a Trojan
But the condom broke behind the first bitch's empty slogan
Survival is a necessity so cocaine is the hustle I handle
Provided by United Snakes under the Iran-Contra scandal
Grinding on the corner my enemy wears a badge
Wanting me to face the black robe who's an undercover fag
He wants to poke me send me to the pokey
Fifteen years of modern slavery but the set up is low key
Getting my people to turn cheating at the cat and mouse
Popping a young nigga's cherry so that I can say ouch
Because the code is but a dream and the life is constant war
Too much of a smart nigga because I wanted more
That twenty-two is caught and I can see where you taking me
I am what I am so it ain't no breaking me

3

INTRODUCTION

In this book I intend to deal with the character study of brothers that hustle in the illegal drug game. Many stories that are told about the dope game have a tendency to go to different extremes in telling the story of a drug dealer. I don't believe that this lifestyle should be glamorized but I do believe that their story should be told. They are usually portrayed as heartless killers with no remorse or mega business men that do everything with ease. This is a fallacy that I hope to at least quell in this novel.

In American society we have an institution that is systematically racist. I didn't make it that way but this is the reality of things whether you accept it or not. This is also a capitalist society which means that the only way it could function is if there is a permanent underclass. So through racism many people of color are either at a poverty level or beneath the poverty level in the United States. Black people in particular have suffered under this condition since the founding of this country. In recent years we have seen the emergence of Black wealth which is good. But many of us are still getting by paycheck to paycheck. This being the case, there are three things that usually get us out of poor economic conditions. These three things are Sports, Entertainment or Crime. Sports and Entertainment is usually the route for those that are trying to be rich and famous. Getting involved and being successful in these fields have many white collar tricks and politics. I don't know all the dynamics but the club is exclusive. The dope game is the one that is the most demonized of all. These brothers on the streets selling dope are not always the villains. In many cases they are products of an underlining rebellion.

The rebellion is against an institution that denies many of us proper education. The rebellion is against an institution that teaches people to get educated to get a job instead of creating a job for themselves. This rebellion is against countless systematic attacks of racism through labor, law, politics, religion and housing. Not wanting to settle for poor living conditions many take to the streets and hustle drugs for a living. I'm not justifying selling dope but I am suggesting that I understand why it is done. Then the rebellion is also fueled by the fact that Tobacco and Alcohol companies are able to operate freely but are the biggest causes of death when it comes to mind altering substances. This rebellion is against the hypocrisy that allows certain drugs to be legal because the government has found a way to tax these drugs. Not to mention that there is overwhelming evidence that has been revealed that the government has been involved in bringing drugs into the country. I personally watched a documentary in which a DEA agent said that 15% of the United States economy is in illegal drugs. So we all can safely suspect that the war on drugs is a sham. But young Black and Latino men fill the jails behind drug charges. Their desire to want more in life has got them imprisoned and they have become the scapegoat. The desire for the finer things in life has them using whatever means possible to achieve just that. Then there is the fact that self preservation is the first law of nature. People that don't know how to escape a poor condition will be forced into a way to escape if they are backed against the wall. This is not only a character study but it is also a sociology study. Black Sociology!!!

I would like you to put yourself in the shoes of a drug dealer. What would you do if you didn't have a way to feed your family but to sell drugs? Not force anyone to take the drugs but offer them for a price to anyone that wants to have them. What would it take for you to see where they are coming from? What would you be willing to do to survive? I don't want to suggest that you would become a drug dealer if you were economically poor. What I want you to recognize is the catch twenty-two that many Blacks and Latinos are forced into. Then imagine walking in their shoes for a day under those conditions. How long would you last?

This book is dedicated to so many people that I can't list everyone. Some names I would feel bad if I didn't mention. First off this story is dedicated to a brother that I would choose to call Modi dot. The game is the game and all I can do is apologize for my wrong doings to you. I sincerely wish our situation would have turned out better.

For people that were involved in this project I am forever thankful. I would like to thank God first and foremost if you call him Allah, Yahweh, Jehovah, Jah, The Most High or simply the Supreme Being. This is for my Mama who always insisted that I become a writer. This is also for my Grandparents who are my heroes. I also am thankful to my entire family.

I also would like to thank D. Gibbs for her insight to forgotten places and areas in the city of San Bernardino. Thank you Beautiful for your help and insight. I also would like to thank Herschel Finger and Latasha Hoffman for posing on the cover of my book. I also want to thank Shay Ensley of Black Star Photography for her brilliant photography and her apt professionalism. I am truly grateful sister soldier. Last but definitely not least I would like to thank one of the greatest Graphic Designers on the West Coast, Rafael Rodriguez. You done it again man. I'm still getting compliments about the cover. You are off the chain.

Sincerely

PaPa Sak
The Kingpin of the Inkpen

TABLE OF CONTENTS

1
PAROLEE

Ain't no need for yo mama to trip!
Snoop Doggy Dogg

This was the day I came home. I took a deep breath as I was being released from Corcoran State Prison. My eyes were instantly hurt from the sunlight but I didn't care. My mama Shirley was waiting outside in her Cadillac I had bought her at an auction five years ago. She was still looking glamorous for a middle age woman with two grown children. I was a twenty three year old twin. Usually my sister Sharon would have come with my mother to pick me up.

"How you doing mama?" I said while getting in the car.

"I'm doing fine baby, ain't you happy you out?" She smiled.

"You better believe it, where is Sharon?"

"Damn Sherwin is she all you care about? You didn't ask me have I visited your grandmother's grave or how your aunts and uncles are doing. First thing you want to know is where your sickening twin sister is." She replied.

I didn't respond right away because I knew my mother. My sister must have pissed her off about something and she wanted to vent to me on the way home. If she has a problem with someone in the family she doesn't expect you to bring them up. It was always my rule to let her bring up everyone in the family, but my bad I had forgotten.

"You know Sharon done moved with that nappy headed nigga Marcus. She is moving in with that black ass nigga to spite me. He probably fucks her real good. Them black niggas can fuck

8

but they make ugly babies. And she done fell hook line and sinker for this nigga. We ain't talked in two weeks." She bitterly replied.

"How is everybody else?"

"Never mind that, how are you doing? Now that you are free what you gone do with yourself?"

"I don't know mama, just yet. I might try and get me a job somewhere. You know, keep it straight and clean so I don't have to see prison again."

"You didn't have to see prison in the first place if you would have been smarter. You too loyal to people that ain't your family Sherwin. When it comes down to it, family and only family you can depend on. If you would have done it that way we wouldn't be having this conversation." She said as a matter of fact.

I laughed to myself because my mother always talked like she knew what she was talking about even when she didn't. She would make you believe that she was an expert in everything she talked about.

The ride was smooth in her Cadillac, which gave me time to look at the mountains from off the highway. Mama gave me time to think which I appreciated. But before long I knew she would start talking and I knew what she would start talking about.

"Have you talked to King James with his black ass?" Mama asked.

"No, not yet. Don't know if I want to either."

"Shit, don't burn ya bridges boy. That's who you should contact, he still moving weight."

"I told you mama I was thinking about going straight so I don't need to be fucking with King James."

"Who the hell you cussing at? Never mind, you better think of something quick because ain't too many jobs hiring felons. He might be your only way to make some real money."

I ignored her comment and kept gazing out the window. I loved my mother but she was too self-centered for me. She was one of those middle aged women that guys in their twenties

9

wouldn't mind hollering at. It bothered me when I was younger but I had grown used to it by now. The middle-aged men that dated her showered her with gifts but she was difficult to get along with. You know the type of women that know they are attractive so the first sign of them giving of themselves makes them forfeit the relationship. That's my mother. Now that she has grown accustomed to a certain lifestyle she is expecting me to hold it down. She's gotten tired of tossing men to the side so now she expects her son to carry her weight. I didn't mind if I had it but now she is putting pressure on me when I don't have it. There lies my problem.

"Sherwin Daniels, what are you thinking about?"

Once again I ignored her. We were now entering into San Bernardino County line. It felt good to see the Inland Empire once again. I represented the I.E. card when I was locked up. San Bernardino is the capitol city and county of the Inland Empire. It is about 60 miles outside of Los Angeles. I love it out here even though it's the desert. I've been here all my life. My mother even grew up out in the Inland Empire. But she grew up in the city of Rialto. I couldn't wait to see key people once I touched down. I would first holler at my road dog Antoine. That was my nigga. Then I would probably go kick it with Vanessa. She was a pretty beautiful Kenya Moore looking muthafucka. She was my heart and I knew she was down for my dirty drawers. My mother didn't like her because of her dark complexion. I never loved a woman more. She was streetwise too. She was the perfect woman to me.

"Boy did you hear me ask you a question?" Mama snapped.

"Have you seen Vanessa around the Dorjil Apartments? I got a letter from her three weeks ago." I asked.

"Why are you worried about that Black ass girl? You need to get you someone closer to your complexion. I swear, you and your sister must get your tastes from ya'll daddy." She sneered.

"Ah mama, she is beautiful and you know it." I finally replied.

10

"For a dark skin girl." Mama admitted.

We both didn't say anything then we looked at each other and started laughing. No matter how mean my mother could be she was still my mother and I loved her. I decided to change the subject so that she wouldn't get on my nerves. I started asking her questions about Sharon's new live in boyfriend. She described him as a short stocky dark-skinned brotha. According to my moms he had put up all the money for the apartment in Riverside. Riverside was a neighboring city. She vowed to never go visit her at their new place.

"If that nigga start beating her ass she better not come crying to me. He will probably start beating her ass so that she could be ugly like him." She sassily vented.

"He's already beating her ass? This nigga is already hitting on my sister?" I snapped.

"Maybe not now but he will real soon. That's what black ugly niggas do when they get a pretty ass girl like Sharon." She sneered.

"How do you know mama, you never dated a dark skinned man?" I replied.

"Shit, my friend Paula use to get her ass kicked by her ugly ass man. That nigga used to leave hand prints on her pretty ass face."

"So that means Sharon's boyfriend gone do the same? What is his name anyway?" I asked.

"Don't be a smart ass boy. I told you his name is Marcus. He was a star running back for that school on Baseline Blvd." She dismissed him.

"Marcus Mosley?" I asked.

"Yeah, you know that nigga?"

"Yeah mama he was the best running back in the county. He was supposed to had went to play college ball for the Longhorns in Texas." I replied.

11

"Well he got hurt in his junior year but got his degree in business from that school you talking about." She replied as if he hadn't accomplished shit.

I just smiled knowing that my mother once again was making a mountain out of a molehill. Sharon had done real well for her self if she was able to make him commit. He was always about his business. They had met about a week before I was picked up on my dope charge. He was out here for the Christmas break in his freshman year. He always was a nigga I respected on and off the football field. He claimed I.E. to the heart. He wasn't a banger or anything but he was proud of where he came from. After graduation he went to college and I went to the dope game. We went to different high schools but we had seen each other when our high schools played each other. I had played Pop Warner football with him when we were younger we just went to different high schools.

Sharon and I went to our old high school to see the game since they were playing against our rivals. We went to Cajon High School while he went to Arroyo. I was surprised he had never met my sister before until that night at the game. Then I remembered that my mother wasn't one of those types that invited kids on the team to her house. My mother probably didn't meet him until Sharon introduced them. I noticed a mutual attraction but I was more concerned about other things. Besides, I always thought that if they did hook up it would be Sharon that would be moving up a notch. So I let them talk for a little while before I walked off and went looking for Vanessa.

My mind was on fine ass Vanessa. She was my girl at the time. Rumor had it that she had a baby while I was locked up. That letter I got from her three weeks ago was the only letter I received from her. But it was a reason for that. By the time I found Vanessa she was in the bleachers and my sister and Marcus was right behind me. We all sat together during the entire game. We had a real good time and it was fresh in my head when I got locked up. I was happy for my sister when I reminisced on that night.

By the time we had made it close to home it was getting dark. My mother still had her three-bedroom apartment in the Dorjil Apartment Complex. She was still on section 8 so she was able to keep up with the rent. I had some money stashed at her house when the police cracked me. But I had a good idea that my money was long gone. I walked into the house and it looked exactly the same except for some new furniture. Mama was pretty basic about how her house looked on the inside. I dropped my bag on the living room floor and fell on the couch.

"Oh no you don't, you better take that shit in the room. You remember where your room is right?" Mama nagged.

I grudgingly got up from the couch and took the bag into my bedroom. I knew I couldn't stay in this house too long. I had to sit down and really map out a plan of how I was going to get back on my feet. When I went into the room nothing had changed. I still had the fold out couch bed in the corner. The plan was to get a place with Vanessa before I got locked up. I had money stashed with my mother, my sister and Vanessa. Vanessa had about eight thousand dollars of mine. My sister had about ten thousand I gave to her when she lived with my grandmother. My grandmother died when I was locked up so Sharon probably had to go back home to my mother's place. My mother and Sharon usually didn't get along. They would argue a lot but I stayed quiet.

I put some of my things away so that I could sort out my belongings before I jumped in the shower. I didn't feel too fresh and a nice shower would do me good. My mother was already blazing some weed when I got out the shower. I thought I would ask my mother about the ten thousand I had left with her.

"Boy, things came up and I had to use that money for different things. You got to understand that ten thousand dollars wouldn't last within five years of time." She explained.

I could hear the guilt in her voice but I expected it to be spent anyway. I put on some clothes and stood by the heater. I wanted to smoke a cigarette outside but I was afraid of catching a cold. I tried to watch a little television but that bored me real fast. Shit I was able to watch television around this time when I was in the pen. I didn't want to do anything that I was able to do in jail. So I waited for about an hour, stole two of my mother's cigarettes and stepped outside. I had to smoke her nasty ass Virginia Slims when I was used to smoking either Newport's or Camels. When I stepped outside it looked different to me. It was somewhat more peaceful than I remembered. I couldn't believe how much things had changed but much had stayed the same. The apartments had been painted. I decided to stroll through the neighborhood to check out the scenery. Man it was good to breathe that San Bernardino air. Looking around I saw things that brought back old memories. When I passed by apartment 21 I thought about how I used to fuck with Tracy. She would let me ditch at her house and run up in her all day. I was like sixteen or seventeen at the time. She had moved out right after high school. She wasn't too cute but she had a body for days. She wasn't the brightest in the world either. When I thought about it she probably was autistic or something. But then again she was smart in other ways.

Once outside the apartment complex the fresh air was soothing. I didn't feel confined as I once did. I walked up the street to look around at my old neighborhood. Nothing had really changed and my emotions were mixed. Part of me was disappointed but the other part was relieved. I knew I was home because of the familiarity. But the same dry ass desert surroundings made me realize that I hadn't gone much farther. I was gangster till I die though. My heart was pumping blood not Kool Aid. I can overcome this.

I did a full circle around the block. It was a time to clear my thoughts. As I paced slower on the last block a figure came towards me in the dark. My senses instinctively let me know that danger was in the air. I decided to focus on the task of making it home. The streets were tricky at times but intuition can get you a long way. Something told me to concentrate on staying tunnel

14

vision and the approaching danger might bypass me. It was something about this person that indicating he was on the hunt. Fear was not an option. Growing up around killers taught me something quick. They were like pit bulls if they sensed fear they pounced on fear. If I disregard him he would be led to believe that I meant him no harm.

He drew closer with his eyes focused on my form in the dark. He was definitely a killer. He was like an owl that can spot a mouse in the dark. He was accustomed to hunting his prey in the dark. When he was within a yard of me I spoke to him as though he was a friendly neighbor. I didn't say anything out of my mouth but gave him a slight nod to acknowledge him. I looked him directly in his eye so he would know I was a man. You have to be less than a man to a killer. That is how they justify what they do. We passed each other without incident but I contained my relief.

"Pooh, is that you dog?" The voice spoke in the dark.

The killer knew me. My name being Sherwin is what made the women in my family call me Winnie. But niggas in the street knew me as Pooh. Like Winnie the Pooh, but Pooh was what the people I grew up with called me. It startled me but I kept my face stone cold as I slowly turned around. I got up closer and looked into his eyes.

"Fabian? Little Fabian Gilmore from over here in the Dorjil's and in the Delmont Heights?" I rhetorically asked.

"In the flesh my nigga. So they let yo hustling ass up out of jail huh?"

"Yeah man, how you been Fab Five." I said embracing him.

Since his name was Fabian, niggas called him Fab for short. But after awhile he started being called Fab Five after the host of YO MTV Raps. Shit it was actually good to see him. He was as clear eyed as I had ever seen a nigga roaming the streets this late. He wasn't high or buzzing off of shit. That was bizarre to me considering the feeling I got when we first passed one another.

15

"What you doing roaming the streets this time of night?" I asked.

"Nothing but heading back to the house. What you doing out so late, don't you know this is a dangerous place to be at this time of night?" He said lightheartedly. I knew he meant it though.

"This is my first day out and I had to get a breath of fresh San Bernardino air my nigga." I replied just as lightheartedly.

I was a friend in his eyes and I knew to keep it that way. I wasn't afraid because he would have sensed that, but I was cautious. I made it a point to relax and be comfortable.

"Since you been home you seen that nigga Greg? You know the chubby nigga that went to Cajon with us? He was about two years behind you and a year in front of me?" He asked.

"Naw, but I know who you talking about. He used to fuck Mimi with the big ass titties that stayed over in Little Zion." I replied.

"Yeah man, I need to get at that nigga for real." He had venom in his tone. He didn't look at me but his facial expression showed scorn.

" I'll let you know if I see that nigga." I lied.

When shit like that goes down you stay the fuck out of dodge. I embraced him again, letting him know it was good to see him. But I wasn't going to be in the middle of that shit. If I seen Greg I would pretend as though I didn't run into Fab Five. It is always safer to mind my business. Once I turned the corner back into the Dorjil Apartments I went straight into the house. I had had enough of San Bernardino nighttime air.

When I made it inside the house my mother was already asleep. She had a smooth womanly snore that indicated she was passed out. I surprisingly missed her snoring. I smiled as I passed her door and closed it. She had left it open to make sure I made it in safe. That was our little way of recognizing that there was love there. If she woke up in the middle of the night and seen the door closed then she knew I had made it in safely.

16

Once inside the bedroom I collapsed on the fold out bed. It took me awhile to take off my shoes. I cut on the television and watched various programs until I was too sleepy to keep my eyes open. It felt good to be home.

The next morning I didn't wake up until ten in the morning. I hadn't slept that hard in a long time. My body must have known I was at home. It was an exciting day for me because it was a few people that I planned to see. I climbed out of my bed and walked towards the bathroom. Once I opened the bedroom door I smelled the aroma of cooked breakfast food. It froze me for a moment but then I continued my course into the bathroom. After washing my face and hands I strolled into the kitchen. My mother was on the couch smoking a cigarette. I followed my nose to the sausage inside the cooking pan and the waffle batter inside the large measuring cup.

"When you done eating, I expect you to clean up that mess. Don't just eat and leave Winnie or I'm gone cuss yo ass out." Mama yelled from the living room.

I didn't reply because that went without saying. My mama was real particular about her house being clean. After living with her for almost two decades I knew the routine. Maybe she thought I had forgotten.

"What time did you come in last night?" She asked.

I heard her fumbling with her keys. This indicated to me she was about to go somewhere.

"I don't even know. I wasn't paying attention to the clock when I walked inside."

"Well I'll be back, I'm about to go over to Paula's house for a little while. Tell your sister to leave that hundred dollars on the table. Clean up now ya hear." She said walking out the door.

"I thought you was mad at Sharon?" I curiously asked.

"That still don't mean she can't help her mother out when she is in need." She smiled closing the door behind her.

She wasn't mad enough not to borrow money I thought. I thought about Paula, which was mama's best friend. My mama

17

got along with her so well because 'she was the only bitch I knew that wasn't jealous of me' in my mother's own words. The crush I had on Paula Armstrong went back to the third grade. Mama once slipped up and told me that Paula was the mistress to someone who played for the Los Angeles Clippers. She was a beautiful woman that always dressed like a million bucks. I wondered if she looked the same.

I threw down on the heavy breakfast. It was better than what I was used to. Once I cleaned up the kitchen I took a shower and got dressed. I had a few places to go but I was without a car. Living in San Bernardino without a car was hell. I didn't remember how the Omni bus lines ran because I hadn't been on a bus since I was about sixteen. I was a little nervous. As I was walking out the door my sister Sharon was walking in.

"What's cracking twin?" I smiled.

"What's up Winnie?" She embraced me.

This was my other half. We were born on the same day right after each other. She came out first. But we were thick as thieves since day one. I never got into a significant fight with Sharon ever. Of course we had disagreements but we were tight as could be. My mother envied our bond because she never had that with her siblings. We held each other tightly for at least ten seconds. We finally let go and just grinned at each other with our teeth spreading from ear to ear.

"Where's mama at; so that I can drop this money off to her?" She asked.

"She went over to Paula's house and told me to tell you to leave it on the table. So I heard you hooked up with the homeboy Marcus?" I asked.

"Yeah, he's outside in the car. He didn't want to bump into that color struck woman we call mama." She laughed.

"He is a good dude, I'm happy for you sis."

"If you want to say what's up to him, you can? He's right outside."

"For sure."

She sat the C-note on the table and we walked outside together. Marcus stuck his head out forward to see my twin and I walking towards him. I could see him smiling when he seen me. He got out the car and we embraced.

"What's up my nigga? You look good and healthy" He looked me over.

"Shit, *I* look good and healthy? You the one rolling up in this pretty ass Lexus truck. You look real good and healthy." I said with enthusiasm.

He didn't even notice his truck like I noticed it. It was second nature to him but to me it was living it up. I was happy for him and my sister.

"So what are you into right now?" He asked to detract from his truck.

"I got a few things to do. I was headed a few places to take care of some business that's all."

"How many places you need to go, we can take you?" Sharon volunteered.

"Better yet, why don't we take you to our pad and let you roll the Honda Civic. Then you can do what you need to do without us all in your business." Marcus suggested.

"I know huh!" Sharon confirmed.

We rolled out in the Lexus and even though I was in the back seat it felt good. We talked and laughed all the way to their home. They took me inside their apartment and it was beautiful. They were paying a nice chunk of money for it but it was nice nevertheless. It sort of disturbed me that they didn't buy a house but drove a Lexus truck. But I made the thought go to the back of my head instead of the front. They were doing good as far as I was concerned. After about an hour of shooting the shit with my sister and Marcus I climbed into the Honda Civic and rolled out.

I checked in with my parole officer first. My sister had given me eight thousand of the ten I had given her which was cool. I knew she wasn't trying to spend my money unless it was an emergency. I went shopping after my visit with my parole officer.

19

Then I went around the neighborhood to inquire about Vanessa. I changed into some of the new clothes I had bought first. After hours I came to the conclusion that no one knew where she was hiding. I caught up with a few familiar faces but when it got dark I went home.

Later that night I stepped outside to smoke a Newport and once again get some fresh air. This time I just walked to the outside of the Dorjil Apartments. I crossed the street to the empty patch of dirt and dead grass. I was in a zone wondering about my future plans.

Suddenly I heard gunfire and it was relatively close. I turned to my right and seen nothing. I turned to my left and I seen a chubby nigga running through the dirt patch. He had a long way to go. Then the gunshots went off again but this time I seen the fat man jerk. Then five more shots came firing right after the other. The fat man collapsed on the ground. About ten yards behind the fat man was Fab Five running up on him. He quickly went into the fat man's pockets and found a substantial amount of money. He kicked the fat man while he laid dead on the ground.

"Lying piece of shit. You gone pay one way or the other." He said.

Suddenly he realized that he wasn't alone. He kept his pistol drawn and looked to see who was the third party. I didn't move a muscle. He walked up on me glaring until he could make out the face.

"What's up Pooh?" He sounded relieved.

"Ain't shit but getting fresh air."

"I see you got some fresh gear too huh? You about ready to push up on these cute little bitches with Antoine." He said referring to my road dog.

"Maybe, but one little female I am curious about is that winner Vanessa that graduated with yo class?"

"Yeah I remember her you used to fuck with her for awhile. She moved over there near Cal State." He replied.

"Good looking my nigga, that is all I needed to hear."

20

We embraced but by this time he had put away his pistol. We both walked away from the scene without another word said. I glanced back at him and I seen him toss the gun yards away from the body.

When I walked inside the apartment I seen my mother was surprisingly still up. She was about to doze off but came to consciousness when I walked in the door.

"I see you bought you some new clothes. If you keep yo mind on your money and not chasing after these hot tail girls you might be able to get back on your feet." She warned.

"I'm knowing mama, I'm knowing." I went into my bedroom and shut the door. I knew whom she was referring to as hot tail.

2
CONVERSATION

Clocking much dollars on the first and fifteenth!
Ice Cube

I finally thought now was a good time to hook up with Antoine. He heard from my sister that I had gotten paroled. I was eager to see my running buddy but things had changed. He and I used to chase pussy together. Don't get me wrong, I still wanted to get me some pussy but I had to concentrate on more important things. My concern was if he was on the same page he was on five years ago. A whole lot had changed for me.

As I was leaving to go visit Antoine I walked outside to see people gathered in the front of the Dorjil Apartments. It made me somewhat curious so I went to investigate. When I got to the front the police were everywhere. They were inside the empty field with yellow tape surrounding them. I glanced over to the side and noticed Greg's mother and sister outside crying.

That made me ponder on that night. Fab Five could have smoked me just the same but gave me a pass. If I were less than a man to Fab Five he probably would have killed me just the same. He was one of the kids that used to idolize my big cousin Melvin. Melvin grew up in Delmont Heights, which was around the corner from the Dorjil's and was a stone cold killer. He had been locked up since I was seventeen for attempted murder. Out of respect for Melvin and him knowing that I wasn't a snitch he gave me a pass. Not to mention that he was always cool with me. In other words I didn't have any strikes against me in his heart. I knew he wasn't worried about me hanging the murder over his head in fact it was probably the other way around in his eyes. I searched my surroundings after clearing my thoughts and slowly walked off.

My sister was still letting me use her car but the plan was to buy one some time today. Antoine would link up with me then we would move from there. My license wasn't current so I took another direction to avoid the police. I was ready to get into something as soon as possible and interruptions wasn't in the plan. An ex-con without a driver's license would have been a serious problem for me. The plan was for Antoine to come and pick me up but he was laid up with this broad. I didn't really know the female he had mentioned. All he told me was that she had graduated from San Bernardino High School about four years after us but she had grew up out in Los Angeles somewhere and her name was Karen. Initially I was pissed off but on second thought I shouldn't have expected better. Antoine was hooked on pussy more than you would believe. He was a light skinned pretty boy that had all kinds of women after him. I was considered somewhat of a pretty boy myself being a shade darker than Antoine but still considered light skinned. I was a few inches taller than Antoine also. But I didn't fiend after women as bad as him

I pulled up into his apartments he had moved into near San Bernardino Valley College. They looked sort of worn from the outside, which didn't sit too well with me. But who was I to complain when I lived in the Dorjil's with my mother. As I walked inside the turquoise apartment complex I easily opened the gate that was supposed to be locked. My eyes darted all around to check my surroundings. It was only an eight apartment complex and he was in number eight upstairs. Climbing the stairs it was easy to tell how worn the stair rails were. They were rusting and loose inside the cement. Once making it to the end of the hall I opened his raggedy screen door then hesitated. The television was booming loud through the door but I couldn't hear any movement. It would be difficult for him to hear me knocking I thought. Nevertheless I banged hard on the front door. After my second parry of knocks the door swung wide open.

23

"What's up my nigga?" Antoine yelled.

He didn't give me a chance to respond. He looked me over like I was something he was about to purchase.

"Damn you done got stocky on a nigga. But a muthafucka like me ain't trying to see the pen. I like pussy too much to see the insides of that bitch." He chided while we quickly embraced.

I grinned from his sly comment. He invited me inside to get comfortable. His wall was all white with one small picture frame on the wall. The drawing with the dogs playing poker hung above the couch. His couch was a lighter brown than his nappy carpet. Then he had a large television sitting on an otherwise empty entertainment center. I plopped down on the couch looking at his meagerly decorated apartment.

"I thought you had a little female laid up here with you?" I rhetorically asked.

"I do, she in the bedroom right now. Karen come on out here so you can meet my ace boon coon." He yelled.

After about a thirty-second delay she strolled out of the bedroom. It was obvious that she was in the bedroom preparing to make her grand entrance. She walked in the living room with her head up high and confident. Her complexion was a light caramel with a mole above her lip. She had a round face and her braid extensions wrapped in a ponytail. She was a cute little breezy with a nice little shape. She wasn't particularly voluptuous but she was curvy and sexy. She wore a black summer one-piece jump suit that extended into a mini skirt. Her matching high heels accentuated her ass. She was about 5'1 or 5'2 in height. I had seen him with better looking women but she looked good.

"Hi, I'm Karen." She extended her hand for me to shake.

"What's up, I'm Sherwin."

"Shit, call that nigga Pooh, like Winnie the Pooh." Antoine chided.

"So what's up Antoine we gone do this or what? I got a gang of shit to do and I want to get my sister back her car tonight." I blurted out with a slight irritation in my tone.

24

"Damn nigga, alright then let me grab my coat."

He took another ten minutes saying his goodbyes to Karen. By the time he had made it inside the car I felt like leaving him. Some niggas never change. He got inside and turned the music up on Sharon's radio. She had some beat in her car and I was playing some old school DMX.

"I'ma rob this nigga when I'm done I'ma slay him." I rapped along to DMX

"For being stupid, like come through after one or two and having gun he couldn't get to, that one'll do." Antoine finished the DMX line.

He then turned the music down so that we could talk. He leaned back in the passenger side acting as if we hadn't missed five years. That was my road dog for real.

"You know that I can hook you up with one of her friends. She thinks you cute my nigga. She got a homegirl with a big ole ass named Stacy."

"I'm straight for right now but maybe later on I can get some pussy. But first things first I need to get back on my feet. Getting a new whip is the first thing on the list." I replied.

"Alright but I got a surprise for you later on. How long you plan on staying at your mother's house?" He asked with a sly smile.

"A few weeks if I do things right."

He started laughing because he knew I wasn't going to be able to stay there long. We got over to the car auction spot my sister had told me about in Rialto so that I could pick me up something nice. I had about six thousand left from what my sister gave me. Antoine interrupted my thoughts of what kind of car I should get.

"You know I be getting my raw from King James. I'm mean James, that nigga act like he wrote the bible and shit." He joked.

"He still walk around with that bible all the time?" I asked.

"Yeah, like he a preacher or some shit. That nigga moving more weight than a little bit but he carries a bible everywhere. What kind of shit is that?"

"Shit most preachers be pimps anyhow so he fit right in." I joked.

"No shit huh. I believe in God and everything but I ain't gone be no hypocrite about it."

"How much of the raw you be getting from King James." I changed the subject.

"A quarter piece."

"It already be cooked or you got to cook it." I asked.

"It's already been cooked. All I got to do is cut that shit up and hustle." He replied.

He said it as if he didn't want to worry about those tedious things. He waved his hand and glanced at me like it was a waste of time.

"Then you ain't getting the raw nigga. King James is deciding how much he wants to cut into your dope. He could be stretching the shit out of that raw."

"Naw nigga, them crack heads be fiending for that raw shit I be getting from King James." Antoine protested.

"Well that's good but we gone see what's going on with that shit. Where do you be serving at?"

"Over there near my crib off of Mt. Vernon and sometimes in the California Gardens but I was thinking about setting up in the Dorjil's. I was waiting for you to touchdown." He said.

"Them California Garden niggas don't be tripping with you?"

"Naw they know I get my dope from King James. He is the one that hooked up the spot over there. Plus they know I ain't into that gangbanging shit. Besides some of them are L.A. niggas so everything is cool."

It was deep in my mind that I wasn't slanging anywhere near the California Gardens. Some L.A. nigga in the mix would really bring drama. They like to set trip even if you ain't

26

gangbanging. Some L.A. niggas is cool but some of them grimy hungry east side south central niggas like to set trip. I don't have a problem killing a nigga if I have to but why invite trouble. According to Antoine it was his day off so checking out his spot would have to take place at a later time.

When we were finished with the auction I had bought me a 98 Caprice sitting on rims and had beat for $4000. Even though it was signed over to me Antoine had to drive out with it because he had a license. I felt lucky that day. I had him pull up inside the Dorjil Apartments so that I could drive my new ride. Sharon had told me to sit her keys on the table and she would pick them up later.

When we walked in the door Sharon and my mother were sitting at the table talking. It was like a small family reunion because they hadn't seen Antoine in a while. Sharon only talked to him periodically over the phone.

"How you doing Mrs. Daniels I ain't seen you in a long time?" Antoine said.

"How you been Antoine baby? Thank You for everything honey." Mama said.

She then got up from the table and hugged him. It surprised the shit out of me. They were always cool but I didn't think they would hug each other. But then again I appreciated the display of affection. Antoine then looked over at Sharon.

"What's up Sharon with yo fine ass?"

"Nigga you crazy!" Sharon laughed.

"Is she the only woman looking good up in here." Mama got up to turn around and display her goods.

"Aw Mrs. Daniels, Sharon just a chip off the block. You a dime piece all the way I just don't say so because I don't want to disrespect my homeboy's mama." Antoine explained.

"Shit never mind Winnie, because he better not have a problem with someone complimented his mama." Mama blushed.

Sickened by the whole display Sharon quickly changed the subject.

"You hear what happened to Gregg?"

"Naw what happened to Gregg?" I lied.

"Fat ass Gregg that drive the Thunderbird?" Antoine interrupted before she could respond.

"Yeah him, he got smoked a few nights back and was laying in that empty field for a few days." Sharon explained.

"Damn, ooh my bad Mrs. Daniels but that's messed up." Antoine said.

He was definitely stunned. I let them talk about all of the suspicions that they had about who could have done it. No one even mentioned Fab Five. I basically participated in the conversation enough to seem interested and concerned. I always had a problem with speaking on murders.

"So what car did you get Winnie?" Sharon asked out the blue.

"A 98' Caprice, black with some rims and some beat." I bragged.

"I told you they had some good deals at that auction. Let's go outside and check out what you got." Sharon replied.

"You buying cars and shit but I know this much, come rent time you better be ready to help with that too." Mama barked.

"I'm knowing mama, I'm knowing."

I knew she was obviously hurt. At that moment she figured out that I must have given Sharon money to hold as well. A tinge of guilt was probably there also knowing that Sharon kept my money without spending it. But I knew she would get over it fast. She was hurt because she couldn't understand why I wouldn't let her hold it all. She was guilty because she knew that I knew why I couldn't let her hold it all.

We walked outside to view the ride with her straggling behind. It was a clean car that Sharon and my mother got excited about. The car must have been confiscated in a raid or something. I just smiled from ear to ear. I had to make sure that it didn't get confiscated in a raid with me. I also wanted to paint it. I was thinking about painting it royal blue to give it a little flavor. We walked away with me promising Sharon that she could roll with me in it one day soon.

"You and your man are rolling a Lexus Sharon why you so interested in rolling in my ride?" I asked casually.

She rolled her eyes at me and smiled. She was pondering on why she wanted to roll in it so bad.

"That's some gangsta shit, that's why." She smiled.

"I knew that's what you were gone say." I chuckled.

"One thing you got to watch out for is the Po-Po in that gangster car. The Sheriffs in San Bernardino will be on yo ass like white on rice." Antoine put in.

"I'm knowing. What I plan to do is get me a bucket to take care of business in but floss in this whip."

"That's good thinking baby." Mama added.

We all were headed towards the house when Gregg's sister Monica called Sharon over to talk. It was obvious Sharon was reluctant because she was having such a fun time with us. But out of respect for Gregg she gradually strolled over to meet her. The rest of us sat on the porch waiting for her return.

When she came back to my mother's porch she looked sad. Her arms were folded and her mouth was poking.

"What's wrong with you?" Mama asked what we all were thinking.

"It's just sad what happened to Gregg and his family. He was the only income in the household. No one else in the house is working. Luckily he has insurance to bury him but that's about it." She explained

"That is some sad shit but niggas get smoked all the time in the I.E. nowadays. A lot of L.A. niggas done moved out here and shit done got crazy. Not to mention the Mexicans that be tripping." Antoine replied.

"I'm saying!" I agreed.

"Well I'm out! Stay up Pooh, Sharon and Moms." We embraced.

29

"Oh yeah, you gone hook up with me later on tonight right?" He yelled back.

"For sure, you said about nine right? I ain't got a cell phone yet but I might try to get one today. I got your home number and I'll hit you when I get one." I yelled back.

"Damn Winnie, I thought ya'll was gone hang out for the whole day. That's odd to see ya'll depart from each other. Yo road dog?" Sharon said in playful surprise.

"Yeah I got some things to do. But we gone link up later on."

Mama was already in the house after Antoine walked out. I walked past her on the couch to jump in the shower. I hadn't taken a shower all day because I had got up to run those errands. Tomorrow was the day when I started hustling with Antoine. It was a few things I would have to do first.

Once out the shower I grabbed my keys and headed for the door. My mother gave me a look as if she was wondering what I was up to. She didn't say a word and I just glided out the door. I wanted to hook up with Ace around four in the afternoon. He lived out in Montclair, which was about twenty miles, or so closer to L.A. I was taking the 10 Freeway to get there and I didn't know how traffic would be. The middle of the week could get hectic right after school let out. It would be best if I started out earlier than later. Ace got pissed off easy about niggas being late. He hated CP time. He was a real muthafucka

Ace was my uncle by blood on my father's side. He was the only link I had to my dead father. My father got killed when I was too young to remember in a dice game. At least that's what Ace told me. Mama never knew how my father got killed so I had to rely on Ace's word, which was pretty reliable. Ace was the only surviving brother of six sons. All five of his brothers had died before their time. Three got killed, one died of cancer, and the oldest died of old age so that left only him. It was always fun hanging out with Ace because he would tell me stories about my uncles and father.

30

"All my brothers were some rough ass niggas." He would brag.

He would always make me drink some cheap whiskey while he told his stories. But he was also one that schooled me to the game. He had been selling dope, coke and weed since he was fourteen years old. He was the second youngest of the Daniels' clan. I couldn't wait to see him. He was someone I truly respected.

I pulled up in my new whip outside his apartment complex. There were trees everywhere. You could still see the freeway from his apartment complex. He had been living there forever and a day. It was always refreshing to be at his house to getaway from the desert of San Bernardino. Plus it was more of a retreat type environment. I knew not to knock on the door to his apartment because more than likely he would be working on a car in his garage. Ace was always greasy from working on cars. He would fix old cars and sell them for cheap. He had been out the dope game now for at least fifteen years. Once I got to the garage I knew my assumption was right. I could hear the sounds of Motown playing on his radio as I turned the corner into the alley. All thirty-two of my teeth were showing at this point. Just as I turned the corner he looked up from the engine.

"Damn nigga you must have gotten you some pussy with a grin like that." He replied.

"No not yet."

"Well ain't shit to smile about." He sharply replied.

I wanted to hug the ornery old man but his entire jump suit was filled with grease. He had a bottle of whiskey barely open sitting on an old kitchen chair in the corner. He went back to fixing on the car as though he had seen me yesterday. I knew he was glad to see me from the way he looked at me. Besides he had a fresh bottle of Jack Daniels specifically for me. Ace expressed his love in different ways. I let him finish what he was doing on the car without any disturbances.

"Take a seat nigga." He pointed to another chair.

31

I sat down still quiet, knowing that he was feeling me out before he would talk about anything. When he finished doing something to the car he stopped instantly to look me up and down. He was sizing me up. I was used to it by now.

"I see they didn't turn you into a bitch. Some niggas don't make it out the pen without being turned into a bitch. You definitely a Daniels' man." He replied.

I hadn't said anything at this point. I was studying him like he was studying me. He reached behind his chair to grab two glasses he had waiting. He picked the Jack Daniels up from the chair and sat down. As he began pouring the whiskey into the glasses his wife Thelma walked in.

"Earnest I'm going to the store you…"

The face for a brief moment didn't look familiar to her. Then she smiled with a sincere cheerfulness.

"Come here baby and give yo Aunt Thelma a hug. Earnest didn't even tell me you was getting out." She said while hugging me.

"I didn't want to jinx the boy, that's all" He nonchalantly replied.

I had forgotten in the last five years how superstitious Ace was. I brushed it off with light laughter. Thelma put her hands on my shoulders and looked me over. After she did her twice over she left us three men to ourselves. Ace, Jack Daniels and myself sat quietly in the garage under the dim light bulb. The sun was still out but it was slowly going down.

"So you gone get put back on or are you going square?" He asked out the blue.

"I supposed to be fucking with Antoine on some shit he got from King James. That nigga buying quarter pieces though and I might want to step it up." I replied.

"How much is he giving a quarter for?"

"Antoine told me Forty five hundred. I'm figuring if we move up in weight we might be able to get a whole brick for seventeen or seventeen five." I replied.

Ace didn't say anything for a moment. His thoughts were racing as he sipped on his full glass of whiskey. His head was basically in his glass. Then finally he looked up at me.

"If you trying to get a full kilo I might can get it for sixteen. The nigga I'm talking about you fucking with ain't gone sell you nothing less than a whole bird. And it's raw." He said.

"I ain't there yet Ace but I'm trying to get there soon, you know."

"The rules are different now. Niggas don't have a code anymore. If you in the game longer than five years, nowadays you are one of four things. You either snitching as a confidential informant, in and out the pen or very discreet with real good luck." He somberly explained.

"What's the fourth thing?"

"Shit you dead!" He looked at me incredulously.

"Well shit how am I gone be discreet and I'm curb serving?" I asked.

"That is when you are under the radar. Have a young nigga start handing people the dope and you just collect the money. A reliable nigga now. Not anyone that is too hungry but hungry enough to do what you tell him. A teenage nigga that still live at home with his mama but might want some new clothes or a nice ride for the bitches." He calmly explained.

"Like King James used to do us. But how am I gone handle the business with Antoine?"

"Give him game on hiring a young nigga and that's it. Then start stacking your bread so you can talk to me about getting a whole bird."

"When I tell Antoine we might have a different connect he might concentrate on saving his money to get a whole kilo huh?" I curiously asked.

"You not gone tell Antoine you got another connect. Use your own money and put that nigga on when you start moving weight. If you use his money then he gone want to know where you copping from."

"Hold on Ace, that's my road dog since back in the day. He putting me on with him but I'm not gone tell him about my connect?" I protested.

"I don't give a fuck if you came out the same vagina nigga. The game is real. If a nigga gets caught up he gone think of himself first. Self-preservation goes way past friendship. No nigga should know everything about you anyway. The one that does is the one that will bury yo ass first. He knows you can cop from King James so just slide that shit in with the rest of the dope."

"How am I gone do that? Eventually that nigga gone catch on that I got more dope than I'm supposed to have." I commented logically.

"When you get to the point where you can move more weight then you set it up so you could have more than one spot. Than you get you a little cute bitch to put an apartment in her name and keep dope there. Don't ever keep a stash of money with a woman though."

"Yeah, I learned that the hard way." I replied.

3

CELEBRATING THE GOOD TIMES

We knee deep in coke, we keep deep in ice, we flood streets with dope, we keep weed to smoke.
Jay-Z

We didn't hit the corner until 7pm. The plan was to get out there around one or two in the afternoon. Antoine was tied up with Karen and that kept him busy until dark. I was a little upset but I didn't want to look like I hated on him. The wisdom of Ace's words was stuck in my head. I liked pussy just like the next man but I was sleeping on a fold out couch bed at my mama's house. It was some things that had more priority. I couldn't ask him to let me take his dope and I meet him out there later. It was his dope. I had to wait until that nigga was ready to hit the block. He promised me he was going to let me put money in the next time he re-copped. That was what I was waiting for then I could make decisions on how we sold this shit. Curb serving was always tricky because the police love to pick up the small time hustlers to look good. I never have seen them really pop someone like King James or anyone on his level.

Once we made it out there it was buzzing kind of quick. We had the block hot for a while but the way we were hustling made it easy for us to get caught by the police. The crack fiends would come around and we would keep a few in our hand to pass it to them. If the police watched us closely they could easily tell we were curb serving.

"How about you collect the money and I serve the dope in the back? Then it won't be straight in Po-Po face that we hustling." I suggested.

"But then you would be way back there and I would be way in the front. Nigga we both can hang out front and still make that money. The fiends be rushing to get that shit I get from King James." He replied.

I smiled without responding but I wasn't comfortable. Here I am an ex-con fresh out the pen hanging out at a dope spot openly. I thought we could do shit better than that. It dawned on me real fast that my homeboy had become complacent. He was trying to survive and that was good enough for him. He had a decent apartment and a nice whip and that was all he needed. But my mind was elsewhere. I wanted it all.

It was Thursday now and he was talking about copping some more on Saturday. He wanted me to go with him but I was reluctant. By now someone had told King James I was out but I still didn't want to be all in his face. I wasn't quite ready to face him just yet. Since I had made a promise to Antoine I would roll with him it was etched in stone.

"Ay Ant, how much you got left on this package?"

"We gone sell out before the night is through. That's good cause then we can have a celebration on Friday. We invite a few females over and get some drink. I got a surprise for you." He smiled.

"Ay what was you and my mama talking about yesterday when she was thanking you?"

"Aw that wasn't shit. I would come by and speak that's all." He dismissed the incident.

"Naw she said she hadn't seen you in a while. What we keeping secrets from each other." I pried.

"Naw nigga it ain't like that. I would help her out with some bread from time to time. Put a little money in her mailbox. You know like Tupac would say. She the closest thing I got to a mother dog." He replied.

Antoine's mother had abandoned him when he was young to his grandmother. His grandmother didn't live too long after he was born so he would move to different relatives. Many of them didn't want to be bothered because they judged him for what his mother was. He was the only one of my friends my mother allowed to stay with us for a while. He would get kicked out one of his relatives' houses and have to crash with us for the night.

His mother on the other hand was a prostitute that fucked with sherm real tough from what we heard. We don't know for sure because she was never around to deny or confirm. He never knew his mother or where she could be. It affected his self esteem to a fault. Females was his way of validating that he was a man. That is the case for many men but it was more deep rooted with Antoine than the average man. He always had to have a roster since we were twelve years old. At least three or four was on his team at all times. I had only been out a week but the only female I seen him with so far was Karen. I wondered about that.

"What's up with you and Karen is that serious? Is that just someone to pass the time?"

"I don't know. She is sexy than a muthafucka to me. Them sexy ass legs and them lips. I don't know what's going on with her." He wandered in thought.

"I've seen you with females' way finer than her. What got you hooked on her so much? Is she putting it down that tight?

"I don't know. It's like she don't give a fuck. A lot of females cater to whatever I want but she refuses. And just when I think she is not gone give me what I want she does. It's whatever with her. She's not all jealous like Shawna or Felicia so we always have fun. You feel me my nigga?"

"Fine ass Shawna whatever happened to her. She was bad then a muthafucka and she was down for your dirty drawers." I reminisced.

"Yeah me and her still talk. She fucking with this nigga that's a supervisor at a warehouse or some shit. They live together and everything. But if I call her up she still will let me hit. But that bitch was jealous than a muthafucka." He emphasized.

37

"What happened to Shamara with the big ass and titties? The one that got pregnant by you but had a miscarriage is she still around? She was bad." I asked.

"Yeah we fuck around every now and then. She moved out to L.A. because of this new job she got when she graduated from U.C. Riverside. When she come to visit her mama she always hit me up. If I was a marrying type nigga Shamara would be wifey to me." He replied.

We laughed and talked until close to one in the morning. By then we had sold out and was ready to get into some more shit. We decided to hit the liquor store and rent a couple of rooms. Antoine had called up Karen and she had a homegirl that she would hook up with me. Now that work was done I couldn't wait to get into some pussy. He hung out in my room until Karen and her homegirl arrived. They didn't make it to our rooms until around two in the morning. We both had a buzz when they came banging on the door.

When I answered the door Karen came walking in with her homegirl. They both had an air of confidence about them. The girl with Karen was fine as hell. Her name was Stacy. She resembled Sunday Carter from the State Property movies but she was way thicker. She had a thick California accent with a walk that was out of this world. It appeared as though she deliberately walked on her toes so her ass would poke out. She was sipping on an Apple Smirnoff when she first came in. There was an instant mutual attraction. Even Antoine had the facial expression like 'DAMN' when she walked in the door. Of course I tried to be cool about it. All I knew was that I was trying to touch on those ass cheeks poking out of those tight jeans.

"Uh uh this is my homeboy Pooh. And I'm Antoine." Antoine stuttered.

"I thought you said his name was Sherwin right?" Karen cut in.

"Yeah but I told you to call him Pooh remember." He waived his hand as if to make her memory resurface.

"Oh yeah that's right girl they call him Pooh." Karen remembered.

"Nice to meet you Pooh my name is Stacy. They call me Lady Stay from Peck Street Crip." She replied.

"Ah shit we got a gangbanger in the house." Antoine clowned.

"Well they call me Big Pooh from the West Side Inland Empire." I added.

"I.E. till I die, I.E. till I die nigga!" Antoine shouted.

I just laughed. I sat next to Stacy and started whispering in her ear. It didn't take long for Antoine and Karen to go in the next room. I was eager as hell but I tried to be as cool as possible. I started off talking a little in her ear then I nibbled on it. She didn't seem to mind so I put my hand on her leg. Slowly but surely I began to touch her in familiar places. Then we started kissing on the bed. My dick was about to rip the denim in my jeans. I started rubbing on her almost flat chest. We began kissing and touching each other until all our clothes were off. When we went to the store I had bought some condoms because I wasn't gone hit this bitch bare back. I barely knew her and she was about to give me the ass. I wasn't complaining but I sure in the hell was careful.

Once she was totally naked on the bed she told me to cut off the lights. I cut off the lights then slid the condom on. I started kissing on her belly button all the way up on her titties until I reached her neck. She folded her knees up and spread her legs wide as I slid inside. I started pushing harder and harder. My dick was so hard that it was numb at the tip. She was groaning in a soft tone as I dug inside her. Then after the sixth or seventh stroke I busted a nut.

Damn I thought; I didn't get to hit it doggy style. I got up from the bed mad at myself. She laid there in the dark without saying a word but I could have sworn I heard her smirk. I pretended to ignore it but my ego was bruised. She decided to soften the blow.

"Karen told me you just got out from doing five years." She replied.

"Yeah it ain't even been a full week yet." I said from the bathroom washing up.

She got up to join me and washed up right next to me. I decided to cut the shower on and wait until it got hot. Within a few minutes of the water running hot I asked her to join me. She didn't want to fuck up her hair so she told me she would stay in the back of the shower until she needed to rinse off. When we finished drying off we were back kissing again butt naked standing on the bathroom floor. This time I eased her over to the bed then grabbed the condom from out the box and fucked her till dawn. When it was all said and done I had busted three nuts and she had busted four.

I woke up the next morning feeling good about myself. I was lying in bed with a fine ass woman. I had just bought a brand new whip and I had money in my pocket. It was only a few thousand but it was some bread nevertheless. It was on and cracking for me and I felt like I was on top of the world. We slept in until eleven in the morning then went to IHOP for breakfast. All four of us laughed and joked like we were friends for years. Stacy and I exchanged numbers then everyone went on their way.

Later that day I told Antoine that I wasn't ready to meet up with King James. I wanted to skip going with him when he told me he was going on Friday instead of Saturday. He expected me to know that since we had sold out Thursday night. I made up some excuse but the real reason was that I didn't want see King James just yet. I wasn't at the level I wanted to be when I seen King James. I suspected that it might be a long time from now. My mother was doing badly with her part time job. My sister was getting by but they were trying to keep up with the Jones's her and Marcus. It was maybe an ego thing but I wanted to face him as a man not as a survivor.

The next night Antoine recopped from King James with some of my money in the pot. He said that King James was surprised that he wanted more than usual. I told Antoine not to mention my name and he told me my name never got brought up. He wasn't too interested in anything because he seemed too preoccupied with other things according to Antoine. Him and his wife Latrice had a stillborn baby and he was dealing with that. Latrice was in the hospital depressed. He was leaving to visit her when Antoine came to recop. Antoine said he had never seen King James look so stressed. At that point I was glad I didn't go. He said King James was rushing out the door so fast that he had Boom-Boom grab the dope to give to Antoine.

Boom-Boom was King James' number one road dog. To be more real about it he was King James' muscle. That nigga could fight is ass off. They say if he didn't knock you out with one punch then the second punch would definitely do it. That's how he got the name Boom-Boom. The thing about Boom-Boom was that he didn't mind smoking a nigga either. He was implicated in a few murders before him and King James got big time.

It was rumored in the streets of San Bernardino that he robbed and killed the last big time roller in these parts before King James. The High Roller that was killed was moving major weight. Then one day the police found him and his girl shot to death and sodomized. They never found any suspects but not even a year later King James became one of the major niggas moving weight in the hood. Antoine personally hated dealing with that nigga because he always gave him a hard time. He would sex play Antoine telling him he was too pretty to be in the dope game. It always fucked with him because deep down I think he believed it was somewhat true.

That same Friday night Antoine threw a get-together with a few people from back in the day. He had even bought a sound system for the music he would play. It surprised me to see how much he cleaned up for the party. The party was cracking by ten o'clock. I sat back and relaxed on the couch and sipped on a beer. It was a celebration of my release from that hellhole. While I downed the rest of my beer Antoine passed me some chronic.

41

After taking a few hits I was really on cloud nine. The enjoyment of watching everyone dance made me stand up when they put on this banging old school Biggie song. Right when the song came on everyone started singing along.

"Hot sicker than your average, Papa twist cabbage on instinct niggas don't think shit stink." Everyone chanted.

Some of us were throwing up I.E. I eased into the kitchen while the song was playing to grab another beer. Came out of the kitchen with a full bottle mellow from the urb. Letting the Biggie song run through my veins I look up inadvertently. There she was standing right by the door just coming inside. I can tell she was wondering where I was from the way she was looking. She was truly beautiful. My heart dropped and I was nervous as hell. Now I regretted smoking that chronic because I didn't feel too sure of myself. If I had a clear head I would have easily walked over there to speak. I stared at her while she looked around slightly frantic. She was hoping that I hadn't left yet. Then she relaxed when she acknowledged in her mind that the party was for me. We were that connected. To the point when she looked up her eyes gazed right by the kitchen door. Her smile lit up the entire dimly lit living room.

Her hair was pressed down on the sides of her face straight without any curls at the end. Her full lips had on moderately glazed lip-gloss. Her pretty mocha colored skin highlighted her pretty eyes. She wore a conservative cream-colored sweater with Black jeans. She had on comfortable looking platform closed toe shoes. I watched her glide over towards me, as I stood stiff in front of the kitchen door. If I tried to move slightly parts of my body would start trembling. She stood in front of me. Her eyes became somewhat misty so she had to cover her nose and mouth with her hand. She kept fighting the tears.

"Give me a hug Winnie."

When my arms went around her waist I felt like paradise had hit me. She smelled so good. The aroma of her perfume was so intoxicating that my knees went weak for a brief spell. Her and

I had something more than intimacy. That's when that Monica song 'You shoulda known better' start playing. We took our Q and joined everyone dancing on the living room carpet. Neither one of us said a word. We were both stuck in the moment and it seemed that everyone else had left the apartment. They played two more slow songs after Monica then we gracefully walked into the kitchen. His kitchen was small with a table in the back with four chairs. To not be as close to the music we decided to talk in the kitchen at the table. Words still didn't come out of our mouths for at least twenty seconds. There was a mutual admiration and attraction.

"I missed you so much, but I didn't have anyway to contact you. Your sister Sharon was hard to find and your moms...well you know your moms. You were gone so long from me Winnie." She said.

"It's nothing like seeing a woman that always has a place in your heart. You don't have to explain yourself to me Vanessa. The moment is now and I don't want to dwell on the past in any negative way. I want to dwell on the present and the future."

"But Sherwin I wanted to talk to you so bad. I wrote letters hoping I could tell you how I missed you. I wanted to be there for..."

"Shhh! You were there for me. Your memory kept me going. Trust me, seeing you now is like heaven to me." I interrupted her.

We talked and talked about life and how everything was that changed and stayed the same. I didn't think that it was appropriate but she asked me to spend the night with her. Vanessa was different. It wasn't all about pussy with her. She was my friend and my confidant. Women will tell you that you can be honest with them but I truly could be honest with her. She was definitely a special type of woman. Before I left Antoine smiled at me pointing at Vanessa and saying surprise. That was a real big surprise and I appreciated it.

When we got back to her house it was already warm inside. She had a nice two-bedroom apartment. She lived by California State University of San Bernardino. I could see the mountains clear from her porch during the day. We stepped outside on her balcony to talk for a while.

"Fab Five told me you stayed over near Cal State. I didn't know to believe him or not but he seemed pretty sure."

"Crazy ass Fabian ran into me in Wal-Mart about four or five months back. You know that nigga had his pistol inside the damn store. I swear some niggas ain't got any tact." She commented.

She leaned on the balcony railing while I puffed on a cigarette. She knew the game just as well as the next man. Vanessa had been involved with hustling since she was thirteen. Her brother was a high roller for a minute but he had gotten killed when he was twenty. Vanessa was only seventeen and we were together at the time. I was locked for the funeral and everything. He taught her and I a lot of shit. His name was Vernell. I could see the pain in her eyes at the loss of her brother.

"Well you know Fab Five got a few screws missing anyway. So you have to excuse that nigga at times." I replied.

"Yeah that nigga need a purpose in life. You want something to drink?"

"Naw, I'm good. Where is your son, I would love to meet him?" I asked out the blue.

"You mean our son. He's at his grandmother's house for the weekend because I wanted to be alone with you first."

"I knew he was my son, I just needed you to confirm it. We should get married Vanessa." I replied.

"You know I love you Winnie but let's get reacquainted first. It's some things that we still got to work out with our families. Besides, you gone want me to help you in this game isn't that right?" She smiled.

"You telling the truth about that." I smiled back.

"Oh by the way!" She ran inside.

44

It took her about two minutes then she came back on the balcony with a brown paper bag. I knew exactly what it was. I had close to thirty thousand dollars saved up before I got locked up. Eight thousand I told my sister to hold, another ten thousand I kept under my bed at my mother's house and the last ten thousand I told Vanessa to hold for me. My bail was one hundred thousand dollars, which meant I only had to put up ten percent. If I had put up the ten percent I knew they would have thrown a tax lien on me. I told my mother where my stash was in her house thinking they might lower my bail. But they never did.

I held on to the stash of money knowing that Vanessa didn't touch it. It was in the same paper bag I used when I gave it to her. We talked into the wee hours of the night. Then finally around three but close to four in the morning we dozed off. We held each other throughout the night. That Saturday morning she fixed breakfast; even though it was a little past noon by the time we both woke up. She let me know she wanted me to stay for the weekend until Joshua got home on Monday night. I was glad she didn't name him after me. I didn't hate my name but I thought giving him my name was too typical. She told me she needed to run some errands and she would talk to me later.

I had most of the dope that Antoine copped from King James. I brought it with me to Vanessa's house. It was already cooked up into crack and I hated that. But I still had every intention to grind. By one-thirty in the afternoon I was on the block. By the time Antoine got there it was like six in the evening. The package that I held on to was almost gone. I had a fifty piece left so he showed up right on time.

"Damn nigga I'm glad you showed up when you did. Where is the rest of that dope?"

"In the car. Nigga please don't tell me you sold out all that shit we had?" He said in astonishment.

"I got a fifty piece left and that's about it. You didn't know this spot was cracking in the day time."

45

"Hell naw nigga I only come out here when it gets dark." He replied.

I could tell he was in total disbelief. The fiends would walk by hoping they could get some of that good dope during the day but no one was out. Forcing them to go elsewhere to get their high. It was money to be made on this spot. We sold out of everything by the rest of the night. I was glad that I had taken most of the dope with me that night. This nigga Antoine had a prime spot that he was sitting on and wasn't milking it for everything it was worth. When we were done for the night I told him to talk to King James.

"Look here nigga," I said while sipping on a beer. "Let's get a whole bird from King James but this time tell him to give it to you raw."

"I don't know dog, he might trip seeing me come back that fast to recop. Maybe we should wait about a week then get at that nigga. Plus if we put all that we made in the pot that's gone leave us damn near broke. His bricks be going for seventeen-five." Antoine shrugged.

"Look here my nigga, if we both put in eighty-five hundred and tell that nigga we got seventeen I don't think he gone trip." I snapped back.

I knew his rate was too high anyway. All King James was trying to do was keep us under his wings. As long as we was getting small shit he could cook it up and he gets paid off the stretch. We would be able to get forty thousand dollars off a whole kilo if we cook the shit ourselves. Since Antoine had been buying quarters all this time he was losing major money. Not to mention the money he could make if he hit the block early. I could tell that thoughts were running through his head. But it was obvious that he was genuinely afraid of King James. He wasn't trying to get that nigga pissed at him in the least bit.

"I'm down my nigga but let's stay on his good side, you know." He replied. The fear was evident.

"I feel what you saying but fuck kissing his ass when we bringing him money. It's always respect but a nigga ain't supposed to work with crumbs forever. This shit can be gone by tomorrow so we should live it up today. Make these the muthafuckin good times so when shit hit the fan we can at least know we celebrated them."

"Damn my nigga you should be a preacher or some shit. Where you learn to talk like that, in the pen?" He joked nervously. "It's just that nigga King James got eyes and ears everywhere. That nigga told me about some shit I was into about a month ago. I was like, how fuck that nigga knew that. Look Pooh, I say we wait but if you want to move right now then we will move right now."

"Right now!" I firmly replied.

"Well we should at least bring the whole seventeen-five."

"Nope bring seventeen so it will look like we scraping all we got. And still ask the nigga for it raw and uncut. We'll cook that shit our selves."

He did as I told him to do and came back with a whole brick of some uncooked raw. I loved it. Vanessa had a homegirl that worked at a dental office who was able to get us a gang of procaine and we started cooking. We had the fiends jumping for that shit. Within two and a half months we had moved up to two kilos every time we copped. I always made Antoine go by himself. But after we had asked for those two bricks, King James wanted to have a sit down with us. With the both of us. It was expected so I had prepared myself for the inevitable. It was time for him to read me.

47

4

THE SIT DOWN

Niggas don't be gangstas when they supposed to be gangstas

Juvenile

King James sat quietly at his office desk. He would have his meeting with Pooh and Ant in about thirty minutes. A few months back Antoine was only copping a quarter every week and a half. Now that Pooh was home from the pen they were moving two bricks every two weeks. He was nervous about the meeting but didn't understand why. Being the biggest baller on these parts of the I.E. he felt like they should be the ones worried. He questioned why Pooh had taken so long to come and see him. He had to believe that the mighty King James would have gave him some dope on consignment. It appeared as though Pooh deliberately avoided contact with him. He swung back and forth in his office chair pondering on these things. Boom-Boom was in the other room but close by. He made sure the lights were dim for the effect King James wanted to have. Fifty percent of this dope game is show he thought. Chuckling to himself he knew that how people perceived you was part of the way on how you were treated. He had Antoine figured out but he never quite understood Pooh. That's what bothered him. Before they got there he thought it would be best that he talk to his road dog about his dilemma.

He slammed his fist on his Oakwood desktop. The nervousness was not part of his personality. It couldn't show in the least bit to either one of them young niggas.

"Ay Boom-Boom, holla at ya boy for a minute. Let's have a few words before them young niggas get here." King James yelled into the front room.

Boom-Boom was on the couch looking at a magazine when he heard his boy's voice. Getting up from the couch Boom-Boom walked in with his chest out and his arms broad. He always had the aura like he was ready to knock someone out.

"What's up James? What's on ya mind?" Boom-Boom asked.

"What do you get from these young niggas able to buy two birds when a few months back they could only buy a quarter? Is that some tricky shit or what?" King James didn't look up from his desk.

Boom-Boom let his boy puff on the cigar that was sitting in the ashtray before he replied. It was as if he was showing an unspoken courtesy. King James blew out the smoke then leaned back in his chair.

"They've been grinding lately that's all. That's all it is. That young nigga Pooh done got out of jail and is hungry. Sometimes it's like that for a nigga."

"Yeah but he too hungry. That low-ball nigga Antoine was cool with what he was moving until Pooh got out. Now he is copping two at a time?" King James questioned.

"You think them pretty ass niggas is working for the police? That shit can be taken care of." Boom-Boom retorted.

"Naw, we would know if they was working for the police. I just think them niggas is moving too fast, that's all."

"Shit but that just mo' money for you. He could be copping from them Mexicans but instead he getting yo raw. Let's get *they* money so we can get *that* money." Boom-Boom arrogantly chuckled.

"But who says they not copping they shit from somewhere else? That's when they gone be moving in on my money. If they can get it for a better price they might go somewhere else."

That wasn't the only thing that made him uneasy. Pooh was hustling for him when he got cracked. The young nigga didn't snitch or anything but he wondered if Pooh held resentment. That could be why he never came with Antoine to cop. The only reason he was coming was because he was requested to come. Boom-Boom interrupted his thoughts.

"You thinking about selling it to them for cheaper than seventeen. Shit if you sold it for fifteen-five you would still make a nice profit."

"Hell naw, but what I'm gone do is practically force them young niggas to take two more kilos on consignment. See how fast they move four at a time and if they cop from someone else they always got to worry about getting my four bricks off. And they know that I'm gone look at them funny if they stop getting the two they already started getting."

"Hell yeah, they know they better make sure they got yo money or it's gone be a problem. You be coming up with some clever shit James." Boom-Boom chuckled.

"Yeah, we give them a lot of weight then put them niggas on a timer. That way they committed to hustling my product. They ain't got time for nobody else's dope. They hustlers huh, well we gone find out." King James gloated.

Leaning back in his desk chair he puffed on his cigar with a sly grin on his face. That's all he had to do was talk to his boy Boom-Boom and he could always come up with some sly shit. They had about fifteen more minutes before the youngsters walked in. They both sat quietly and patiently waiting for the two hustlers to get inside. Pooh was always punctual when it came to business. He made sure that his habits were on the up and up. King James always respected that about him. In fact he thought he respected the young hustler too much. Now it was time to take him through some trials. See if he really had the heart for this grown man shit.

Pooh walked into the office followed by Antoine. Antoine looked pitiful to King James. He knew that he was easily influenced by trivial shit. He decided at that moment to have all his dealings with Pooh. Pooh wasn't scared when he walked inside. In fact he had an air of confidence that made King James unsettled.

"Take a seat." King James said.

They both sat down in the two chairs adjacent to the desk. Standing behind them leaning on the doorframe was Boom-Boom. Antoine gasped when he looked behind him to see the massive man. Boom-Boom smiled as though he was up to something. Pooh felt him behind him but didn't glance back. He understood what King James was trying to do. It wasn't going to work with him. He made sure he was careful enough not to do any reckless eyeballing. But whenever he spoke to King James he wanted to be firm and sure of himself. He would give him eye contact only when he spoke to him.

"Ya'll young niggas want something to drink?" King James asked.

"Naw I'm straight." Pooh replied.

"Me too." Antoine followed.

"Well how have you been Pooh? You've been out for a few months now and you just now coming to see me. I was wondering about you, hoping you landed on your feet. I wish you would have came earlier, because you know I would have taken care of you." King James lightheartedly replied.

Pooh wasn't a fool. He knew that King James was about business and if there was any small talk he was usually trying to get something out of you. Pooh decided to play along with his game. If King James hears some shit about him let it be mostly from his own mouth.

"I couldn't come to you in the condition I was in. I couldn't come begging when I hadn't shown you that I was worthy to even be in your presence. I wanted to prove I was worthy to be on your team, that's all." Pooh replied.

"A hustler to the bone." Boom-Boom proudly interjected.

King James hated that Boom-Boom had said that. He also knew that Pooh was catering to his ego with the whole worthy line.

51

But he wasn't convinced because of some words. He wanted to know motives. That was his concern. He remained silent allowing the compliment Boom-Boom gave Pooh to resonate. He threw it out there let's see if I can use it to my advantage.

"You a true hustler huh?"

"I'm one who does what he got to do. I'm true to getting my needs and wants met. And all I want to do is grind that good shit you got." Pooh replied calmly.

King James smiled at how Pooh was subtly suggesting his loyalty. He stared at the young hustler hoping he could get more than what was being said. But Pooh remained humble.

"Well I'll tell you what, since you want to grind this good shit of mine this is your lucky day. Not only am I going to give you the two bricks you want I'm also gone give you two more bricks on consignment."

"Are you serious? Man we gone grind..." Antoine was interrupted.

"Naw not yet. We ain't ready for all that weight right now. If we take all that weight we might be sitting on yo money longer than we want to. Plus I don't want to have to hold on to that raw that long. I appreciate the offer but we gone pass." Pooh replied without looking in Antoine's direction.

"I'm offering you a deal of a lifetime and you want to turn it down. What kind of shit is that Pooh?" King James' voice sounded rigid.

"I don't mean any disrespect. But us sitting on that much weight at one time is too much for us right now. You might think that we moving weight like that because we copping a lot more than before. But the truth is that I had a little money saved up before I got locked up. I put most of it in plus what we made when we first hooked up. It ain't what you think OG homie we ain't there yet." Pooh explained.

"So you don't want to take this free dope I'm offering?" King James asked again.

"Not just yet, but give us time and we will be there soon." Pooh insisted.

"Ya'll still over there on that spot off of Mt. Vernon?" King James asked Antoine.

Antoine nodded in agreement. His eyes quickly looked downward after he responded. The tension was in the air. No one wanted to move or budge from his position. Pooh was making it difficult for King James. Antoine couldn't understand why Pooh wasn't taking such a sweet offer when the spot had been cracking for some time now. He knew he would get an explanation so that wasn't what bothered him. What bothered him was wondering if Pooh had pissed off King James for turning down his offer. He glanced over at Pooh and his best friend was stone faced. He had to play along or it would show weakness.

"I'll tell you what; I'll only give you one kilo on consignment. If you handle two than one more won't do you too bad. And to show my generosity I'll only ask you to give me back seventeen for it." King James offered in an upbeat voice.

"If we could we would King James but we can't." Pooh knew that he loved it when people called him 'King' James.

"You got to believe me when I say I don't want to play with your money. We gone work this down maybe two or three times and then we will get that third brick on consignment. But if we do it now ain't no telling when we gone bring back your money. I ain't trying to not have your money." Pooh feigned fear.

It was convincing enough for King James. Truthfully he was tiring quickly over the discussion. The young hustler appeared genuine enough for him. He looked up at Boom-Boom who was still flipping through his magazine. King James shrugged his shoulders when Boom-Boom looked up.

"They only want two so give the young niggas two." King James surrendered.

It made plenty of sense when he thought about it. He probably had some money saved up and after a few hustles he was able to get two bricks. King James didn't really remember that Mt.

53

Vernon spot really being hot like that anyway. Plus they were curb serving so that was slower money than if they were selling more. He knew that Pooh was getting more money off of stretching the dope but that wasn't too big of a loss for him. He decided to let them walk with the two they had and see how fast they move from there. When he really thought about it they weren't any real threat anyway since they didn't have any guns to back them. Knowing Pooh he would be able to protect himself from getting robbed but he wouldn't have the manpower to call shots. This was the first time since Pooh had gotten out that they met. He figured he would read him better the more he came around. When Boom-Boom walked up and gave the raw to Antoine he excused them.

"Ay Pooh let me holler at you for a minute alone." King James said.

"Yeah what's up?"

King James waited for Boom-Boom to close the door behind Antoine to leave them two alone.

"From now on, I want to deal with you and only you. When it is time for ya'll to recop I want you to pick up the dope from now on. You can bring Ant if you want to but from now on I'm only dealing with you." King James rigidly replied.

"That's cool. We can do it like that for now on."

King James held his hand out for Pooh to shake. When Pooh reached out to shake his hand he got up to hug the young hustler and put his mouth to his ear.

"Glad you home young soldier, now go and get that paper."

Pooh nodded to confirm and walked out the office. King James stared at him walking out the door with his arms folded. He had to admit that the young hustler showed much respect. Nothing pleased him more than a nigga knowing his place. King James smiled but there was still inner turmoil. He usually could read niggas pretty good but Pooh was still just as difficult to read as before. He dismissed his suspicions only for a brief moment. He just wants to live that's all. But a nigga in my position got to be suspicious about everything. Boom-Boom walked into the office after they left. He looked up at King James with a slight smile on his face.

"So what you think?" Boom-Boom asked.

"I don't know what to think."

When I walked outside of King James's office my legs must have damn near buckled. It was hard to feed that niggas' ego but I did it nevertheless. I was dwelling on him trying to lay two more bricks on us. He had to think that we or I was a dumb muthafucka. Antoine was in the driver's seat with the motor running when I hopped into the passenger side. Once I sat down I was relaxed as hell. Antoine waited until we got down the street and around the corner.

"That nigga was offering us two more bricks on consignment and you turned it down? I couldn't believe that crazy shit you did. You know how much money we could of made. That spot is cracking right now. I don't understand you sometimes Pooh damn." Antoine sounded frustrated.

"That nigga was putting us on a timer. He was trying to see how much we were gone hustle. Once he knows how much we can move he watch how we buy our dope. Let's just keep that nigga thinking we moving small shit."

"Yeah but he still gone know how much we moving every time we recop with just two kilos." Antoine replied.

"Yeah but we can cop with our shit whenever we feel like it. If we holding on to his shit we gone have a certain amount of time to get his money to him. But instead of not giving us consignment, he gone keep giving it to us but putting pressure on us to get him his money." I explained.

"Why would he do that, when we making money for him every time we cop from him to buy our own shit?"

"So we can be too busy with his shit to buy our shit from someone else. He hooked you up with a little spot. It ain't too far from yo house so that you could bring money to him. If we get too big he knows we might can get weight from someone else for cheaper. The game is the game." I shrugged my shoulders after my explanation.

"Yeah but we ain't gone fuck with another connect except for him anyway. He shouldn't even be tripping off of that." Antoine replied showing is naivety.

"He don't know what the fuck we gone do. Three months back you were buying a quarter of a kilo and now you buying two whole ones. He got to see where we coming from. Let me deal with him from now on though, okay?" I asked but meant it as a matter of fact.

"Why my nigga, I can still make the buy when it's time to? You think I'm scared of that nigga or something."

I wanted to say to him that he was scared of King James but chose to refrain. I didn't want to bruise my best friend's ego.

"Because he asked me to deal with him directly from now on. You can come with me but he wants to deal with me." I despondently replied.

"That's fuck up! What I do to make him be like that?" Antoine took it personal.

"It ain't anything against you it's more about watching me. Don't take the shit personal. Look at it as you don't have to see Boom-Boom's big ass." I chuckled.

"Fuck that big fat muthafucka." He retorted.

I laughed to pacify him. We didn't say much on the ride back to his house. We rode down Baseline Street getting to Mt. Vernon because King James' office was off Baseline right next to Rialto. He had the west side on lock and we were stuck right in the middle of his territory. We were able to buy one more brick but I told Antoine that we would save it and put it to the side but I was actually waiting on Ace's connect. He was selling the raw for sixteen thousand even. This would work out good for me as long as I kept it secret. I was somewhat relieved when Antoine let me do most of the talking. At least he knew that much. The silence is what allowed us to stay in our own thoughts. When we pulled up in front of his apartment complex words still wouldn't come out after he turned off the engine. I knew the reason for his silence. He was pissed off about not being able to connect with King James anymore. What bothered me slightly was the thought of whom he blamed for what happened. He should know that I kept avoiding the man. But you never know with Antoine. Sometimes his emotions were like that of a woman.

"I know that nigga asked you to stay behind so he could tell you that. But what bothers me is that he could have told me if he had a problem with something I was doing." He interrupted the silence.

"I told you not to dwell on that dumb shit. That nigga just funny like that sometimes. He's more familiar with me than you that's probably all it's about." I tried to downplay the situation.

"Whatever nigga. What you about to do; because I'm about to have Karen stop through for a minute? Maybe even spend the night."

"I'm about to check on Lonnie and shoot the shit with him for awhile. Then I plan on heading over to Vanessa's house."

He smiled then got out the car. Lonnie was a young hustler that always looked up to me. He was curb serving for us by now. He used to keep my stash back in the day before I got locked up. He was only fourteen at the time but now he was nineteen and hungry. I got him and a couple of his homies to hold down the apartments close to Antoine's house on Mt. Vernon. Lonnie's mother and my mother both stayed in the Dorjil's. I knew him since he was a toddler. He always had heart.

I wanted to get it cracking with some raw in the Dorjil's. It had been years since the brothers with the suit and bow ties been in there soldiering. I knew I wouldn't be able to hustle shit while they were around. Since they were gone I was thinking about setting up Fab Five in the apartments. It was a little too close to King's James' office but I didn't give a fuck. I grew up over there not him. I was hoping to hustle some of that raw I got from Ace's connect over there. It would be wise to put a shooter over that stash just in case someone wanted to buck. There was no doubt that Fab Five wouldn't hesitate to peel someone's cap back if they tried to lean on him. And if one of King James' people came asking questions they would assume he got the dope from King James once my server told them they were hustling for me. Besides, most of his hustlers were in either California Gardens or the Delmont Heights. It was territory that needed to be reopened.

After talking to Lonnie for about thirty minutes I headed towards Vanessa's crib. Lonnie handed me twelve grand on arrival. He was a youngster after my own heart. I handed him a bonus on the spot. I knew he was saving up to get him a new car. He had a little bucket to get him around but he was trying to get something to floss in. We embraced and I shot to my final destination.

When I got there Vanessa was in the living room watching television. My son was in the bedroom sound asleep. She had introduced me as his father and we had developed a close bond. Some nights I would spend the night over there but for some reason Vanessa didn't want me permanently staying there. She would tell me that I didn't need any distractions. Some nights though, she would yearn for my company. This was one of those nights. I had a key so I sat a short distance away from her on the couch. Neither one of us spoke as she was watching the last minutes of a sitcom.

"Let's go on the porch so we can talk." She said.

We went on the porch after she handed me a beer. I sipped on it without saying anything.

"So what happened?" She said impatiently.

"He just wanted to see how I was doing. He was wondering why I hadn't come around sooner. And from now on he wants me to cop the dope instead of Antoine."

"I figured that. Did he try to get you to sell some of his dope?" She asked already knowing the answer.

"On consignment for seventeen even. But I wasn't trying to hear that shit."

"Where was Boom-Boom big ass?" She glanced at me.

"He was standing in the doorway right behind Antoine. That big muthafucka be getting a kick out of intimidating Antoine." I replied.

"He's like a pit bull, if he senses fear he gone attack. Ant shouldn't show his hand so openly." She reflected.

I smiled without replying. She was right but that was my boy through and through. It was hard to teach a grown man how to handle himself. He already believed he was a man; so it's hard to swallow when another man tells him something to do, especially if he considers you his peer. I had to play it by ear.

"When are you going to hook up with your other connect?" Vanessa asked.

"Early next week."

"You ready?"

"About as ready as I'm ever gone be. He fifteen hundred dollars less than King James but I don't know how good his raw is." I replied.

"But it ain't even about the price as much as having another connect besides King James. If you got to depend totally on that nigga he will always have you under his thumb. You don't want to give any nigga that much power over you. Especially a nigga like him." Vanessa venomously replied.

It was nothing left to say at that point so I changed the subject. I didn't want the entire conversation between her and me strictly business. In fact I was hoping that it was mostly pleasure.

5

HUSTLING

I got a wheel of fortune cause I flip O's like Vanna White!
Ludacris

About two hours before I was supposed to meet with Ace's connect a problem occurred. Some man was looking for his wife apparently. Of course she was smoking dope and he came walking the streets looking for her. He was a middle-aged workingman that appeared to be a functional crack addict. He was about six-foot-one, which was only a couple of inches taller than me. I guess he had come home from work and she wasn't home. So he decided to come over there at the spot talking shit to my boys and me. He made sure he copped him a twenty piece before he started talking shit. I was leaning against the mailboxes when he approached me. I was working the corner so that Lonnie could handle some business.

"Any of you young muthafuckas seen Lorraine around here?" He said loudly.

"I don't know anyone by the name of Lorraine. How does she look?" I asked.

"Never mind how she looks. If you don't know who I'm talking about then there ain't shit else to say. But you probably do know who I'm talking about cuz she cops from ya'll." He snarled

"Look man I don't know a Lorraine so the only way I would know her is if you described her." I replied.

"Fuck you, why you keep worrying about how my wife looks?" He snapped.

"Hold up homie you better watch who the fuck you talking to. It's probably best you go home and handle yo business somewhere else." I warned.

"Or what? One of you young niggas probably got my wife somewhere fucking her. Ain't no little pretty ass nigga gone run me away from finding my wife. So fuck you!!"

With one swing I caved his mouth in with a right hand punch. One of his teeth loosened from the punch and left an imprint in my knuckles. I hesitated briefly then followed up with a punch to his nose then to his stomach. He folded over and dropped to one knee. I paused again and gave him another one right in his mouth. That loose tooth fell out this time. I hated that I had to beet his ass because it was always bad for business.

He yelled as he fell to the pavement. I thought about stomping him but I wanted to see what his next move would be. He had managed to get up on his knees again holding his stomach. His fallen tooth flew a couple of inches from my foot. His eyes had watered and his words were stammering. By that time one of Lonnie's young comrades had walked up. Chucky was his name and he was a soldier. He had his three-eighty drawn coming towards us.

"You want me to peel his cap homie?" Chucky asked.

"Naw it's cool."

I pointed my finger at the disrespectful man then looked him in his eyes.

"You gone show some respect from now on, ain't you? Cuz some pretty niggas don't play that shit."

"I'm sorry about that my man. I thought you knew where my wife was man but that shit won't happen again." He pleaded.

"How we know this nigga ain't coming back?" Chucky asked me.

"I'm giving you a pass so are you gone make me regret it?" I asked him with my finger still pointing at him.

"Naw it ain't like that at all. I get my high from ya'll and I ain't trying to fuck that up. It's cool I swear."

"Alright then get the fuck out of here." I demanded.

He scurried off still grabbing his stomach as he walked away. Chucky immediately started laughing. He was laughing so hard that it made me laugh a little.

"You did that nigga like Big Red did that one nigga in 'Five Heartbeats'. You should have asked that nigga what was your working hours." He laughed.

I chuckled when I thought about. The game is the game and there is always someone willing to test you. I hated when a muthafucka called me pretty. I always took it as they were calling me a bitch. It always brought out the worse in me. I couldn't wait to get off this spot and make my move towards the new connect. I knew that Lonnie would be walking up any minute so I had to be patient.

"You know that crack head bitch he was talking about gave me and Lonnie head yesterday. I didn't even know she was married. When he said the name Lorraine I thought about it and she did tell us her name. She looked good to be a crack head. She had ass and everything. Lonnie wanted to fuck but she said she was only giving us head." Chucky replied.

"Ya'll niggas be careful about that kind of shit. There are three things you don't fuck with a man. His woman, his money and his food will get him to acting different. Some niggas go crazy over that kind of shit."

"I feel you. But we didn't know the bitch was married until just now. Wait till I tell Lonnie about this shit."

Right when he said that Lonnie and Antoine walked up. I didn't know why Antoine was there but it didn't matter I had to roll. Everyone embraced then I jumped into my ride. Antoine came to the passenger side window for me to roll it down.

"What you about to get into my nigga?" He asked.

"Shit I'm about to run a few errands then take my ass to sleep. What, you gone hang with these niggas for a while?"

"Yeah for a minute. Talk with the young niggas and watch how they hustling our shit, that's all."

"Alright then I'll holla at you later." I replied.

I rolled the passenger window up and drove off. We were still close but I could tell he was still hurt over that King James shit. But I made a mental note to hang with that nigga real tough for a couple of days. Put his mind at ease.

I arrived at the hotel Ace told me to be at eight o' clock sharp. He told me to go to room 203. I knocked on the door a particular way that Ace told me to and that's when he opened the door. When the door swung open there was a big extremely dark skin Black Man in front of me. He had muscles but he also had a gut. He had to be about 6'3 in height. He had a perm that was fixed in a ponytail. He face was filled with a mustache, beard and handle bars. He looked me down as if he might fire on me or something. I must admit I was a little nervous. But I stood my ground and didn't budge, as he looked me over.

"What's yo name?" He frowned.

"Pooh!"

"Alright nigga come on in." He said closing the door behind him.

I looked around and seen that the room wasn't used at all. Only thing that was out of place was two sweat suits lying on the bed. He walked over to the edge of the bed then glanced at me one more time.

"You ain't a fag or nothing are you?" He firmly asked.

At first I was offended but I felt that his question was going somewhere.

"Hell naw I ain't a fag." I sharply replied.

"Good then, you can take off all ya clothes in front of me while I take off all my clothes in front of you." He replied.

"You know that Ace is my uncle right?" I protested subtly.

"You being his family is the only reason I'm fucking with you. Now when you get totally naked I want you to squat and cough. We'll do the shit at the same time you dig what I'm saying." His deep voice resonated with force.

"For sure!"

I got undressed and complied with everything he said do. Then he handed me a sweat suit and he told me to follow him to his car. We drove around the corner to another hotel. We got inside the parking lot and he parked. Then we walked a little ways before he said a word.

"What you got for me?" He asked.

"I got thirty-two for two." I replied.

"I thought you was only getting one?"

"I thought so too but I realized that we could put in for two."

"This time that shit is cool cuz I brought an extra one just in case. But next time know what you want cuz." He replied.

He looked at me to see my reaction. Ace had already told me that the nigga was an OG Crip from Main Street he thought. But I wasn't tripping off any gangbanging shit. He sat in his car and counted the thirty two thousand in his car. I made it easy for him because I had Vanessa hitting up the banks to change the small bills into big bills. She wore a business suit every time she went out. It didn't take him long to count everything.

"You a organized young nigga." He commented.

He then took me to another hotel where he had the two kilos sitting under a bed. He tossed me the bag and there they were. He handed me a knife and a roll of moving tape. I tasted the product and it was to my satisfaction so we rolled out. We went back to the original hotel and he handed me the key.

"You can grab yo shit from upstairs but turn the key in to the clerk when you done." He replied.

"How much I owe you for the sweat suit?"

"That ain't shit. But this is the number you call when you need to recop. Put in 909 then put in the ten digit number so I'll know that it's the nigga from San Bernardino." He replied.

I nodded and got out the car. I could feel his eyes following me up the stairs. It didn't matter much to me. Once my clothes were gathered I took a deep breath then walked out the room. He had already drove off by the time I came outside. I made sure to put the dope and my clothes in the trunk before I turned the key into the clerk. I rung the doorbell twice and waited for someone to answer. After a few moments an Arab man came to the gated window half asleep. I handed him the key and he looked at the room number and looked puzzled.

"Young woman already checked out? She only been in room for two hours but she pay for whole night."

I shrugged my shoulders and he did the same. Then he handed me a five-dollar deposit for returning the key on time. I chuckled to myself. I was ready to go back to San Bernardino. I had drove all the way to Azusa, which was a city closer to Los Angeles. I hopped on the 10 Freeway and headed back to my new apartment in a city next to San Bernardino called Colton.

I had gotten up early the next morning because my mother wanted me over her house that next day. She wouldn't tell me what for but that it was important. There was some money I wanted to give her anyway. When I got home that night I cooked up those two bricks I bought from Big Black. That was the name he wanted me to call him. He had to be in his forties or late thirties in age. I was up until two in the morning cooking up all that dope. I wanted to holler at Fab Five that day so that we could discuss how we would work this dope. It was easy to tell that Big Black's dope was more raw than King James' shit. King James must have stepped on his dope a few more times or his connect was putting out some weak shit. I believed the former more than the latter. He probably was stepping on his dope just so he could get much more money but settling for weak shit. Now I had a connect that gave me the real raw.

Once I opened up the door to my mother's house it was obvious she was wide-awake. It was ten in the morning, which was early for me. That meant I had to be up by nine to make it to her house. She must have been talking to someone because she was laughing and talking. There was also someone else laughing right along with her, which indicated she had company. This made me skeptical. Then I walked into the living room to see the prettiest woman sitting next to my mother laughing and joking. It had suddenly gotten quiet when I walked inside.

"Just in time, come over here Winnie and meet my co-worker Janice. She has been working with me for a few months now while she goes to cosmetology school" Mama explained.

The way my mother introduced her was obvious that she was trying to hook us up. She was fine as hell to me. She was a redbone with thick lips and dimples. She was simply breathtaking but she still wasn't finer than Vanessa. At least not to me she wasn't. But I wasn't going to complain because she was fine than a muthafucka to me. I smiled and reached out to shake her hand.

"Nice to meet you Janice."

"Nice to meet you too? Sherwin isn't it?" She asked.

"Yeah girl his name is Sherwin but we call him Winnie. I forgot to tell you all about that. Some of his knucklehead friends call him Pooh because my nephew Melvin started calling him that." Mama explained.

People in my opinion weren't too privy to that information but mama talked on. My mother gossiped on as if I wasn't even there. I slid her an envelope with money while she talked to Janice. Janice would glance at me and smile. She was digging me and I was digging her.

"So how much longer you got before you finish school?" I cut in once school was brought up again.

"Two more months and I'm finished. I'm waiting to get my license so I can work at my cousin's shop. Then one of these days I'm going to open up my own shop."

"Good thinking girl. You got to have your own business." Mama complimented.

I talked with Janice alone when I told them I was about to leave. We went outside so that we could get to know each other. While we were talking Stacy called me but since I had my phone on vibrate I ignored the call. I would always take her to a hotel room whenever we hooked up. There wasn't enough trust for me to take her to my new spot. She was calling to see if we were

66

hooking up tonight. I planned on keeping my date with her but Janice was now in the picture. If I could do something with Janice tonight than I was going to cancel with Stacy. After talking for about twenty minutes outside on the porch the man I wanted to see came walking by.

"Hold on for a minute Janice."

She didn't get a chance to respond because I was already walking towards Fabian. It appeared as though he was wandering aimlessly. I had to jog lightly to catch up with him nevertheless.

"A Fab-Five, holla at ya nigga for a minute." I yelled.

He turned around with that fierce killer instinct. When he seen it was me his face suddenly lightened up. No doubt he was a killer and just the person I would need for my experiment.

"Damn Pooh, you hollering my name got a nigga wondering whom the fuck was creeping up on me. You know how it is." He replied.

It was evident that he was relieved. He held out his hand then we embraced briefly. I turned around seeing who was observing and I noticed Janice still on the porch watching what I was doing. In my head I considered that a problem. But I did tell her to hold on for a minute.

"Look here Fab-Five you a down ass nigga that I got much love and respect for. So I want to work with you on something." I began.

"What's up?"

"How much do the fiends be coming around here nowadays? I see people around here that smoke dope but I don't ever see product." I replied.

"Cause it ain't shit around here. Muthafuckas got to either go to the Delmont Heights or the California Gardens if they want some dope. That base head Lenny was complaining about that shit just the other day."

"What if a nigga had that dope over here how do you think it would move?" I asked, like it was out of curiosity.

"Shit if a nigga was moving weight over here he would clean up. All these muthafuckas around here be on that dope real tough. But most niggas that got a little bit of product will take they happy ass somewhere else." He replied still not catching on.

"What if you was that nigga with the raw? How would you move that shit?" I asked, slowly luring him in.

"First thing I would do is set up by the recreation room and work that shit from there. I'll get a few of the little homies to stand look out and serve them niggas that want that raw." He imagined.

"What if I told you I could get that raw for you? I give it to you upfront and you pay me the going rate for the amount I give you after you sell out."

"How much you talking about giving me?" I had his full attention.

"I'll start you off with a half kilo. We see how you work that shit from there then we will see what happens."

I figured that I could take a loss if shit didn't work out with half a kilo. I could work the other half on Mt. Vernon and still break out even. Even though Mt. Vernon was buzzing I wanted another spot to expand. Once a few niggas got a whiff of this raw then I would be selling good.

"When you talking about doing this shit?" He interrupted my thoughts.

"I got the raw right now. It's already cooked and broken down into bags. That shit is street ready and everything. I even got a little extra so that you could have some test runs with a few of the smokers. See how they like it and if they want some more you the man to holla at." I replied with a sly grin.

"You ain't said nothing but a word my nigga. How you want to do this?" He started looking around.

"You see that cute little piece I'm on the porch talking to? I'm gone be over there talking to her and you go in my back seat under the passenger seat and grab a black duffle bag. The back door is already unlocked so all you have to do is grab the raw and work it." I smiled.

"Good looking my nigga." He said walking over towards my car.

I gradually walked over to Janice who was still waiting on the porch. She looked as if she was paying attention to my entire conversation. She gave a lighthearted smile when I walked up on the porch. Damn she was fine and she had a nice ass. I couldn't wait to get up in that.

"I apologize for the hold up but I had to holla at my homeboy for a hot minute."

"I ain't tripping. You could tell he had much respect for you." She replied.

"You think?"

She nodded to confirm. When I turned around to look at Fab-Five he was already across the apartments with the duffel bag in hand. Seeing his movements made me chuckle. I knew he was hungry plus he was a killer. See King James wasn't about to mess with young niggas that was hungry but broke. That wasn't his thing. Helping other niggas come up wasn't what he was into. You had to be already doing something for him to feel he would give you more to get ahead. Then he would hold his thumb on you so you won't move further than him. I had peeped game a long time ago I just had gotten myself into a rut. Going to the pen was the best thing that could have happened to me because it made me think long and hard.

Janice and I sat on the porch chairs enjoying the sun being out. My mother brought us both a cup of lemonade when she seen us still outside talking. My mother set this up for real. The lemonade was a clear sign of it. I had the type of mother that would tell her company as well as myself to go get what we want to drink ourselves. She was trying to leave a good impression. She smiled gracefully and winked at me when she walked inside.

"Your mother is so sweet. She is one of the coolest people I have ever worked with. She told me that I remind her of herself when she was younger. I hope I look as good as her when I'm her age." Janice said.

"You probably will. As good as you look now I can imagine that you gone have it going on for a long time." I smiled.

"You ain't bad looking yourself. I see good genes run in your family."

We exchanged numbers after talking on my mom's porch for about two hours. She was light hearted and even a little silly in conversation. I appreciated the way she took everything so jovially. I knew that we would be seeing each other real soon.

I called Stacy back on my way over to Mt. Vernon. I knew Antoine wasn't going to hit the block until it got dark but Lonnie and them might have sold out. I told Stacy I would hook up with her in another thirty minutes to an hour. She talked shit for a brief moment but I didn't care. I let her run off at the mouth then as plain as day I simply said.

"I was dealing with some shit with my moms."

She pretended to understand but I didn't care one way or another. When I made it to Mt. Vernon Lonnie and Chucky was already standing outside of the apartment complex. Their faces had a look of relief when I pulled up. I jumped out the car with a grin on my face wondering what was going on.

"Damn Pooh, we damn near sold out and we didn't think you was gone be over here in enough time." Lonnie said.

"When have I let my niggas down? I was running a little late but you should know that I was gone have some shit ready for you." I laughed.

We walked towards the back of the apartments. Lonnie handed me a wad full of money and I handed him a grocery bag I had gotten out of the trunk. Lonnie was in good with a middle-aged base head named Tina. Most of the time she would let them come crash upstairs or keep the stash in her apartment. In return she would get some free dope. I thought that was smart of him to involve the natives. What I didn't think was smart was the fact that he would get sexual favors from Tina as well.

"Don't shit where you eat nigga." I warned.

70

Recently he was claiming to not be fucking with her anymore. Lonnie was a true hustler who I believe loved money more than he loved pussy. Unlike my road dog Antoine who was probably laid up with some pussy. But Antoine was happy because now he was making more money without having to work harder. Hustling was on my mind through and through. Females and everything else was secondary.

Two nights later Fab-Five had hit me and told me it was done. That was all he would say over the phone. I drove over to the Dorjil's and seen him over by the recreation room. He had it set up just like he told me he would. He pulled me over to the side of an apartment patio.

"You got some more of that good shit? I need some more as soon as you can get it." He said.

He handed me a wad full of money just like Lonnie did a couple of days ago. He was grinning from ear to ear. He looked at me and told me to count it to make sure it was there. I told him I would count it later. Then I told him the same thing I told him the other day.

"It's under the passenger seat."

He was elated when he realized I had some more. I smiled as he scurried off to grab the new package. I tried to do a brief count and it looked like it was all there. I would count it in detail when I went home. He went to the side and stashed his shit and was ready to serve all over again.

A week later I drove him and two of his homeboys down to Los Angeles and treated them to a strip club. I remembered the two youngsters when I was younger but they were real young at the time. This was my way of showing them I appreciated the hustle. I had treated Lonnie and his boys to the strip club months ago. I had to get fake ID's for Chucky and Lonnie's cousin Chris. Fabian's crew had to go to Barbary Coast because they were barely eighteen and the Barbary Coast didn't serve any liquor. We had fun until the club closed. One of the girls stayed in a city called Rancho Cucamonga, which was close to San Bernardino. She

71

thought I was cute. She could also tell that I had money to burn. Her stage name was Princess but her real name was Nakia.

6
FAMILY WOES

Stop smiling, cause still don't nothing move but the money!
Rakim

The first thing I did was set up Princess with an apartment in her name. All I did was pay her rent and she would pay her own utilities. She was living at home with her mother before she started fucking with me. I would fuck her every now and then but she was really someone for business. My only problem with her was that she was a sex addict. Every time she was home unless she was on her period she wanted to have sex. It got to the point where I would cook the dope at her house when I knew she was at work. That was where I kept the dope. I kept a bulk of my stash money with Vanessa who still didn't want a relationship with me. She would always tell me that she loved me and we would make love every now and then but she didn't want more than that. She was the one I would assign to changing the money into one hundred dollar bills. She would take fifty to a hundred thousand dollars and cash them all in for one hundred dollar bills. This way the money was easy to store and it could eliminate any marked bills by narcotics agents. It was her idea. By this time I was getting three bricks from Big Black and still buying two from King James.

As for Janice, after a few months she had moved in with me at my place in Colton. She had graduated from school and had plans to work at her cousin's shop.

"Why don't you open your own shop? Then you can set it up the way you want to. You can even name it what you want to." I suggested.

"Where am I going to get the money to have my own shop?" She asked.

"You look for a building you like and I'll worry about the money. If you want a shop anywhere just tell me and we'll check it out." I replied.

She was elated after hearing that. She had a facial expression as though the wheels were turning in her head. She put her index finger on her mouth while she thought.

"I got a few homegirls that would love to work at a shop with me. We all got clientele that come to us from the school already. This shit is gone be off the chain." She giggled.

"You gone think of a name?" I asked.

"I'll think of something sexy but classy. Oooh baby this is going to be a dream come true." She hugged me.

She got up from the bed to get a pen and pad. I yelled to her not to forget to start looking for a building. It wasn't a problem for me to pay rent on a shop that I could wash my money through. I had it all figured out. Since she was the girl my mother chose for me then she would be my squeaky clean girl. The one that all my legitimate shit would go through.

About three or four nights later I was lying up in Stacy's bed. We had just got through fucking when she started complaining. She felt that I wasn't spending enough time with her. She was complaining in a playful whining sound that irritated the fuck out of me. I didn't want to be bothered with her bullshit especially after I busted a nut.

"Seriously, Sherwin why don't you spend more time with me? We can have all kind of fun together. You just got to give a bitch a chance. You sure liking fucking me when we're together." She commented sharply.

I sat up in the bed looking at her. She was a beautiful creature in the standards of many men. She had all the physical equipment that would make most men wife her.

"You don't want to know why I don't spend time with you. You just want the time without the truth." I commented nonchalantly.

"That's Bullshit!" She exclaimed. "I do want to know the truth why you won't take the time for me. I think you and I would be a bomb couple."

"What else do you have to offer me but some pussy?" I remarked.

It was a question but it was said more like a statement. She glanced at me with surprise and awe.

"Every woman in my life plays some kind of roll besides fucking me. She might be fucking me but she definitely is doing something else. What else can you bring to the table that's gone make me say you should be my bitch?" I calmly replied.

"Who the fuck is you to be asking what I'm bringing to the table? I'm bringing *me* to the table. Everything I am is coming to the table nigga." She fired back.

I remained calm knowing that she couldn't handle the truth. I wanted her to hear it in a harsh way so it would have the effect that it did. She would at least have to ponder on that question if not now but later. I figured her arrogance would prevent her from thinking on it now.

"What is everything you are? Tell me what it is about you besides the way you look that makes you the one in my life?" I arrogantly replied.

"Who are you that I should make you the one in my life?" She lashed back.

"I'm not asking to be the one in your life, you are asking me to be the one in your life. But that poses another question. If you don't know why I should be the one in your life then why do you think we would be good together?"

"Fuck it then Winnie? If you don't see what I see then forget about it." She surrendered.

"My name is Sherwin or you can call me Pooh." I sharply replied.

"I don't give a damn what they call you. I just heard that they call you Winnie sometimes."

"Who told you that?"

"I don't know, um I think Karen overheard Antoine say that is what they call you."

At that point I was up and out the bed getting dressed. I had had enough of her shit. It boiled down to me not trusting her.

"Damn Sherwin you just gone up and leave? That's fucked up! We have a little disagreement and you off to one of yo other bitches."

I was practically dressed by the time she was finishing her last sentence. She ran up behind me and wrapped her arms around my waist. She started softly rubbing on me all over my stomach and chest.

"You shouldn't leave just yet baby." She said seductively.

"Just think about what I said then we can talk."

We kissed and then I gracefully walked out the door. I wanted to pick up some money from Lonnie before I went home. I knew Janice was going to have some food cooked for me. Only way I wasn't going home to that fine ass woman was if another fine ass woman called. Vanessa was the only woman that had rank over Janice when it came to being my girl. Not only was we friends but she was also someone I could go to for council. I could trust her with my money and I had known and loved her since I was a teenager. But she didn't want me as her boyfriend.

Janice was wifey material that wasn't in the game. She was the female that could keep me clean and give me a home. She could preserve the kind of environment that a household might need. My mama knew that when she chose her for me. Not to mention she fit the complexion my mother preferred.

Nakia on the other hand was the one hand washing the other girl. She was a stripper, which was the dope game for females. She probably did whatever it took to get the money she wanted. As long as she was in that game she understood why I was in my game. She was a hustler like I was a hustler, which gave me the room to do what I needed at her place. She got a financial benefit while I got a stash spot apartment in her name. We were all a family and everyone had a roll to play.

The following morning I had linked up with Fab Five to pick up some money. My sister was at my mother's house when I pulled up. I noticed the Lexus in the parking stall as I got out the car. I wanted to holler at Fab-Five but I didn't see my sister that often so I went inside. My mother was at work so I knew we would have a chance to talk alone. We really hadn't had a chance to really do that since I had gotten out.

It was daytime but it was dark inside my mother's apartment. Sharon had the blinds closed and it appeared as though she was sitting in the dark. She smiled when I walked in the door. It looked as though she had been crying when I had gotten closer. My first thought was that she had just fought Marcus. They probably had an argument because he knew better not to hit my sister. I sat at the dinner table while her head was lowered.

"What's up Sharon, you alright?"

"Yeah Winnie, I'm just having some domestic issues that's all."

"You and Marcus got into a fight?"

"Naw nothing like that. He lost his job and we supposed to get married in six months. He was making sixty thousand dollars a year and unemployment ain't shit. If I tell mama she gone be on some I told you so. Just because he ain't light enough for her tastes."

"Then don't tell mama then."

"We can't afford that apartment and the car note with the money we bringing in. We might have to move in her apartment. She got a three bedroom and we will be needing a place to stay soon."

"Go ahead and stay in the apartment you are staying in. Here is five thousand dollars to hold you for a while. Tell Marcus to get at me so we can talk." I replied.

"Winnie I'm not trying to get Marcus in the game. He's a straight-laced nigga that done fell on some hard times. We about to get married and everything." She shook her head.

"C'mon Sharon I'm not about to put him in the game. I'll have him doing legal shit for me and I will pay him for it. That way if anything goes down I can keep him out of it. Just until he finds another job." I explained.

Her face lit up. She got up from the table and hugged me. My sister was my best friend. We were born on the same day and everything. I sure in the hell wasn't about to let her fall to the wayside. I peeled her off five grand and then we talked about other things. She told me that she had gotten a letter from our cousin Melvin. He was glad to hear that I had gotten out of jail and he was hoping to get out soon. Melvin was a cold piece of work when it came to shooting a nigga. I wondered what page he would be on once he got out this time.

We talked for a little while then I went to get paid by Fabian. He was ready for me when I walked up. He was selling quickly. I wondered to myself why King James hadn't never really tried to set up over here. I was glad that he didn't. The Nation of Islam used to be over here real tough back in the day so he probably always thought it was unsafe territory. I hadn't seen the Muslim brothers over here since I had gotten out. Things had changed a lot while I was in jail.

Later that day when I visited Lonnie on Mt. Vernon he looked perturbed. He was noticeably angry about something. My first thought was to give him space but I looked at him as family. He was leaning against the mailbox collecting money with a fucked up disposition. I strolled up on him after getting out of my car.

"What's up Pooh? I got some bread for you upstairs in the apartment." He greeted.

"What's up with you Lonnie? You look like somebody pissed you off. I know you ain't letting these crack heads fuck with yo head?"

"Naw it ain't shit like that. You could tell some shit was bothering me by just looking at a nigga?" He asked surprisingly.

"That shit is written all over your face. What's going on little homie?"

"Man this punk ass nigga from California Gardens shot my cousin Chris. He jacked him then shot him in the leg like he wasn't shit. Niggas is saying we can't push up on that nigga because he cops from King James."

"Whose this nigga you talking about? Shit I cop from King James too. So fuck that nigga if he running up on family." I sharply replied.

"You know that nigga Kay-Kay? His real name is Kevin something." He asked.

"Yeah, that nigga always robbing niggas he doesn't know. Kevin uh, uh...Kingston that's his name."

"Yeah, ole grimy dirty dick nigga that will steal a nigga's shoes. I want to serve that nigga or at least get my cousins shit back."

"What hospital yo cousin in?"

"Arrowhead Regional Center."

"We'll go visit that nigga after we done taking care of Kay-Kay." I replied.

"We might have to smoke that nigga. He don't want to give up shit, from what I heard. And we gone have to walk up in California Gardens to serve that nigga." Lonnie explained.

"I figured that much."

Once a couple of phone calls were made the homies met up in the Dorjil. I wasn't really tripping about firepower because I had been stacking up on straps. That spot on Mt. Vernon was really in Mexican territory but we were hustling over there anyway. It was easy to figure out that if enough customers start fucking with us that's gone take money out of their pocket. I just made sure when the shit went down my homies were prepared. Now we were ready to handle some other shit. This was complicated because we was going to another nigga's hood to check him. Many people done died up in the California Gardens so we had to be ready.

We rolled four deep in a five hundred dollar bucket I had bought from a crack head. I hadn't planned on using it after that night. We rolled around looking for this nigga and he was easy to find. He was serving in front of this vacant house that appeared as though they were rebuilding it. It was hard to tell in the dark. We rolled past with everybody ducking down like it was only one person in the car. Then we parked it a half block away from where he was serving. We parked close to Rio Vista Park. We made sure our straps were loaded and ready to go.

As plain as day Antoine, Lonnie and myself walked up on Kay-Kay. He had a name around the west side so he was more than likely strapped. But he stood alone on this day. We knew he had a road dog named Booby but he wasn't in the vicinity. He seen all three of us and he sort of recognized me.

"What's up nigga what can I help you with?" He spoke directly to me.

"You remember taking some shit from a little young nigga around sixteen years old the other night? You took his jewelry, his money and his Nike shoes then shot him in the leg."

"I don't know what the fuck you talking about nigga." He replied.

He started shaking nervously, which indicated he was lying. He pulled out a Newport to play off his sudden mood change.

"All we asking for is his money and his jewelry back and we on our way." I replied.

"I don't know what the fuck you talking about. You niggas need to get away from here with that shit." He growled.

"This nigga got on Chris's ring right now!" Lonnie blurted out.

Simultaneously everyone drew they straps. He was nervous and we were nervous with our weapons drawn. He had

80

three straps pointing at him while he had one pointing at Lonnie. Nobody made a move. We were at a stand still.

"Look nigga a lick is a lick. If a nigga gets caught slippin that's on him. Now ya'll might kill me but one of ya'll gone die besides me. Plus ya'll don't really want to fuck with me, I got connections." He blurted out nervously.

I knew he was referring to King James. At this point I didn't give damn about King James. This nigga just admitted to taking the homies' shit and refused to give it back. But fuck it I said out loud.

We began lowering our weapons slowly. Antoine and I did ours a little faster than Lonnie did. But when Lonnie lowered his gun a sly smile went across Kay-Kay's face. I could see the wheels turning in his head as he began to walk away from the spot. He wasn't going to let anyone catch him slippin like this again. He kept his gun somewhat pointed at us but indirectly. He wanted to have his weapon in range just in case we changed our mind. He must have thought I was referring to him when I nodded my head once.

PLAAH-PLAAH!!!

Kay-Kay's body fell to the ground. Fab-Five emerged from the back of a car shaking his head.

"I knew that nigga was gone buck." Fab-Five replied.

Lonnie was already going through his pockets and taking off the jewelry. When he was done going through his pockets he found twenty-five hundred dollars and some dope. We all looked at each other thinking he was a dumb ass nigga serving with the dope still on him. We crept away to the bucket then drove to Baseline Boulevard and dropped it on the road. I made sure that Fab-Five dropped his strap in a sewer somewhere then I gave him another one of my guns. We hopped in Antoine's car then rolled back over to the Dorjil Apartments.

Once in the Dorjil's everyone went his separate way. I decided to go home to Janice. I didn't walk in the door until one in the morning. The house smelled good from her cooking some lasagna. She was sound asleep when I peaked into the bedroom.

On the dining room table there was a bunch of notes and ideas she had jotted down. It felt good to know that she was taking this beauty salon so serious. I shuffled through her notes and read what it said at the top.

"THE PLEASURE PALACE beauty salon."

When I said the name aloud it sounded really good. I smiled to myself seeing things coming into fruition. I was really pleased with what she had done.

"I found a building near the Carousel Mall." She softly replied.

"Damn Janice, you caught me off guard. I thought you were asleep."

"I was…but I heard you come in and woke up. Let me fix you something to eat." She walked past me towards the kitchen.

"Is it nice?"

"It's my lasagna; you always liked it as far as I know." She looked puzzled.

"No, I'm talking about the building for the Pleasure Palace."

"Oh, yeah it needs some work but it will do. The rent is twenty-five hundred a month."

"I can handle that."

"I swear I should be able to pay rent with the clients within a month. I even plan to have a barber in my shop. I'm going to have a room for pedicures and facemasks. I'm even thinking about hiring a masseuse." She gleefully explained while fixing me a plate.

I figured life had a few problems but everything would eventually work out if you prepared for the bad. I made love to Janice that night after she talked to me about her dreams. I had some worries on my mind because things were going good but I knew a storm was brewing. People in my family had problems but I was expecting some problems of my own to come knocking at my door. But soldiers overcome I thought. Let me brace myself for the seven skinny cows that are going to devour the seven fat cows. All the signs were there so I knew it was coming. Just when and how was the question.

7

SAVING HIS MONEY

You gotta learn how to shake them snakes nigga!
2Pac

The wind blew hard against the windowsill of King James' office. He was slightly more irritated than usual. He had just learned that morning that one of his hustlers was killed last night. He held his chin in his hand feeling that valley breeze of San Bernardino weather come through his window. It was hard to put someone in the spot where he had Kay-Kay posted. Kay-Kay wasn't much of a hustler but more like a thief. But he had enough respect where he could serve in the California Gardens without someone running up on him. Someone finally got the heart to kill him though. What bothered King James was he knew that it would be difficult trying to pinpoint who killed him. He did so much dirt that it was no telling. He had his people seeking out information but he knew it was probably useless. People didn't speak up on murders. Plus if the person that killed him knew he was copping from King James he might fear the consequences. There were no suspects but at the same time there were plenty of suspects.

His information came from a few different sources but he had sent Boom-Boom to find out for real. Boom-Boom walked into the office looking as if he had lost a friend. For a few moments the two friends didn't say anything. It was written all over Boom-Boom's face. He sighed as if to surrender while leaning against the doorframe of the office.

"That nigga is just as dead as they say he is. Someone said they seen four niggas walking away from the scene. They supposedly jumped into a raggedy Toyota Tercel or something that looked like one. I'm telling you James it could have been anybody that smoked that nigga."

"I'm knowing. I thought our name carried enough weight that niggas would stay off him though. Shit but I remember when niggas was scared shitless when you mentioned the name Macon. Now that name doesn't hold any weight. I guess niggas is trying to test me now." King James replied.

He had to show some flex to somebody so niggas would know he was still for real. He lifted his head up from the desk and smiled.

"We gone serve some nigga for that shit. I don't know who just yet but somebody gone make a mistake we start hurting some niggas." King James said.

"Yeah but that nigga Kay-Kay was soon to have someone run up on him. We probably shouldn't jump on niggas until we know who and why. Kay-Kay crossed the wrong nigga that's all." Boom-Boom retorted.

"Fuck that though! Everybody on the west side knew he was connected to us so if we don't light somebody up they gone think anybody copping from us can get smoked. We got to raise some panic. That is what makes niggas talk. It also makes niggas make mistakes."

"People dying brings about police. Now you know I'm down for whatever but I just think we need to be more specific." Boom-Boom suggested.

"Maybe you right. We might want to have a nigga checking on who hustling on the west side and see who they copping from. That way we can do a process of elimination. Rally up the troops so we can see what's going on. And get at that punk ass nigga Noony so I can holla at him." King James said.

"Foe sho!"

Boom-Boom walked out the office making calls on his cell phone. King James went back to sorting out his paper work for his real estate business. It was only a front but every now and then he had to do some work. He didn't mind as long as he was preoccupied with other things besides the dope game. He had his head into his paperwork when he finally got tired of the hard wind. He stood up to close the window when he heard the door swing open from behind him. He quickly turned around to reach for his large King James Holy Bible.

"What you grabbing for that thing for? You ain't about to read shit in it." Latrice came waltzing in.

Latrice was his beautiful wife. She was drop dead gorgeous to many. She had hazel eyes, a golden brown complexion, pretty thick lips and the body of a goddess. She had been pregnant three times by King James but she could never come to full term in her pregnancy. She was Mrs. Sophisticated with her constant wearing of high heels and form fitting dresses. King James couldn't remember a time ever seeing his wife wear pants or jeans. She always carried herself like a lady. Except for her mouth because there were times she could curse like a sailor.

"What the fuck are you doing with all that paperwork?" She asked.

"Trying to see what's up on buying these apartments in Fontana. How you been?" He leaned over to kiss her.

"I'm doing just fine. I wanted to know if you wanted to get some lunch together then maybe we could go shopping." She replied.

"Yeah that's cool. You hear about Kay-Kay?"

"That California Gardens nigga? Naw, what happened to him?" She asked. She said it and meant it like she didn't really care.

"He got smoked last night. We don't know who did it or what the fuck for."

"Damn, I thought you was gone say the nigga got arrested or something. And ya'll don't know who did it. Boom-Boom probably gone get to the bottom of that shit."

"Yeah that's what I got him doing right now. What's up with yo cousin, she doing what she supposed to be doing?" King James inquired.

86

"Don't worry she got that nigga on lockdown. We leaving or what? We might be able to catch a movie or something." She snapped.

"Slow yo muthafuckin role on how you talking to me." King James snarled.

He stood up and reached for his coat hanging on a coat stand. Latrice looked around the office trying not to roll her eyes at her husband. She knew how to push his buttons and she knew in her heart that this wasn't the right time. Not only was she trying to get him to spoil her today but it was also a day when he found out one of his hustlers got killed. She didn't want to infuriate her already irritated husband. They walked out the door with no more quarrels. He locked up his small office and he decided to drive his Black Mercedes. Her blue Jaguar would stay in the parking lot probably until tomorrow.

Once inside the car King James put on his oldies music as usual. 'Be my Girl' from the Dramatics was playing when he started the car. Latrice turned the music down so that she could gossip to her husband. Surprisingly he rather enjoyed her gossip. It gave him insight to people and things going on in San Bernardino.

"You know I ran into Sharon day before yesterday. I forgot to tell you. I hadn't seen her in over a year. She doesn't even live in the city anymore." Latrice said.

"Sharon, Sharon?" King James attempted to remember.

"Sherwin's twin sister."

"Oh Pooh's sister Sharon. Where did you see her at?"

"Over by the carousel mall. She was checking out some building that was supposed be turned into a Beauty Salon. She invited me out for the grand opening."

"Oh for real where she get the money to start up that kind of shit?"

"I don't know but her fiancé Marcus or something like that was rolling a nice little Lexus truck so he must have some bread." She replied.

"Did you ask where Pooh was at?" King James eyed her slyly.

"You know I did. But like I expected she don't know what the hell be going on with her brother. They twins but they are totally opposite." She gossiped.

"You go down there any chance you get and see what her fiancé is into for me. Can you do that for me?" He suggested.

"That bitch ain't about to let me get in good like that with her. In high school I was two grades ahead of her so we didn't really hang out like that. It's a say hi when passing type of thing, that's it." She remarked.

King James didn't have anything to say at that point. He allowed his wife to gossip without any interruptions. He had become extra attentive when she mentioned Pooh's name. From that time on he concentrated on spending quality time with his woman. He knew once he did all the things that made them a couple for a day she would end the day with some wild sex play. He was playing his role with her for the day. She was fine as hell but he had only married her because she had gotten pregnant. King James never looked at himself as the marrying type. But it was what it was. He felt relieved that his beautiful wife was in a good mood because then she would cater to him. At least until the weekend he didn't have to worry about any other pussy.

Saturday morning King James went out to Marino Valley to visit his sister and do some shopping. Every Saturday morning Latrice would pamper herself in the morning by getting her hair, nails and feet done. She would take someone in her family or she would take one of her homegirls. Since she was preoccupied with that for most of the day he could take a little time for himself. He was into leisure suits and Alligator shoes. He always tripped off of young hustlers looking like they sold dope. Wearing sweat suits, gold chains, sneakers and white T-shirts was so stupid to him. He had his jewelry as well but it was much more discreet. He even had business cards that went along with his façade. James Stuart-Real Estate Consultant is what read on his card. He walked with his head up to reflect the regal aura that came from his 6'0 frame. He had in mind to buy him three or four outfits for himself since he had spoiled Latrice earlier in the week. It was his turn to make sure he was looking right. He never went to barber shops especially after watching a mafia documentary. It was about Albert Anastasia the boss of Murder Incorporated. Not the rap crew that Ja-Rule is in but the real Italian Murder Incorporated. This powerful boss found himself dead lying in a barbershop chair. So he always had his barber meet him at his office and he would pay him handsomely.

King James was walking out the mall when he bumped into someone. He nudged her sort of hard and she almost stumbled to the ground. He caught her hand before she could fall.

"Excuse me Ms."

"No problem!" She replied.

He looked at the pretty middle aged woman and was stunned. She was fine as hell when he glanced at her face. Her light brown face and light brown eyes left him in a daze. He could tell the way she carried herself she was either in her forties or close to it. But she didn't look a day over thirty-five. Her eyes met him and she did a once over with her eyes and smiled suggesting she liked what she saw. He smiled then decided to do the same thing with his eyes. She was amazing. She had on a brown dress with a gold-yellow belt that wrapped around her small waist. Even though the dress was to her ankles she still couldn't hide the well-rounded ass protruding from the dress. The dress was supposed to be loosely fitted but it was practically impossible for her to hide her shape. She was a middle-aged sex toy that attempted to down play her frame. Her lips were full and thick with a light glaze of lip-gloss. Her hair was a sandy brown conservative press and curl hairstyle that went about shoulder length. After she smiled his knees buckled slightly as he shuffled to put his three suits over his left arm to cover his wedding band.

"How are you? My name is James Stuart." He said.

"My name is Paula, Paula Armstrong. It is a pleasure to meet you Mr. Stuart." She replied.

"The feeling is mutual! Do you live around here?" He inquired.

"Actually I don't! I'm down here visiting a friend but I live in Victorville."

Educated and sophisticated he thought. It was a welcome change from Latrice's ghetto acting ass. His eyes kept studying different parts of her anatomy. She didn't get her nails done at a shop and if she did she made them appear as though they were naturally immaculate. Her expensive two inch closed toe heels matched her dress. She made everything look casual and easily put together. She delicately down played her dressing preparation but King James could notice the subtleness. She was a grown woman with class and poise. Her feminism was her strength as she relished in being an attractive middle-aged woman. He was captivated.

"I must admit that you are breathtaking. Your beauty, your elegance is very attractive." He said.

"Why thank you. You are quite a handsome young man yourself. How old are you, about thirty-seven, thirty-eight?" She asked.

"Isn't it impolite to ask a person over twenty-five how old they are?" King James smiled.

"It is impolite to ask a *woman* how old she is." She corrected him.

"I didn't know it only applied to women. Well if you must know I am thirty-seven like you originally said." He replied.

"Ah-hah, a young man!" She teased.

"But that shouldn't stop you from getting to know me. We can laugh talk and learn from one another sweetheart."

"That's Ms. Armstrong to you." She laughed.

"So be it Ms. Armstrong. When can you and I see each other again?"

"You are very assuming. What makes you think that I am interested in seeing you again? I've lived a pretty prosperous life thus far without you." She said.

"That is true. But it is always good to meet new friends that can revitalize your life in many different ways."

"How would you revitalize my life?"

"I can show you better than I can tell you. The next time we meet up you will see how I can revitalize your life. Everyone can always use a good friend." King James explained.

"Are you sure that is all you want to be?"

"How about we let time decide. But first we have to continue our initial contact."

She pretended to be reluctantly interested but King James knew better. Her eyes gave him every indication that she wanted him like he wanted her. Linguist say that 70% of interpersonal communication is non-verbal. Her words said one thing but her non-verbal movements said something entirely different. He entered her number into his cell phone under P. Armstrong. They spoke for a brief moment longer then he rolled out in his Mercedes.

He couldn't keep the woman off of his mind. She was something else to him in so many ways. He smiled as he got on the freeway heading back to his house. He had a grin that could have lit up the entire freeway. King James wasn't one to get too excited about a woman but she was different. Finally a woman that could teach him a thing or two. He wanted a change of environment and surrounding for himself. There were a lot of things wrong with the young women in his life. They were fresh but they were dumb about a lot of things. Now he felt like he had a chance to talk to a woman that was on his level. He was excited. It was around three o'clock in the afternoon by the time he made it back to San Bernardino. He decided to go to his commercial building he had set up like an apartment in Fontana. He had almost forgot he was supposed to meet someone there at four.

There was a shower and kitchen in his hidden spot because it used to be a restaurant/bar back in the day. He had it renovated and remodeled on the inside. Latrice didn't even know about this place. He would take females here when he needed to get away from home or the office. It wasn't too far from the house he and Latrice owned in Fontana. He had it all decked out for his other women. His other women didn't know about his house, the apartments he was buying or the office he had on the west side of San Bernardino. That was how he stayed a step ahead of everything.

When he pulled into the parking lot she was already waiting outside for him. She got out of her Black Altima switching her little ass for him to notice. She was a sexy little young bitch. She walked around as though she knew it. He unlocked the door and she waltz inside his hidden refuge. She smiled at him as he went to the bar to fix him and her some Remy Martin. It was quiet while he poured both drinks. She seemed somewhat excited as though she had something juicy to tell him. She was sitting on his brown suede couch with her legs closed as if she had to pee. He still didn't say a word. When he got over to her he handed her the drink and she took a few swallows then sat the drink on the end table. He stood in front of her sipping on his drink.

She grabbed his slack pants and unzipped his zipper and dug her hands into his crouch. She pulled out his dick and start darting her tongue on the tip. He didn't make a sound. It felt extremely good and she began to slide her lips up and down his hard on. She then made her way to his balls. He jerked his head back trying to conceal how much he enjoyed her oral sex. She stroked his dick with her hands slow and hard while her lips sucked away. Right when she thought he was nice and hard she unbuttoned his pants and unlatched his belt. His slacks dropped to the floor. She stood up while still pulling on his dick and turned around. She pulled her dress up showing that she didn't have any panties on. Then she bent over the couch and guided his dick right inside of her. King James finally moaned once he penetrated without a condom. The lust overwhelmed him to the point where he forgot about protecting himself. She started pushing her ass into his pelvis faster and harder. She wasn't slowing down one bit. King James felt himself about to cum and decided to release inside of her. Fuck it; if she gets pregnant she will probably get an abortion he thought. She felt his semen shoot inside her and she moaned loudly. King James pushed his dick inside of her a few more times before he collapsed on her back. He waited for a moment then lifted himself up. He pulled his pants up, picked up his drink and walked into the bathroom. He already had a wash towel waiting for him so he began washing up.

"So what do you got for me? You seemed excited and I know you weren't excited over some dick." He yelled from the bathroom.

"I'll wait to you get out because I want to wash up too." She replied.

Shortly after she got out of the bathroom she walked back to the bar. She went behind the bar and poured her another glass of Remy Martin. She looked around the place admiring the décor.

"When you do it big you do it really big. Latrice ain't ever mentioned this spot to me." She remarked.

"That's because she don't know about this place and don't need to know about this place. Ya hear me now?" He sharply replied.

"There are a few things that Latrice don't need to know about." She slyly grinned.

"So what were you so excited about? What is it you have to get off your chest?" King James asked.

"That nigga Pooh been ready to buy more than two bricks from you. He can probably buy five at a time. They running through that dope on Mt. Vernon." She replied.

That was some shit King James was starting to figure on his own. He knew the young nigga was probably just stacking his bread. Saving his money for a rainy day. But he knew two ways how to fix the young nigga. He was going to first get the Mexicans over there on Mt. Vernon to give him some problems then force him to take more bricks on consignment through Antoine's weak ass. She gave him time to let the revelation marinate. She sat quietly looking at him like she had just revealed the word of God.

"Did that dumb nigga say anything else? Did he say anything that Pooh might be up to? And how is your homegirl Stacy doing with that nigga Pooh?" He pried.

"She hit a brick wall with that nigga. She said they got into a big argument about she don't do anything for him but give him some pussy. He told her that he needs a woman that does more for him than just that. She ain't spoke to the nigga since." She retorted.

"Okay well you need to tell that young bitch to put her emotions to the side and get back in with that nigga. You understand?" King James replied.

"Okay James but why you worried about that nigga anyway? He ain't a threat to you. He even cops his shit from you." She remarked.

"Look Karen some niggas got potential to be problems and I don't need any problems. You keep doing what you doing and you know I will take care of you."

"I know. I got that nigga Antoine wrapped around my finger though. That nigga done told me he loved me twice. I always go along with that bullshit." She laughed.

"How you know he's not feeding you bullshit? Are you wearing a condom when you be fucking that nigga?"

He just fucked the nasty bitch and he wanted to consider it now. She nodded her head like he should know better. He was still skeptical. But his mind quickly jumped to him wondering why Pooh has only been taking two bricks bi-weekly when he knew he could take at least four. If he was just saving his bread he could have bought a lot more than two and doubled his money. His head began to hurt.

"What is that young nigga up to?" He inadvertently said aloud.

Karen recognized it as a rhetorical question and was wise enough to be quiet. She continued drinking her Remy Martin allowing his mind to wander. After rubbing his eyes a few times he looked up.

"Is that all he said about Pooh and that Mt. Vernon spot?"

"He says all kinds of shit at different times. He is real open with me especially after we have been fucking. He pillow talks so much that I be feeling like I'm a psychologist."

"You mean a psychiatrist?" King James corrected her.

"Whatever, all I know is I'm the one that he wants to tell all his problems to. He even thinks that nigga Pooh must have said something to you to make you not want to deal with him anymore."

Now this was getting juicy King James thought. He probably can use that to his advantage. Maybe get them niggas to turn on each other if need be. But he knew that Pooh was probably carrying Antoine. Antoine wasn't a real hustler he was a pussy chaser. When he gave it a second thought he couldn't see Antoine turning on a nigga that was feeding him.

"Is that all you could remember?" He continued to pry.

"Not that I can think of really. When I get some more shit for you I will let you know." Karen promised.

"Okay sweetheart." King James surrendered.

Karen began walking out the door after gulping down the rest of her Remy Martin.

"You welcome Daddy…Oh yeah I forgot to mention he said something about him and his homeboys had to serve a nigga for stealing one of the little homies' shit. He didn't say what he meant by that but he told me this the other night. It probably don't mean shit to you but that's all I can remember." Karen said.

She waived goodbye while walking out the swing door. King James quickly walked up to lock the door behind her. He was actually stunned about her last revelation. The puzzle was coming together. He could see Pooh having the heart to smoke Kay-Kay because it probably involved business. Pooh wasn't a stone cold killer but he was the type of nigga that would do what it takes to get shit done. This King James knew to be true. He would have to get with Boom-Boom early in the morning for some plans. He sat back on his suede couches thinking about everything. Pooh, Antoine, Karen and what brought pleasure to his heart was the thought of Paula. Ms. Paula Armstrong.

8

LOVE AND LUST

All I did was shook it off, yeah you heard me shook it off!
DMX

Antoine wanted to meet with me as quickly as possible. I didn't have any idea what was so urgent but I rushed over there as soon as I woke up. I had my phone off because Stacy had been calling me a lot lately. It was becoming a problem because Janice was looking at me funny. The grand opening for her shop was coming up and I wanted our relationship to be smooth. We weren't having any problems as of yet but I didn't want to make waves. Marcus had made sure everything was up to code. He set up the business license and all the details to everything she might need. To keep it on the safe side I put it in Janice and Sharon's name. At first Janice was against the idea but I told her I didn't want my name on anything just in case the police got to knocking. I believe she would have preferred my mother instead but I went with whom I preferred.

When I knocked on Antoine's door he was half sleep. He opened the door with his hair matted and sleep in his eyes. We were suppose to hang out today anyway so I was there early. I had picked up some coffee and donuts from Winchells before I arrived.

"What's up nigga? You called me three times last night leaving messages and shit. I come by here early and you sound asleep. It's nine in the morning and you ain't even chasing after the worm." I teased.

"Whatever nigga pass me some of them donuts." He replied with a deep morning voice.

"What was so important that you had to holler at me last night?"

97

"Boom-Boom called me in to meet with King James last night around eight at night. Karen had just gave me some pussy then that nigga Boom-Boom started blowing my phone up about fifteen minutes after she left. So I threw some shit on wondering what the fuck was going on. So I called your cell phone to see what was up. You wasn't picking up so I said fuck it and went over there by myself." Antoine explained while sipping on his coffee.

I knew what he was about to tell me but I had to hear him say it for some reason. I stood there captivated hanging on his every word.

"So what happened when you got there nigga?" I impatiently asked.

"He asked me about business and how was the spot on Mt. Vernon. I told him it was cool but he said he heard that it was cracking. I tried to downplay what we were moving but he wouldn't hear of it. He then dropped two bricks on the table for consignment. I tried to tell him we wasn't ready man but he wouldn't take no for an answer." Antoine replied.

He had a pathetic look on his face. I loved him but he was a weak nigga I thought. I let what I was feeling for the first time charge through my body without suppressing it. I had out grown my road dog Antoine. But I still had love for him so I would have to swallow his weakness for the time.

"So we gone move that shit or what?" He asked.

"Where is it at right now?"

"I got it in the trunk of my car. It ain't been cooked yet or nothing. It's raw!" Antoine replied.

"Keep it in the car and we will deal with that shit later. Get dressed and we will roll in my car."

"Where we rolling to now?" Antoine asked while walking in the bathroom.

"We are going to look for you a new apartment. We should probably look over near Cal State for a nice one bedroom."

"What the fuck is wrong with where I'm at right now?"

98

He sounded dumbfounded when he asked me that. I just waved my hand for him to hurry up and take a shower. When he got out the shower he sat in the living room getting dressed.

"Look my nigga, don't let anyone know where you live once you get into this new apartment. Especially that Karen broad." I suggested.

"Why not?"

"Because she knows you in the game and she ain't who you gone be with. If you pull a female into your household make sure she is a square broad or a female that you have known all your life. You have known this female for more than six months and you don't even know where she lives. She always comes to yo house. Find a female that goes to school or some shit like that. But don't let a female like Karen know everything about you. That's why we moving because you don't know who King James got watching you right now." I explained.

"You think he got someone watching me?"

"How did he know when to call you last night? Someone must have seen Karen leave yo house so they knew when to hit you."

"You don't think it's Karen that told King James do you?" Antoine asked with disbelief.

"That hoodrat bitch wouldn't know anything about a nigga like King James. And King James wouldn't waste his time with a hoodrat like Karen. He just probably got someone watching the spot but since you stay so close they're probably watching you too."

He finally got dressed after an hour and a half. He always took his time about getting dressed. That was one thing about Antoine that I would never outgrow was his ability to dress. We were both considered pretty boys but he was much more delicate about his dress than me. I would copy a lot of his styles to blend in with his flavor but I made sure niggas knew I didn't have the heart of a pretty boy. I looked good but I wasn't a nigga to be running up on.

99

We checked out three apartments in the Cal State area, which was right next to the San Bernardino Mountains. I wanted him to leave the city or away from the West Side. Once we found a place he liked he put the money down for it and we went shopping.

"I should probably move all my furniture at night huh?" He asked out the blue.

"Naw nigga leave that shit there and buy you some fresh shit. Only thing you should take is yo clothes and that flat screen."

"That furniture is new my nigga?" He retorted.

"Yeah but you can get some new shit for the new place. Get you a little cute female to help you design the spot." I appealed to his lust.

"Yeah I met this square female that goes to UC Riverside. She majors in communications. She fine then a muthafucka my nigga. I met her mama and everything and she on the up and up. That's a little winner I can fuck with for real, you know what I'm saying?"

"Yeah I feel you. It's good to know her background like I did with Janice." I said while eating French fries.

We were in the food court at the Riverside Galleria mall. It was a place where a lot of white people hung out. It was cool for both of us because we were away from the drama.

"But I'm gone miss fucking Karen. You don't think that I should let that bitch ever come over to my new apartment?" He slightly pleaded.

"If you feel you got to fuck with her take her to a hotel. Tell her that you staying with some people that ain't too cool with company. If she can't role with that then fuck the bitch. That's how I did her homegirl Stacy who been calling me a lot lately. What's that shit about?"

"Karen told me she been asking about you. You should hit a few more times because she got a bomb ass body." He lustfully replied.

"Yeah but all pussy ain't good pussy." I snapped back.

100

"If you get burned or something but I know you strapping on condoms tight when you hit that right?"

"It ain't just that though. She pretends like she is really needy when she fucks with me but I know better than that. She ain't the needy type. But she puts on this act for me when I know niggas is lining up to get at her. It makes me think she up to something." I replied with disgust in my tone.

"You ain't got to trust her but you can still hit a few more times."

We both started laughing. It was a bittersweet laughter for me because I knew what Antoine loved. Most men did. But I had to read between the lines if I was going to survive. I tried my best to help him see between the lines because I had love for him. But for the most part we had a good time together. We headed back to the spot on Mt. Vernon to see what was going on with Lonnie.

When I pulled up Lonnie looked as if he was relieved to see me. I smiled when I got out the car. His cousin Chris was out the hospital and helping him to serve. Lonnie walked up to me as though he had something important to tell me. Sometimes I wondered why they never went to Antoine because this used to be his spot alone. But I would always rethink this complaint knowing what I knew about Antoine.

"Ay Pooh, let me holla at you for a minute?" Lonnie whispered.

What the hell was the problem now? We just got through taking care of some shit and now something else came up. Nevertheless I smiled as though I wasn't worried about shit. We backed away from Antoine, Chucky and Chris then headed towards the back of the apartments. He didn't waste any time once we made it to the back.

"Some Mexicans is tripping about our spot. They claim we taking their business from them and something is gone have to be done." Lonnie said.

He was a little startled behind the whole ordeal. It was understandable since we were really in their territory. This issue

101

kind of bothered me but I chose to ignore it for the time since no problems had arose. He looked at me as though I was the problem solver. I knew that I couldn't let him down. My head was down as I pondered on the new dilemma.

"When did they say they was coming back?" I asked.

"I told him that we ain't trying to beef but I ain't the nigga to get at. I didn't put you on blast so I just suggested he comes back tomorrow so we can talk about this shit. He wasn't fucked up about it but they were strapped. I think since I was cool about it they didn't trip either but they were ready…if you want us to ride on the essays then we can but I didn't want to make the spot hot and not check with you." He explained.

I liked how level headed the young nigga was. Niggas his age would have let they ego get the best of them but he thought first. He probably thought about the money we would lose if it got too hot.

"You did good! What time are they coming through and I will get at them."

"He said around three or four. I don't think he wanted to give an exact time because he didn't know what we were up to." He replied.

It made sense to me. Tomorrow would be good for me because I had plans to meet with Big Black later on tonight. Antoine still didn't have any idea that I was copping from another nigga besides King James. But my decision not to tell him was confirmed when he let King James give him those two bricks.

I met with Big Black later on that night around midnight. He was in a good mood. We had begun having small talk here and there and overall he was a real cool muthafucka. He was extremely cautious though. He would give me pointers from him being in the game for so long.

"Most niggas in the game longer than five years is working for the police. Ya own homeboys will turn on you over money, pussy or jail time. Niggas don't have a code." He would repeat.

I was buying so many from him that he was giving them to me for fifteen five on most days. He had major love for my uncle Ace.

"That's a real muthafucka. When I was yo age he would school me to shit like I'm schooling you." He would say.

This night I had a lot on my mind. Figuring that he could help me I talked to him real. He always listened with respect.

"I'm gone be needing some artillery real soon. You know where I can get a hold of some shit that can back some essays off of me?" I asked.

He looked at me and noticed the perplexity in my facial expression. I tried to smile hoping to down play the urgency. He appreciated that.

"Don't go to the gun too fast. But if you need to I'll take care of you in about three days from now, some Mexicans ain't got no problem killing a Mayate. Tell me what you looking for and I'll get it for you." He replied.

"Some real heavy artillery with a few automatic hand guns and that should be enough." I replied.

"Be careful young hustler. I'll get the straps but be careful. I been in wars before and they don't ever bring money. But they bring jail time. I did eight years for manslaughter back in the day. They at first tried to charge me for a murder one charge but they dropped it to manslaughter. We was beefing with some slobs on the East Side. East Side of L.A. that is. Ya'll San Bernardino niggas sympathize with the Damus (Bloods) huh?" He asked out of the blue.

"It's Crips and Bloods in San Bernardino but I try to stay out of that shit. I'm down with getting paid." I sincerely replied.

"I hear that nigga. It always boils down to what you love. Some niggas love money, some niggas love pussy and some niggas love fighting. But what makes wars dangerous is that most niggas is willing to fight to survive. You can back a coward against a wall and he'll start swinging. The first law of nature is to survive and that what makes a nigga dangerous. So I'm saying all that to say that when I get you these guns you consider if you the one backing someone against a wall. And if not still see if you got yo back against the wall. That's the only time you should be pulling out yo strap. Don't let the lust for power make you lose what you love. You hear me cuz?"

I nodded. But at this point I knew I would need those guns. I appreciated the advice though. My back wasn't against the wall but I wanted to be ready if it got there. The way Big Black carried himself was a clear indication he had been in some wars. A wise old soldier was what he was. Ace warned me that Big Black still had that Crippin in him. But only in mannerisms and disposition did you see that old gangster come out. He had some wisdom that young hustler should heed. The words resonated and he allowed it to do such. It was an unspoken mutual admiration we had. My reasons were the fact that he had been in the game for so long but hadn't been compromised. His principles were in tack. His admiration for me was the wisdom I had for my age. He would compliment me here and there. Somehow I had managed to impress him. It couldn't have been an easy feat to impress a man that's been in the game more than twenty years. I bought six kilos from him this time around. Business was good and he could tell. He had to realize that I wouldn't fuck up a cash cow unless there was no choice but to. We shook hands as usual and went our separate ways.

The next day I called up Fab-Five to meet me over at the spot on Mt. Vernon. He hung with me for most of the day. Especially from two to six in the afternoon was when I wanted him around. A little bit after three was when three essays walked up on us. I seen them walking up about a block away. It was obvious that they had straps on them. They were attempting to hide them under their big button up shirts and long khakis pulled up to their stomach. They were Cholos for sure. I didn't really worry about it because I knew we were just as strapped as them. Fabian was ready to let the triggers go but I told him that I wanted to talk to them first. They walked up with as much bravado as one could have with a gun. They calmed down slightly when they seen everyone standing out front ready for anything. It was Fab-Five, Antoine, Lonnie, Chucky, Chris and me posted out in front of the apartments. The one with the blue khakis on was the first to speak.

"Which one of you I need to talk to homes?" He asked firmly.

"I'm the one you need to talk to." I replied.

I reached out to shake his hand. He was reluctant at first so he glanced down at my hand. He looked up at me and seen the disarming facial expression and agreed to shake hands.

"Let's you and I talk in the back about yo problems." I suggested.

"Wait a minute homes..." The one in brown khakis said.

I was nervous for a second but tried not to show it. Why in the fuck is he stopping us from talking. I looked around at my homeboys but none of them were fired up. Not even Fab-Five was in an attack mode. I slowly turned around to face the second Cholo and see what the problem was.

"Didn't you go to Cajon back in the day homes? Your name is Sherwin something from the West Side. You used to run with this fool." He pointed toward Antoine.

"Yeah, we both went to Cajon. Now that I think about it you do look familiar."

"Yeah, ya'll was the pretty boys at the school. Me and you had Mrs. Davis together for English homes." He said to me.

"Snap, that is you from English. Gangster Oscar Magana, we used to clown in the back of the class all the time. What's up fool?" I replied with enthusiasm.

I walked over to him and we embraced. We were both genuinely glad to see each other. This lightened up the mood tremendously. At this point I had invited all three of the Cholos to come back to meet with me. My homeboys had stayed in front of the apartments looking out.

They told me that they had been getting rumors that some Mayates were moving into their hood. The rumor was that we was

105

moving weight and trying to push them out. I couldn't believe the bullshit when I heard it. I told them that we had been hustling at this spot for months without trying to cause problems. When we were finished talking they were talking about copping from me. I told Oscar that if he makes sure that we don't have any problems that I would give them a whole bird for sixteen even. They were going to L.A. getting them for seventeen-five to eighteen even. They were a little ways away from the Mt. Vernon spot so we weren't really stepping on anyone's toes. But when they heard some Black dudes was trying to take over they had to see what was up. Oscar and I did some reminiscing for a while and they were gone. I told him to have the sixteen ready in a few days and I will have the bird ready for them. And that was the end of that.

I had contacted Big Black and he had the guns ready for me. He also had that extra brick that I had asked for. He took me through the motions of changing clothes this time. He didn't bother with it the last time. I figured he didn't want me to get too comfortable whenever he was in a good mood. He was cool this time around but he made sure to let me know he was still sharp and on guard. He had some heat for me though. I was making five hundred dollars off the brick he sold me because he still gave me the price of fifteen-five. I promised myself I would buy something nice. He laid the weapons out on the bed and gave me a flat rate for everything. I had two tech nines, a sub-machine Uzi and seven assorted handguns. From nine millimeters to six shot thirty-eight pistols. With all those weapons lying on the bed I thought to myself was it worth it. Big Black must have caught the look.

"You still think you need all this shit?" He blankly asked.

"I might need this shit real soon. I'll keep it close by then bring it out if it is really needed." I replied.

"Well don't get to showing yo homeboys this shit until it's needed. Niggas find reasons to need it when it's staring them in the face. You know what I mean?" He said with conviction.

"I feel what you saying."

He gave me a nice sized duffle bag to put everything in. He dropped me off at my car and he took off. Once everything was stashed away in the trunk I stood outside to puff on a cigarette. I was already getting tired about what came with the game.

The oldies station was playing Stevie Wonder's 'Ribbon in the Sky' on my way back to Nakia's house. She liked it when I called her Princess. Her apartment had a little storage room I planned to put all the guns in. I wasn't going to cook the raw dope for Oscar and them. I wanted him to get it raw at first then if he wanted me to cook it I would. But they probably knew how to cook it themselves anyway. I just didn't want them to think I stepped on they dope. They had plans to meet up with me the next day.

After everything was put into the storage space I contemplated going up to see Princess. I wasn't in the mood but I went upstairs against my better judgment. When I walked into the house I could hear the music playing from inside the bathroom. She was playing Mary J. Blige with the door wide open. She heard me walk inside the house.

"Sherwin is that you?" She yelled.

"Yeah it's me. Soaking in some suds huh? Ain't anything wrong with that." I yelled from the kitchen.

"I'll be out in a minute." She yelled back.

I didn't pay her any mind. I was tired and I didn't expect to be there that long.

"I was able to get five of my homegirls to do that party for you when yo cousin get out." She yelled again.

"That's real cool. Tell them to give him whatever he wants and I will take care of them." I replied.

"Shit they are already knew that when I told them. How long you say yo cousin been locked up, ten years?"

"Yeah something like that." I said.

I had grabbed some juice from out the refrigerator and was sipping on it when she walked into the living room. All the lights were out and she had the candles going all over the house. She was on that aromatherapy vibe. She walked into the living room totally naked and oiled down with Body Oil. Her pretty golden brown complexion glowed from the reflections of the candlelight. She knew what she was doing. Her plump ass shining while the nipples on her titties were hard and perky. For that moment my troubles went away. She walked into the kitchen and opened up the refrigerator. While the refrigerator was open she bent over trying to find something to either eat or drink. Be cool Sherwin, be cool. I hadn't fucked her in a few weeks because our schedule was too different. At least that was how I made it seem. I fed her some story about me having to have a job to satisfy my parole officer. I had my sister to make up check stubs so I could show my Parole Officer a long time ago. But as far as she knew I worked during the day. I knew she was off today because I had seen her car when I went to put the straps in storage.

She smiled at me as she arched her walk so that she would only be walking on the palms of her feet. She walked past me with her ass switching and everything. She wanted me to chase after her. I got up from the table and walked over towards her. By the time I had made it over there she was lying on the couch with her feet on top of the coffee table. Her legs were crossed while she playfully sipped on her water. I wanted to fuck her bad at this point. She knew it.

I sat next to her on the couch and began rubbing on her legs. Then I began kissing on her neck and sucking her perky nipples. She lifted her hands up in ecstasy with the water bottle still in her hand. I worked my lips from her neck to her belly button. Little twirls of my tongue on her belly button and she was lifting my face up to kiss her. We started passionately kissing with hard lip sucking. She began tugging at my clothes. I backed away from her to quickly undress. Once I was totally naked she wrapped her mouth around my dick. She began moaning loudly as if she was having an orgasm from giving me head. I pushed her back against the couch and she gave a joyful shriek.

"Be rough with me nigga!"

There was no need to respond. I spread her legs to opposite ends of the couch and plunged right in. She shrieked again once I penetrated. I held her legs out at her shins and beat it down. That was just the way she wanted it too. Then I picked her up and let her ride me while I stood up holding her ass and legs. I took her into the room and finished my deed with a bang. She had cum at least twice. I was tired. I got dressed and left an envelope on the bedpost.

"This is for rent this month and a little extra to do something special." I replied.

She smiled without saying a word. I smoked some Cush with her then got dressed and headed home. I knew Janice would be home sleep by now so I crept in quietly. Her grand opening for the salon was coming up soon. She was tiring herself out about the whole ordeal. It was a serious business for her while it was a way to clean my money to me. But whatever made her happy was good to me. There was love there no doubt.

9
COLLISION COURSE

But this is worse than the Dow Jones, ya brains is now blown, all over that brown brome, one slip you are now gone!
Jay-Z

The phone rang on my home phone around eight in the morning. I usually didn't rise until nine. Janice was already up and about so she answered the phone. I was still slightly sleep when she came in the room and tossed me the phone. She was still upset with me coming home late in recent times. She didn't say anything until I asked her who was on the phone.

"It sounds like Ant. Why don't you pick up the phone and find out." She snapped.

I picked up the cordless half sleep in my deep morning voice. It had to be Antoine because he was the only one besides my cousin who had the home number. Everyone else had the cell phone. I just recently told my sister to tell Melvin he could call collect.

"Damn nigga she mad at you. What you did yo ass do now? Fuck another bitch or something?" Antoine began.

"Coming home too late."

"Quit telling my business to yo friends Winnie." Janice yelled from in the bathroom

I ignored her because I wanted to hurry up and end the conversation on the phone.

"What's up nigga? What you doing calling me this early in the morning?" I asked.

"I was calling to tell you King James wants his bread. He been blowing me up about his money for the last two days." Antoine warned.

I could hear fear in his voice over the phone. You would think that he knew this was coming because I told him. You would think that he was prepared for some kind of backlash since the dope had been sitting in his trunk for the last two weeks. I didn't say a word and allowed the phone to remain quiet for a few seconds.

"Pooh you there my nigga?"

"Yeah I'm here. You didn't think that he was gone put pressure on us once we took his dope on consignment. It's been two weeks and you still ain't caught on that he gone want his money." I lashed out.

Then it got quiet because it just dawned on me that either one of our phones could be tapped. The home phone was in Janice's name because I always used my cell phone. But I didn't know what was going on with Antoine's phone.

"Look nigga, holla at me in about an hour and a half so we can talk. We gone meet at that place. You know the one we like." I replied hoping he would catch the hint.

"Oh for sure my nigga."

The fast food restaurant I was talking about was Baker's fast food on Mt. Vernon across the street from San Bernardino Valley College. Now that I was awake I started stumbling out of bed. Janice had peeked in when she heard me yelling at Antoine. I walked into the bathroom and came up behind her while she was pressing her hair in the mirror.

"You gone stop being mad at me or what? Come on Janice you know you my baby I just have to handle business late at night." I replied.

"I ain't mad about the coming in late I'm mad about the perfume I smelled when you came in." She replied while I nibbled on her neck.

111

"Ah that wasn't shit. I seen my homegirl from the Dorjil's and that was her perfume. We hadn't seen each other since I had been out so we hugged. You paranoid. I am too busy to be worrying about chasing pussy. I know what I got at home." I lied.

It felt like idiots surrounded me. She had to know that different women came with the game. These females get with a nigga with money from hustling and they expect us to be faithful. Cheating comes with the territory. But it also was the fact that some of the women in my life had roles to play. But keeping up the façade was part of the game also. I never tried to disrespect her.

"Next time you better tell yo homegirl not to wear perfume when she hugging my man." She playfully pouted.

That let me know that she wasn't tripping anymore. But she was only cool about it because she wanted to know what I was yelling at Antoine about. Her being nosy superseded her being jealous.

"What were you yelling at Antoine about? Ain't that yo best friend?"

That very moment I understood what Michael in 'The Godfather' felt when Kay asked him about his business. It would have been good to vent to someone about all my worries. But pillow talk can get you killed. It just wasn't a smart thing to do. So once again she forced me to lie to her.

"Naw he just pissed me off about some money he owed me. He didn't know when he was gone pay me back and it pissed me off."

"It's been two weeks now huh? Don't let money come between ya'll friendship. Mama Shirley say ya'll been close since ya'll was kids." She replied.

I loved how naïve she could be at times. In this game money can be one of the biggest of three reasons that friendships can end. Women and jail time being the other two. I kissed her goodbye but she didn't want to give me any pussy because she didn't want to sweat out her hair. She had been using the curling iron while we were talking in the bathroom. I jumped in the shower right after she left to meet up with Antoine. Some shit was common sense in my opinion. You get tired of schooling a nigga time and time again and he doesn't catch on. It would be good if people could think shit through and I could be stupid for a second.

Antoine looked nervous when I walked into Bakers. He was nibbling on some fries while his leg was shaking. It was obvious he was anticipating my arrival. I strolled up as cool as ice pretending I didn't have a worry in the world. I sat down across from him and grabbed a couple of his French fries.

"So how we gone handle this shit? Boom-Boom done called me twice since I got off the phone with you." He whispered.

He was truly paranoid. He kept looking around to see if anyone was listening. There was a Mexican couple about three tables away but they weren't paying us any attention.

"You done moved right? We gone sit on his shit and I will have a talk with him real soon. This time you ain't coming with me. Change your cell phone number so Boom-Boom can't call you." I explained.

"You gone get me killed. That nigga gone look at that shit like straight disrespect. That nigga be already doing that sex play shit with me." Antoine bitterly replied.

"Because he know you scared of him. It's one thing to respect a nigga but it's another thing to be scared of him. He knows you scared and just like a predator they attack muthafuckas they know is scared of them. Fuck that nigga and everything he stands for. If you don't change that fucking number then don't say shit else to me about him calling you."

"I ain't scared of that nigga. I just don't be wanting any bullshit. I want to make my money and be gone." Antoine replied.

"Well the next time he sex play yo ass you check him on that shit. He gots to see you as a man in order for him to respect you. You feel what the fuck I'm saying." I passionately explained.

113

"I'm knowing."

Later that day I called King James at his office. He sounded as if he was in the middle of something so I told him I'd hit him back later.

"Naw nigga, come by here tomorrow around eleven in the morning so we can talk." He commanded.

I had to glance into the phone for a moment. It bothered me that he wanted to treat me like one of his underlings because I copped from him. I had my mind made up about a couple of things. But I had to check with some of my niggas to see if they were down through and through. Some things you want to avoid though. In my heart and mind though I knew that some things were inevitable.

After hanging up the phone with King James I went over to the West Side to talk with Fab-Five in the Dorjil's. It took me about fifteen minutes to get over there but I didn't tell him I was coming. They had the Dorjil Apartments buzzing when I crept inside. It was the middle of the day and it was buzzing. Then it dawned on me that all the business that was cracking in the California Gardens had came over to us. I walked over to Fab-Five and he was grinning from ear to ear. We embraced.

"Man we got it cracking over here. I'll be sold out by tonight. I think that business we took care of helped us in more ways that one." He chuckled.

"I'm knowing. I'll bring you a fresh new package later on tonight. Be ready for me and tell yo young homies that the shit will already be chef'd and ready to work. No later than eight tonight." I replied.

"That's cool. Ya'll still having that grand opening of that Beauty Salon or whatever by the Carousel Mall on Saturday?" He asked.

I knew why Fab-Five was asking about that. He wanted to check out some of the females in the shop. He had bought him a new whip and some fresh clothes as of lately. He probably wanted to show it off a little.

"Yeah, we supposed to cut the ribbon at noon time. Come through, I got this little female you might want to fuck with." I replied.

His eyes lit up. His whip was a Cadillac Escalade sitting on twenty-fours. He paid twenty-two thousand cash from off the street. It was a pretty royal blue color with beat on the inside. He had the look of a Baller. It bothered me a little because I thought it was too flashy. The police or someone on King James' team might take notice. And knowing Fab-Five he definitely was gone have a strap. On the other hand I thought the little young nigga should have some fun. I'll have to school him in increments. But I had seen this cute little female I thought would be good for Fabian the moment I saw her. She would calm him down a little because of her conservative nature. He was a killer but he had a soft side that many people didn't see.

"So what's her name my nigga?" He eagerly asked.

"Shanell! She has a cute little shape and a real pretty face. Her eyes are hazel brown. Her complexion is about two shades darker than mine. But not only is she pretty she also got a head on her shoulders. She only eighteen years old and she is going to school to be a cosmetologist."

"Damn nigga where did you meet her at? And why ain't you got with her?" He asked in surprise.

"She went to school with my girl Janice but my girl has already graduated from the college. But they good homegirls and she asked me to hook her up with one of my homeboys." I replied.

"That's cool then a muthafucka. I'll be there no doubt to check out this bitch you talking about." He replied.

"Well I'm about to bounce. I'll holla at you later my nigga."

"Let me give you this money before you bone out Pooh."

He went into the bushes and pulled out this paper bag. It wasn't sorted out so it looked like a whole bunch of money. I estimated it was close to fifty grand.

"What we talking about?" I asked while he handed me the bag.

"It should be forty-seven-five. That's straight right?" He glanced up at me.

"Like a muthafucka. All right I'm out, ya'll niggas be safe. I'm gone have that dropped off for you but I won't see you till Saturday." I said while walking away.

"For sure!"

"Ay Fab-Five don't speak up too much about the salon on the West Side, ya feel me?"

"Okay!"

The next morning I prepared to have a talk with King James. I expected it to be a little uncomfortable. It wasn't much of a thing to me. He still didn't know what was going on in the Dorjil's so I still had a card to play. I kept copping the same amount as usual and I didn't have any flash to my shit. The night before I had Lonnie make the drop off to Fabian and told him to not tell anyone. Fab-Five knew him so I knew it wouldn't be any problems. Plus I hit him ahead of time to let him know whom to expect.

That was heavy on my mind when I walked into King James' office. I felt good and knew that I couldn't be intimidated. Boom-Boom was standing outside when I walked in. As long as he doesn't know about the other spot I can negotiate. I smiled when I knocked on his office door. He was shuffling through some papers when he looked up. He only glanced at me for a split second.

"Sit down nigga!" He demanded. His tone was edgy and confrontational.

I sat down without saying anything while he continued to shuffle through some papers. I stared at that big ass King James' Bible he had on the edge of his desk. He was gone make me wait to see if I panicked. C'mon King James I'm smarter than that.

"So what's up with my money nigga?" He growled. He still hadn't looked up from his papers.

"What money? I pay you up front for dope every time I cop." I replied.

He stopped shuffling through his papers and gave me a cold stare. I gave him brief eye contact so he would believe I was scared. Maybe I was a little. I knew Boom-Boom was right outside with a strap. My strap was in the trunk of my car.

"Now you acting like Antoine ain't told you about the two bricks I gave him on consignment?" He calmly asked.

"I ain't saying all that. But what's between you and him is between you and him." I replied.

"So you gone hang ya boy out to dry like that? You don't take me as that type of nigga Pooh." He leaned back in his chair.

"I ain't that type of nigga. But I thought we had an agreement, with all due respect, that you would deal with me directly? Antoine wasn't supposed to be in the picture at all concerning what you and me was doing."

"That don't negate the fact that I gave that nigga two bricks and he took it. That debt has got to be paid." He snarled.

"I can get it back for you. But we can't afford to hustle our shit plus two more on consignment. That was the reason I told you I didn't want that shit." I protested.

He slammed his fist on the desk. I had pissed him off I guess. I was fidgeting in my chair. At this point I had to appear to be coming from a position of weakness. In my heart I was like fuck this nigga. His lips curled up viciously.

"Nigga I don't give a fuck what you can't afford. I sell the shit nigga, what the fuck I look like taking it back. Ya'll niggas got three days to bring me my muthafuckin money."

I sat there for a few seconds without saying a word. There wasn't any negotiations about to happen with this nigga. I expected some anger but not this kind of backlash. It was like he was daring me to not have his money by Sunday. He had gone back to shuffling through those papers that fast. He glanced up at me for a moment.

"You still here nigga?"

117

I got up from the chair feeling dizzy. Respect is a hell of a thing in the streets. If someone shows a little disrespect they will eventually show you more and more. As long as they can get away with it everything is fine with them and they will keep doing it. My eyes watered for a brief moment. I was infuriated. I waited to get in my car and as if to taunt me.

"Damn Pooh, what's up nigga, you alright?" Boom-Boom asked.

"Yeah I'm doing cool!" I replied.

He smiled as if he knew something I didn't know. I quickly drove off screeching my tires when I took off. I went straight to Nakia's apartment. She might have been home but at this point I didn't care one way or another. My head started hurting when I pulled out the duffel bag of guns. I don't know who the fuck he thinks I am. But I ain't ever been a mark(punk). I walked upstairs to the apartment and to my surprise Nakia was gone. Knowing her she probably went shopping or something. I dozed off for a moment on the couch. I had become exhausted because of my anger. My cell phone started ringing but when I seen it was Janice I ignored it. She probably wanted to talk about the grand opening or something. I wasn't in the mood. The ring of my phone broke me out of my slumber. I called up Lonnie, Antoine and Fab-Five and told them to meet me at Ama Polo this Mexican restaurant we all frequent.

We all showed up at the restaurant around nine that night. I had calmed down by then. My mind was on being tactical more than being angry. Lonnie and Antoine were already up there when I arrived. Fab-Five pulled up a few minutes later. That nigga was playing some old school Tupac full blast when he came into the parking lot. We were inside the restaurant and heard him. I thought it was too flamboyant but the song made you feel good.

"Forgive me I'm a ridah, still I'm just a simple man."

He walked in with his head up. I noticed that Fabian smiled a lot more than before. He looked good being a Baller. I smiled when he walked through the door. I stood up to embrace

118

him as well as Lonnie and Antoine. We sat down and ordered some food. Janice had called me again but I turned my phone off this time.

"What's cracking my nigga?" Antoine asked.

I paused for a moment. I began chewing on my burrito before I replied. Everyone was staring at me at this point. I wanted their undivided attention.

"What do you niggas fear the most? What is your biggest fear?" I asked.

"Damn Pooh, you getting all deep on us and shit." Antoine muttered.

"For a nigga to kill me and I'm not able to fight back. If I get murdered let me get murdered fighting. If I'm helpless then that is more fucked up than anything." Fab-Five pondered.

He caught everyone off guard with that statement. I looked over at Lonnie and Antoine.

"I don't know, someone trying to harm my family. That scares me more than anything. I'll die for my family." Lonnie pondered.

"Not being able to get any more pussy." Antoine blurted out.

Everyone started laughing. It was a joke but I considered what he said. After everyone calmed down from laughter Antoine spoke up again.

"But for real my nigga what is this all about?"

"I wanted to know what ya'll was afraid of because some shit might go down. King James says we owe him thirty-five large and I ain't paying him shit. What that means is after awhile he's coming after us. Now the question ya'll got to ask yourself is if you ready for this shit. If not, I understand and everyone can go their separate ways." I explained.

"What kind of shit is that? Fuck that, we got yo back down and dirty." Fab-Five replied.

"Don't speak for everybody Fabian but I appreciate what you saying. Every nigga got to speak for himself on this one though." I replied.

"I always got yo back through and through no matter what. If we got to war with King James then that's what we gone do." Antoine replied.

"I'm down then a muthafucka, just let me get a hold of some straps and it's on and cracking." Lonnie replied.

"Don't worry about guns. I got plenty of guns in the trunk of my car. So we gone go in the back and I'm gone show you what I got." I replied.

"So we gone stop hustling for a while, since we not gone be able to cop from King James?" Antoine asked.

"Naw, I got another connect now. I will have Fab-Five hustling for me in the Dorjil's from now on." I said.

I said it like I was just about to start hustling in the Dorjil's. Fab-Five and Lonnie both knew that I had already started but they caught on that I hadn't told Antoine and kept quiet. They both had heads on they shoulders, I thought.

"That reminds me, no one speaks about what we plan to do or anything we plan to do. Not to ya mama, ya sister, ya woman or anything. We can't afford to pillow talk at this point. King James and Boom-Boom gone put some pressure on everybody so we can't let our women feel what we going through." I explained.

Everyone nodded their head in agreement. I was especially concerned about Antoine talking to any of his women. Lonnie and Fab-Five didn't take me as those types of niggas but I had to put it out on the table. I let them know that we were going to wait until someone made a move on us then we were going to start blasting. It was all about making sure no one crept up on us or caught us slipping. I wanted King James to think that we were dodging him. Then once he tried to get raw we were going let whoever he sent have it. Once I told them everything we went out to the parking lot so that I could show them the guns. They began laughing and talking after seeing the artillery. They knew we were ready.

A couple of days passed without any problems. We had the grand opening of the Pleasure Palace that Saturday. I told Janice I wasn't going to stay too long. She was too much into her world to really mind. As long as I had the money to get it going she wasn't complaining. The reason I told her was because I had to see my parole officer. The truth was that I had seen King James' wife Latrice there and I didn't want her to know how involved I was in the shop. In fact I made sure the night before that Janice didn't get to bragging that I gave her the money for the shop.

"Oh so I'm gone brag that my shop was started up with dope money?" She said sarcastically.

Latrice flirted with me for a brief moment, which was somewhat odd to me. King James didn't discuss business with her so she wouldn't know what was going on. It was too obvious if she was trying to set me up. I just smiled at her and left the event once the ribbon was cut. I had introduced Fab-Five to Shanell when we first got there and they hit it off instantly. When I left the shop I decided to go to Nakia's house because I knew she would be there and would be ready to pamper me. She was expecting me to come through so she had everything ready. All the sex toys and all the catered food for us to relax and for me to hibernate. We would have fun for a few hours then she had to work that night at the strip club.

I knew Janice wasn't getting in until late so I would probably be home before she got there. 'The Pleasure Palace' would have her consumed for at least a few weeks now that it was open. With all this taking place I would have time to relax and prepare for the war that was about to take place. My estimation was about two or three days I had to relax and be dead to the world.

The following night Antoine, Lonnie and Chris were outside grinding at the Mt. Vernon apartments. They were having a good night and was about to sell out by one or two in the morning. It had to be about eleven or eleven-thirty when an army green 72' Chevy Caprice pulled up on them. The car looked familiar to Antoine but he couldn't put his finger on where he knew the car from. Then a massive figure poked out of the driver's window with his hand in the air.

"What's up pretty ass Ant? Come here and give me a kiss."

Antoine recognizing who had just pulled up suddenly became nervous. He pulled out his nine-millimeter before the large man could get out his car. Without hesitation he started blasting into the windshield of the driver's side. The large man ducked, but from the yell you could tell that he had been hit. Antoine started dumping more bullets into the windshield before Lonnie and Chris could react. The engine was still running so he took it out of first gear then hit second and pushed on the gas. Antoine, Lonnie and Chris looked around to see if there were any witnesses. Lonnie told Chris to grab the dope and they jumped into their separate cars and spun away from the scene. I didn't hear about it until that Monday morning.

10
BIG MEL

I ain't that nigga to be fucked wit!
Scarface

The sun beamed down on Melvin Taylor as he reached the final gate to be released from prison. He had talked to his cousin Pooh a few times over the phone and it appeared as though he was doing big things. He chuckled to himself when he seen the brown Lexus truck parked outside waiting for him. Pooh always had a way of downplaying everything. The last time he had seen Pooh his little cousin was only fourteen years old. He was twenty at the time and on his way to prison. He had a little female named Tracy to run and tell his cousin Pooh that he was getting locked up. He wanted him to take a few things before the police took him away. He could see that Pooh felt like crying but he held back his tears as he took a few miscellaneous items from his big cousin. At least the police was cool about. The memories flashed through his head as he walked up to the passenger door of the Lexus. When he opened the door right before him was his cousin Pooh as a grown man. It made Melvin hesitate for a brief moment before entering the car.

"You getting in or what?" Pooh smiled.

Melvin jumped into the passenger seat and they shook hands man to man. They were both very glad to see each other but they were two men from the street. Some things were known but left unsaid. Melvin's thoughts were racing as he kept glancing over at his little cousin who was now a man.

"You hungry? We can stop to get something to eat." Pooh offered.

"Yeah that will be real good. Anywhere you want to go is fine with me. Eating prison food for ten years doesn't make you too picky about restaurant food, you know?" Melvin replied.

"I'm knowing."

"That's right you was down for five years. You had a good little run, what happened?" Melvin asked out of curiosity.

"I was hustling over in Delmont Heights for this nigga named James. I had sold out all of his dope when the police swept up on me. James told me that I could have the rest after I paid him his seventeen thousand. I would have made twenty three thousand off the work but got caught. They knew where the stash was and everything. It was my first offense and they didn't get all the dope. But it was enough to get me eight years and I did five of that." Pooh explained.

"Who you think turned snitch on you? If they knew where the stash was someone told on you." Melvin replied.

"I think it was this punk muthafucka named Noony. I think he's been snitching for years."

"You handle yo business with that nigga when you got out. I mean, he ain't breathing to snitch on anyone else is he?" Melvin asked.

"I don't know for sure if it was him though. I've only saw him once because I ain't been in the Delmont Heights that much since I've been out. I got a young nigga hustling for me in the Dorjil's right now." Pooh replied.

"You only got one spot? You must be moving a little weight to be pushing a Lexus truck. And the Muslims don't be up in the Dorjil's like they were back in the day?"

"Naw they don't be up in there anymore. I had two spots but I had to lay low on the one on Mt. Vernon. Antoine blasted on this nigga named Boom-Boom early last week. So I got Fabian hustling for me in the Dorjil's." Pooh explained.

They pulled up into a Sizzler's parking lot. Melvin was dumbfounded off of what Pooh just told him.

"You mean to tell me that Lil Ant is blasting on niggas now?" Melvin shockingly asked.

"I know the shit tripped me out. But the nigga didn't finish the job and that's gone be a problem later on." Pooh sighed.

"And you got Fabian hustling for you now. Shit how old is he now? He had to be about nine when I got locked up and he had heart even back then. He's the one that told me the police was coming but it was too late." Melvin chuckled.

"Yeah he told me to tell you what's up. He's glad you home."

The wind started blowing hard as they walked into the restaurant. A pretty Latina girl was their hostess. She escorted them into an empty dining area and took them to a booth. She smiled and handed them both a menu. Melvin hadn't seen an attractive woman in person for ten years. It was a few cute Correctional Officers but they were always in uniform. He took in the aroma of her perfume and breathed in. Pooh laughed while the Latina hostess blushed before she walked away. Her nametag read Maria. They took a little time then ordered their food. It was dark inside the restaurant, which made them squint their eyes when they looked outside. Some elevator music softly played to set up a relaxed mood.

"So who is this nigga that Ant had to blast on? He had to do something to make little Antoine want to kill him." Melvin asked.

"You know Boom-Boom; you went to High School with him. I think he graduated a year or two before you. He stayed over there near the California Gardens. His name is Barry something but ya'll went to Cajon together." Pooh explained.

"Not Barry Phillips who used to lift weights at the high school gym after school. Always fucked with them old school cars? That nigga?" Melvin retorted.

"Yeah, he still fucks with them old school cars. He was in one when Antoine bla…"

125

Maria walked up with their dishes interrupting Pooh from finishing his statement. She sat both plates down and smiled at Melvin. Melvin took note and put it in his head he would holla at Maria before they leave. She left and briefly came back to take their salad plates.

"Man that Mexican girl bad then a muthafucka. I'm gone have to hook up with her real soon. But you were saying that Ant blasted on him while he was in his car?" Melvin asked.

"Yeah so we now about to go to war with James Stuart. He was my connect but he tried to keep me on lock by giving me dope on consignment. He got most niggas copping from him on the West Side. He got some muscle with Boom-Boom being his main boy." Pooh explained.

Melvin hesitated before responding. He had gotten knee deep into his steak and he was enjoying the flavor. Some real food for a change he pondered. He chewed slowly trying to savor the taste of his food.

"Man this steak is off the chain." Melvin pointed at his food with excitement.

Pooh understood the feeling. He paused for a moment allowing his older cousin to speak.

"We ain't got to worry about Barry or Boom-Boom or whatever the fuck you want to call him. He knows what time it is with me." Melvin waived his hand as if to dismiss him.

Pooh didn't really respond. He thought that his cousin was being somewhat arrogant but he didn't dare question him. He knew Melvin was known and well respected but so was Boom-Boom.

"I didn't know if you wanted to get involved, you being fresh out and everything. You getting to be an old man big cousin." Pooh joked.

"Yeah but this old man can still get in yo ass." They both laughed.

"Seriously though Pooh, I ain't got a problem with killing a muthafucka. If we need to straighten some niggas out then that's

126

how it's gone be. I don't know this James cat you talking about but if he got guns we got guns. Ain't anybody gone touch my little cousin." He smiled.

"When we get out of here we gone have you crash at mama's house, is that cool? Just long enough for us to find you an apartment." Pooh commented.

"How is my Auntie Shirley? That's my favorite Auntie out of all of my aunties on both my mama and my daddy's side. Where is her fine ass homegirl that's built like a stallion? What's was her name Pauline, Pam or something like that?" Melvin reminisced.

"Mama's doing good. I tried to get her to move out of the Dorjil's because of the war but she is afraid of losing her section eight. I'm like you can get section eight somewhere else nicer but you know how stubborn she is. Her friend Paula is still around and fine as hell. She came out here last weekend to talk to moms. She stays out in Victorville somewhere."

"What's up with Ace's old ass? He still is fixing up old cars?" Melvin asked with a hint of mockery.

"Yeah, and he told me he want to see you to feel you out. See where yo head is. He told me to bring you down there this weekend." Pooh laughed.

They finished eating their meal making small talk. Before Melvin left he made sure that Maria slid him her phone number. She acted a little reluctant at first because she was at work. But after he coerced her for a little while she surrendered the digits. He walked out to the car that Pooh was already in feeling good inside.

"Ten years and I still got it." He said aloud to himself.

They still had about an hour and a half drive before they made it back to San Bernardino. Pooh remembered how he felt when he first got out. He wanted a little time to himself to think about his plans. He decided to give his cousin that same amount of respect. They cruised back home listening to the oldies station because Pooh knew that was what Melvin liked. It was quiet

127

music listening time until 'Love, Need and Want You' from Patti Labelle came through the stereo.

"Man I love this song. Turn that shit up." Melvin said.

Pooh used the remote to turn up the music while Melvin bobbed to the song.

"You really gone like the party that we gone throw for yo ass tonight. You gone have the time of your life, we plan to have food, drink, weed and some fine ass females to make you feel good tonight nigga. That's when you gone meet all the niggas that's rolling with us." Pooh smiled.

"That's tight. I could use some pussy right now. But I feel sorry for the bitch that's gone have me first. I might wear her ass out."

"Hell naw nigga. You gone bust that first nut quickly. Then you gone get into the groove of things." Pooh commented.

"I might have done ten years but I still know how to hold in a nut." He replied.

"Whatever big cousin." Pooh chuckled.

King James walked down the long hallway of the hospital. He could hear the heel of his shoes echo all around him. King James hated hospitals. He always considered them places of death. He had been in the hospital both times Latrice was pregnant and hated every moment of it. He left his house after talking to Latrice, Karen and Stacy. He was a little disappointed about the news he had heard but he knew he would think of something. He turned into the room and knocked before he entered. Boom-Boom was lied up with the cast covering his right shoulder and arm. He looked upbeat when he seen King James peak through the door. He walked inside carrying a white paper bag. Boom-Boom smiled instantly knowing what it was.

"Damn James, this Ama Polo's is just what the doctor ordered." Boom-Boom replied snatching the bag.

"Yeah I figured yo big ass would be hungry. Looks like you done lost a little weight too. Can't hang with the hospital food huh?" King James commented.

"That ain't the half of it. Being laid up in this bed been hard as hell too. But I will be going home tomorrow." Boom-Boom sighed.

"Yeah sometimes things don't go the way we want them to. But we gone be alright and you will heal real soon. Then we gone put these little young niggas in they place." King James retorted.

"So what's up with Karen? She fucking with that nigga or what? We can catch up with that nigga tomorrow." Boom-Boom said with a stone face.

"Naw you heal and let us take care of that young dumb pretty muthafucka. He gone go real soon, I got some niggas on him as soon as Karen hook up with him."

"Why she can't hook up with him tonight or something?" Boom-Boom asked impatiently.

"He couldn't hook up with her tonight because Pooh's cousin or something just got out of jail. His name is Big Mel or something like that. Karen tried to get him to take her but he told her it would be like bringing sand to a beach. They probably gone have hoes and everything up there. We gone have to wait." King James replied.

He then looked up at Boom-Boom who was unusually quiet. For the first time since he had known the man he seen fear in his eyes. They went to the same elementary and Junior High School but went to different Senior High Schools. Since they were children he couldn't remember too many things Boom-Boom was afraid of. There was a brief moment of terror that flashed in Boom-Boom's face.

"You sure he said Big Mel got out? Melvin Taylor from over in the Dorjil apartments. When did he get out?" Boom-Boom said with an urgency in his voice.

129

"Tonight, from what Antoine's bitch ass told Karen. What, you know this nigga or what? I heard Pooh mention him before but that was about it." King James said. He sensed the urgency.

"You remember Dirk and Chay from over near the Delmont Heights area?" Boom-Boom asked.

"Yeah, them rough niggas that was moving major weight before they got killed. That shit that happened to them was pretty bad. All those buck shots on different parts of their body. Yeah I remember them... naw!" King James said in surprise.

Boom-Boom nodded his head. He was finishing the last remnants of his food. He quickly gobbled the food down so that he could elaborate.

"Man he was only seventeen at the time. I personally saw him knock out Samoan Gully with one punch when he was a sophomore. He's a problem James. If he gets involved we gone have problems. He got a lot of respect on the West Side. I..I mean any nigga can get got but I ain't ever seen ruthlessness from a nigga so young unless he's gangbanging or something."

"Why ain't you ever told me this shit before? I would have gotten rid of Pooh a long time ago if I would have known he had a crazy ass cousin like that. That's the same Melvin Taylor that shot a nigga outside the club in Moreno Valley?" King James asked. Now Boom-Boom had his full attention.

"Probably so! I don't know about that incident. They say his mama and daddy was a little off they rocker so that was why he ended up like that. But I didn't think he was getting out after that attempted murder charge. I heard they had a murder case pending on him too. I just thought that he would never see daylight that's why I didn't mention it. But maybe he ain't the same, maybe he different." Boom-Boom attempted to lighten the mood.

"Well we gone find out because they gone catch the blues in a minute. And now they not about to have any dope so they gone be struggling off of what they got. The clamps is coming down on them if Big Mel is out or not. But I'll pass the word that if we see the nigga then peel his cap back on sight." King James growled.

"Yeah they probably got a few straps but we got some heat. We gone handle our business no doubt..." Boom-Boom was suddenly startled.

Peaking his head into the office was a familiar face to both men. The man made both of them stiffen up in his presence. He wasn't intimidating in stature but he still had an aura. He was still a brilliant detective that had eyes and ears everywhere. It was uncanny how he could get to the bottom of things. King James believed he had more than a few confidential informants working for him. He gave King James a glance then went straight to Boom-Boom.

"I heard you were shot so I came up here to visit you and see if you were okay." Detective Barnes said.

He was scanning the hospital room without looking in Boom-Boom's direction. He acted as if he was investigating the room for contraband. But both men knew better than that.

"You hear about things too fast for my taste detective." Boom-Boom replied.

"Ain't that what I'm supposed to do. Investigate leads that help me catch suspects that need to be off the street?" Detective Barnes smiled.

"Yeah I guess. But that ain't part of the game. Snitches get stitches where I come from. So if you came in here to ask me who shot me, you wasting your time." Boom-Boom remarked.

"C'mon now Barry you know I know better than that. I know you live by the code and I can't knock you for that. I just wanted to make sure you were alright. See if you got plans of one day backing out of this lifestyle." Detective Barnes sighed.

"What lifestyle, I am a model citizen that lives a good clean life. I even go to church. So what are you talking about?" Boom-Boom said in a condescending tone.

King James chuckled. It sort of startled Boom-Boom because he rarely ever see King James laugh. He wasn't that type of nigga. He assumed King James was laughing off his uneasiness about the detective being present.

"Insult my intelligence if you want to. But the game doesn't have any friends and if you don't get in and out you will eventually submit to something. Either you will get killed, face prison for forever and a day or violate the code you claim to live by. It's a trap and only the ones that know when to quit can get out and live." Detective Barnes explained.

He had a smirk on his face that made Boom-Boom and King James uncomfortable. No one made eye contact and the tension was thick in the air.

"Okay, Okay just tell me what happened when you got shot. I will spare the speech but at least let me make a report." Detective Barnes surrendered.

"I was driving down the street and someone shot through the window. I don't know why and who. All I know is that bullets hit me probably from a few strays." Boom-Boom replied.

"That's it?"

"That's it! You got your report detective, now have a nice day."

"You do the same and take care of yourself. And you also be safe Mr. Stuart." Detective Barnes said while leaving.

King James nodded his head and then breathed out slowly. Both men looked at each other with concern. It wasn't cool when Detective Barnes started snooping around.

"Maybe you should have mentioned Melvin Taylor had gotten out of jail. We can have that muthafucka on him instead of us." King James said.

"Naw, he don't need to know shit. I don't want him to get the idea that I would even consider snitching. I don't like that Big Mel got out either but I'd rather deal with him in the street then sick the police on him." Boom-Boom replied.

"Real talk! But he snooping around for something. Somebody's talking and we need to find out what they saying." King James replied.

Outside of the hospital room in the hallway Detective Barnes listened attentively. He couldn't believe his ears when he heard the name of Melvin Taylor. He must have beaten that murder one charge, he thought. He wondered how long Big Mel had been out. That might explain the recent shooting of Barry. Only a crazy muthafucka like Melvin would cross him and James like that. He pulled out his notepad to write down his recent revelation. He tried to listen more but they had changed the subject. He slowly crept off with Melvin Taylor on his mind.

Later that night Pooh escorted Big Mel to a spot he had rented. When Big Mel walked in the small office space he was impressed. There were at least twelve women climbing the walls dancing seductively to 'Stairway to Heaven' from the O'Jays. He smiled and looked at Pooh displaying his satisfaction. He walked in and was handed a drink from Fabian.

"Damn, little Fabian is a grown ass man. Come here nigga, it's good to see you." Big Mel embraced him.

"They call him Fab-Five now." Pooh whispered in Big Mel's ear.

"Oh shit Fab-Five my nigga is a real nigga like I knew you would be. We gone turn this muthafucka out tonight." Big Mel announced.

Fab-Five was smiling from ear to ear. Big Mel was like an idol to him. Now he was hanging with him at a party with money, drink and hoes. Pooh shook hands with Fab-Five then pulled Big Mel away. He wanted to introduce him to the entire crew. He took him around the room introducing him to Lonnie, Chris, Chucky and Moe. Then he introduced him to Cornell and Little Eddie who worked under Fab-Five in the Dorjil Apartments. Then sitting by the bar Antoine was smiling when Big Mel approached. Big Mel held out his hand then snatched Antoine up and they embraced. Big Mel gave him a once over then whispered in his ear.

"I heard you putting in work now."

"Just on niggas that's trying to hate on what we doing. I know you glad to be out." Antoine replied.

"Hell yeah, now look at all these bitches up in here. My little cousin is doing good for himself." Big Mel said with pride.

The party was cracking until early in the morning. Each of the homeboys had access to two strippers apiece. But Big Mel had first dibs on the females of his choice. Pooh told him to choose the two he wanted and take them in the back room. Big Mel escorted two Amazon women built like stallions towards the back room furnished with a king sized bed. No one seen him until the next morning. Big Mel had made it home with a bang.

11

IN THE LIFE

I would say fuck you, but go and get ya own dick!
Lil Wayne

I woke up around twelve or close to one in the afternoon after my cousin's big party. It was like an orgy up in there. Niggas was fucking bitches in different corners of the room. It was only two rooms in the back that were both occupied. My cousin had one and I had the other. I knew Nakia wouldn't mind me fucking a few of her co-workers. In fact they probably got a kick out of fucking me because they knew I lived with Nakia. At least that is what she told them. They kept referring to her as Princess and since I had a buzz I always had to think about whom they were talking about. Both of the females made sure they gave me their number so we could one day soon have another ménage a trois. I didn't have any problem with that since they were L.A. girls. If they were from the Inland Empire I might have been a little skeptical. But I knew I still had to watch my back.

When I did get up I took a shower and got dressed and waited for my cousin. He was moving a little slower. He must have had a ball last night. There was another surprise waiting for him before we went to visit my mother. She had been calling for me to have him stop by because her and Sharon were waiting to see him. My mother had him crash in my room when I was young when his mother passed away from breast cancer. Aunt May (short for Mable) used to fight her husband like she was a man. My mother would always comment that her no good husband was behind her getting breast cancer. He would hit her in her chest and face on numerous occasions before he got killed out in L.A. So my mother was like his second mother and he loved my mama

135

immensely. Sharon and I always thought she treated him better than she treated us. I believe she felt sorry for him when he lost his mother and father. I didn't really mind because my cousin was like a god to me. And I was the little brother he never had. He had siblings on his father's side but he never knew them.

"Damn Pooh what time is it? What time did you tell Aunt Shirley we was gone be at her house?" Big Mel asked after getting out the shower.

"I didn't tell her a time but she don't have to work today so she should be at the house when we get there. But hurry up nigga we got a few things to do before we get to mama's house. I'm thinking about having the spot near Mt. Vernon changed to right around the corner. I even know the apartment complex we can hustle out of. It's one of the few places where Black people still be at on this side of town."

"Alright here I come." He yelled from the backroom.

I didn't know what size he wore so I just bought him a few sweat suits with matching shoes. It was comfortable and easy access. In about ten minutes he was ready to go. He came out looking like my cousin of old except for the fact he needed a haircut. When he walked outside to the bar he looked and raised both his arms as if he was asking me how he looked. I nodded my head in approval then handed him a bag with a box inside.

"What's this?" He asked while opening the box.

"About a hundred." I replied.

"What's this, money to recop?" He looked dumbfounded.

"Naw nigga, it's yours." I shook my head.

"Man you got it like that where you can hand me a hundred large. You doing big things."

"Yeah well let's roll because you got a long day. After talking to mama for hours you still got to get you a car, some clothes then go with me to holla at Ace." I replied.

I headed straight for the Dorjil's apartments because my moms and sister had been blowing my phone up since ten. I had cut it off just in case Janice called. But I was straight with her because she was preoccupied daily with her new shop. When I told her I wasn't coming home that night she didn't even trip. But my family had left a gang of messages. I was pushing down Baseline Blvd. When my phone began ringing again. I knew it was my mother or my sister being impatient so I answered the phone quickly.

"Mama, I'm on my way right now."

"You on your way where?" A familiar voice asked.

"Who is this?" I asked in bewilderment.

"This is Stacy! You don't remember my voice anymore. Baby you done forgot all about me?" She said in her innocent voice.

"I thought we didn't have words after that last conversation. I didn't think you wanted to be bothered with me." I lied.

"I've called you since then though but you are always busy. I thought about what you said and we should talk."

"I'm busy right now. So it probably ain't a good time right now. I'll talk to you later." I quickly said.

"Well I'll call you back later baby so we can hook up. I know you and me both miss doing what we be doing." She flirted.

"We sure need to get back into that again." I replied.

I hung up the phone. There she goes trying to tempt me with pussy again. I like pussy a whole lot but I am not the one to believe that she wants me like she pretends. She probably wants me to trick off some money with her. She must be desperate for money I pondered because she keeps coming at me when she knew that I was straight with her.

"Who was that? One of your little bitches you got in the line up?" Big Mel interrupted my thoughts.

"Naw, this little broad that I dropped from the line up because all she could offer me was some pussy. She didn't have anything to bring to the table." I replied with slight irritation.

"That's smart! Its only two things a bitch can do, that is either bring you up or bring you down. And if all she got to offer is a piece of ass then she is a waste of your time. I wouldn't have believed that ten to twelve years ago though. But you have always been smarter than me little cousin." He contemplated.

"I wouldn't say all that. I just learned from mistakes that were made and tried to do it different." I attempted to downplay his words.

"Naw Pooh, give credit where credit is due. You got the ingredients to be a real baller in the game. You always had the brains to know and learn the rules of the street. You were always smarter than the rest of your young homies. You fit the right build to be a boss nigga running shit." He replied.

"Why do you say that?" I replied. I was actually flattered by his comment.

"It's an ingredients you have to have in this game. When you in the life there are components to make you the nigga everyone must answer to. You got it. Like the brains you have helps you get over with money and how to manage it. Then you a cute nigga but not so cute where niggas think you a bitch like Antoine. You cute enough where niggas can respect you, but you rugged enough to where niggas won't be too mad if you doing big things. You are ruthless enough to take care of a nigga if he crossed you. You ain't extreme like me who would peel a niggas' cap without mercy. Little Fabian looks up to me and he reminds me a lot of my self when it comes to blasting on a nigga. But niggas like us instill too much fear for us to last long in the game. We good for muscle but we ain't good for being bosses. Then you are low key about yo shit which keeps you under the radar. You catch them without them seeing you coming. Niggas might underestimate you when everything hits the fan. You got the ingredients." He smiled.

I didn't really respond but I smiled back. By that time we had pulled up into the Dorjil Apartments. I figured that King James might have some niggas parked outside. I told Big Mel to be prepared and we walked into my moms' house watching our back. I banged on the door a few times and my mother quickly opened the door. My mother screamed loudly after seeing her nephew walk through the door. She hugged him and kissed him on the cheek like he had just gotten back from Vietnam.

"How is my favorite nephew?" She looked him over.

"I'm fine Auntie Shirley, how have you been?" Big Mel smiled from ear to ear.

Sitting at the dining room table was Sharon and my moms' best friend Paula. Sharon got up from the table ready to embrace her big cousin. He was the center of attention for a change. I had been the center of attention being the only male family member now it was Big Mel's turn. I was relieved because I needed the break. I decided to let them grill him while I go in the room and make a few phone calls. They had him in the living room for a good hour before we heard a knock on the front door. Everyone was enjoying themselves until they heard the door. It was so loud it made me get up from the bed and walk into the living room. I told my mother to look out the window and the peephole before she answered the door. I didn't want her to answer the door but she insisted that she could answer the door to her own house. This time though she listened to what I told her. After looking out the window and the peephole she realized it was a man that was unfamiliar to her. He was in regular clothes but he looked like a cop. Mama opened the door with the chain still on the door.

"How are you ma'am? I am Detective Joseph Barnes, I was hoping I could talk to you for a minute?" The Detective calmly asked.

"What about?"

"Some things that are going on in the neighborhood that's all." He replied.

I had never let my mother know I had a some homies hustling for me in her apartments so she let him in. If she would have known that she probably wouldn't have let him in. It was times I thought my mother was too naïve. You wouldn't think that she was once married to a nigga in the game. You could hear a rat pissing on cotton it had gotten so quiet. Sharon turned down the television just to hear what he had to say. Moms left the door open to indicate he couldn't stay long.

"We've had a few shootings in recent months that are still open homicides. One that took place in the California Gardens and one that took place in that open field right across the street. If you see anything could…" He stopped talking in mid-sentence.

"I remember you, you are Melvin something right?" He asked Big Mel.

"Yeah Melvin is my name. But I remember you too. You used to roll up in the black and white back in the day now you done moved up to detective huh? What you drive a Crown Victoria now?" Big Mel smirked.

"Right outside. How long have you been out? I thought you were locked up for a long time." He ignored the smart remark.

"It was a long time. Ten years ain't a short time. I just got out yesterday so you can't put anything on me." Big Mel smiled.

"Naw I wasn't trying to do that. But if any of you have any information that could help with these unsolved murders it would be appreciated. Here is my business card if you have any questions or leads." He handed my mother his card.

He then glanced over at me. I didn't really make eye contact with him but was staring at him through my peripheral.

"What is your name young man?" He asked.

"Well Detective Barnes we were having a good family day before you interrupted. We would like to get back to that if that is okay." My mother firmly suggested.

"My apologies." He walked out the door giving me a quick glance.

I ignored him as though I was distracted by something on television. When my mother closed the door behind him the mood had changed. It wasn't the same anymore. That was perfect timing for me to suggest that Big Mel and I had to take care of some business. He still needed a whip to drive around in and he needed a wardrobe. Then after all of that I was going to take him to visit Ace. Big Mel got up and hugged everyone. He even

140

hugged Paula. But I knew why he really hugged her. He pretended like she was family but she still looked good. He had other thoughts about her when they embraced.

Once we got inside the Lexus truck I clowned him about hugging Paula. He grinned as if he was exposed for some crime. We both started laughing aloud. I looked around to see if someone was on us. I was paranoid but I knew it was a good enough reason. The police knocking at my moms' door and King James having his boys on the prowl. I had to be careful. Once I seen everything was clear I sped off.

We decided to stop at the swap meet so that Big Mel could get some accessories like drawers, socks and Pro-Club T-Shirts. It was beginning to get dark outside. We had done a lot of shopping at the mall so now we would rap it up with this small indoor swap meet. We came back out laughing and joking with bags in our hands. We were having a good time when I noticed footsteps approaching us quickly. I seen someone moving close on us through my peripheral. I dropped my bags and pulled out my nine millimeter and Big Mel followed suit. We ran behind a car and they started shooting. Nothing hit us but they were aiming for the head. The parking lot was one of those rough ground lots with rocks all over the place. It was easy to make noise with your feet. I was frustrated but decided to stay put. My cousin had already ran around two cars. He was going into the source instead of keeping away from it. I decided to follow behind him. If we was going out then we was going out together. Whoever was trying to kill us wasn't that good. They should have waited until we got in the car. They were either nervous or impatient.

Suddenly Big Mel spotted one under the car. They were pretty much posted in the same place they started shooting. Yeah they were nervous. Big Mel came around the side of a Buick and let off five shots. I heard a body hit the ground.

"Ah shit." Somebody yelled.

Then I heard a car door open and close. The ignition started up and I poked my head up to see a Bronco moving. I jumped up and started firing into the driver's seat. Glass shattered everywhere and the car went out of control. I walked up closer to see him crash into the wall. Big Mel touched me on the shoulder and I turned around quickly.

"C'mon now we got to get out of here." He said.

We jumped into the Lexus and sped off into the night. We made sure to grab the bags we had so know one could trace anything back to us. Even though they had guns California has a no self-defense law. We would still have had to do time for defending ourselves. Then it was the fact that we were both felons also. I was shaking a little bit as we drove down the street.

"We have to get rid of these guns. And Sharon and Marcus will have to get a new car. As for Auntie Shirley I'm gone talk to her about moving." Big Mel remarked.

I just nodded my head. It bothered me a little because I knew that King James hadn't sent his best. He probably wanted to see how we would stand up to his lightweights. We were officially at war. It was something I knew but something that I hadn't realized. Now the reality of the situation was seeping in. Now it was time to get on the offensive. I wanted my homies to be prepared for an attack but now we had to let them know we meant business.

For the next few weeks I was preparing the new spot not too far from Mt. Vernon. We would get the word out by serving a few people around the way for free and then tell them where to cop from now on. I told Oscar that we were in war with some niggas and he told me he would help if we needed any. He was still copping from me but I felt like he wasn't obligated to help me in the war.

"Naw homes, we go back to high school. We'll be watching for those pinche pieces of shit." He said.

We shook hands and I was headed back to the West Side. I had movers moving my mother's belongings in a spot in Redlands. Big Mel must have said the right thing because she didn't hesitate to move after he talked to her. He had just gotten himself a spot in

Rialto not too far from the West Side of San Bernardino. He had to live near the hood. But I could tell from his demeanor after that day he was focused for a war. He told me he had gotten out just in time.

I rescheduled a day for us to go down to Ace's house. When I picked up Big Mel in my new Range Rover he seemed upbeat. By now he had hooked up with the Latina Waitress Maria. He told me she was from Guatemala. She had spent the night for a couple of nights. She was fine as hell with her little accent. He was telling me how much she catered to him. She would clean up the house and rub his feet. He was on cloud nine.

As for me I was hibernating with Janice as of lately. Nakia was a little pissed at me about her co-workers giving me their numbers. They must have been bragging about the shit to her. She was pissed at me for about a week and a half. So I was coming home to Janice for the most part. On Friday and Saturday I would chill with Vanessa because Janice was so busy. The past weekend Vanessa told me she wanted to be involved in the war. She was determined for some reason. I dropped this on Big Mel to see what he thought.

"I remember her brother and he was a down ass nigga. She probably got that shit running through her veins. Think of something but be smart about it." He replied.

"Yeah we got to be smart about it." I said as I pulled into Ace's apartment complex.

I didn't bother knocking on the door because I knew where to find him. He was fixing up an eighty-eight Cutlass Supreme when we walked back there to his garage. We walked into his garage with smirks on our faces.

"What's so funny to both you young dumb niggas?" He asked nonchalantly.

"You doing the same shit, all the time." I replied.

"For more than ten years as I can see." Big Mel commented.

"So they let yo crazy ass out the joint huh? I hope you here to stay this time." Ace said without looking his way.

"I don't plan on ever going back." Big Mel stated firmly.

"So what you gone do about it then?" Ace sharply replied.

"Do about what?" Big Mel said in Bewilderment.

"You not going back. No one has plans of going back, but what will make you any different from most convict niggas? Take a seat nigga so we can talk." Ace pointed to the three chairs.

Sure enough he had the bottle of whiskey with three plastic cups waiting for us. I wasn't surprised. He expected us to drink it straight like him. I wanted to grab some Coca Cola this time around but I stood firm. Big Mel wasn't driving so he took his glass eagerly.

"So you done got yourself into a little war I'm hearing? You sure you ready for that kind of heat? If you make it out alive you still might be locked up for forever and a day." Ace directed his question and statement to me.

"It's either him or me. He tried to get Mel and I the other night. I didn't want to talk too much about it over the phone. But two of his boys was trying to peel our cap back." I replied.

"Yeah they would have gotten us too if they were smarter." Big Mel added in.

"Why he coming after ya'll like that? A nigga in his position ain't gone start some shit for no good reason. What did you do to cross him?" Ace scolded.

"Antoine picked up some dope on consignment and I decided not to sell it. I told James that we weren't going to take anything on consignment. But he gone call in Antoine behind my back and force two bricks on us."

"Why didn't you just hustle his shit? That would have saved a whole lot of trouble." Ace replied.

"Because he was trying to make us be in the hole with him. He would have kept giving us shit on consignment to the point we would have been hustling for him instead of ourselves." I replied.

144

"And what is wrong with you hustling for him? Was the money right or was it bad?" Ace pried.

"It was cool but I wanted my own. I didn't want to be totally dependant on that nigga." I fired back.

"Now we getting somewhere. Now you ain't beating around the bush. Now ask yourself if being independent is worth going to war with this nigga." Ace said.

Big Mel hadn't said a word. He was observing the exchange Ace and I were having. He sat back swigging his whiskey. I glanced at him but I was too focused on my conversation with Ace.

"Yeah because he was trying to keep his clamps on me. I wasn't about to be his boy anymore. It was time that I took control over my own shit or I would never be able to get where I'm trying to go. That was the reason for another connect in the first place." I explained.

"So little Antoine jumped the war off huh? Don't let that little dumb nigga blow yo head up into thinking this should be more than business. And you, don't you go be trigger happy to the point where you fucking up business." Ace directed his last statement to Big Mel.

Big Mel nodded his head in agreement. You could tell the whiskey had gotten to him a little but he was still sharp.

"Self preservation is the only reason I'm pulling my gun out nowadays." Big Mel replied.

"The first law of nature huh? When you feel you in that predicament then the rules might change. You feel that way too Sherwin?" Ace asked.

"No doubt! King Ja...I mean James wouldn't ever let me get to the status where he at as long as I am under his thumb. If the only way to break free was to go to war then we go to war. That's self preservation like a muthafucka." I explained.

"Well make sure it's only that because in this life wrong decisions will get you in the morgue or in the penitentiary for life." Ace stated.

145

"I'm playing chess like a muthafucka." I replied.

"So what about that detective that came by your moms' house the other day? What did you say he wanted?" Ace asked.

"He was asking about a couple of murders. He appeared as though he was going door to door but I know better than that. Especially what took place later on that night? He should have seen them niggas staking us out unless he was with them." I firmly stated.

"But you didn't see them so what makes you think he had to see them. Don't jump to conclusions, but ain't anything wrong with considering all possibilities." Ace said.

"Well since we in war I was considering the possibility of going on the offensive. I want to hit that nigga at one of his spots. It's time for bodies to fall for real." I said.

"Well don't be like Antoine and shoot a nigga without killing him. Don't give any of them niggas a chance to come back." Ace replied.

"I'm knowing."

It was pitch dark outside about two hours after we left Ace's house. Ace had an entire speech for Big Mel but since we were in war he knew that Big Mel's expertise would be needed. That was the talent of my cousin he knew how to make niggas disappear. I decided to send Lonnie, Big Mel and Fabian back over to the California Gardens. I only needed Big Mel and Lonnie but Fab-Five wanted to go because Big Mel was going. I thought three was better than two in most cases so I told him to roll. Being cautious they went through Rio Vista Park that separated the Dorjil's from the California Gardens.

Fabian hit the back yard to the vacant house where they slung. There was two niggas working the spot. One was collecting the money while the other was curb serving. King James had some older niggas that lived up in the California Gardens hustling for him now that Kay-Kay was dead. Fab-Five jumped over two gates waiting for anyone of them to run his way. Lonnie walked right up to them with a twenty in his hand.

"I ain't serving you nigga, you ain't from around here. All I know you might be 'One Time'."

"I understand!" Lonnie replied.

He put his money in his front pocket and pulled his pistol from his waist. Before he could grasp for breath Lonnie had plugged him in the head. His body dropped to the ground. His homeboy that was serving the dope reached for his gun and went after Lonnie. Before he could take three steps off the porch Big Mel came from behind a bush and shot him in his chest and abdomen. He whined then slumped to the ground. Big Mel and Lonnie walked up on him to make sure he was dead. Fab-Five had been watching where the stash was and grabbed it. It wasn't much so they emptied the pockets of both and ran off into the night.

12
WE CAN DO IT!

Who ever thought that fat girl would turn into Oprah!
Rick Ross

We did him the same way over at his spot near the Delmont Heights. Niggas that was copping from him started coming up missing. It was getting bad for him because I knew where his spots were. Boom-Boom had gotten out the hospital but they didn't know where to find us. I always had to consider that Latrice might come up to the Pleasure Palace to locate my sister or me. I knew them niggas wasn't past kidnapping so I made sure that Sharon wasn't anywhere near the place. Marcus would come up there from time to time but he was a civilian that was dating my sister as far as they knew. It wouldn't be much gain in kidnapping him.

Now that King James knew that I had some muscle to flex I decided to relax a little. Let my money build up and keep things moving. I just wanted him to understand that I can find him but he can't find me. He needed to know if he went against me there would be some consequences. He was still the Top Dog on the street but it was coming clear to a few people that he could be touched. In fact the thought that he could be toppled ran through my mind. But King James had resources that an up and coming didn't have. His money was way longer than mine so he could always get more muscle. He had the means to put money on my head a lot easier than I could put money on him. Then the police would rather get the up and coming than the one on top. It was too much trouble to get the one on top. The up and coming was more liable to make mistakes. Also he had so much money he could disappear for a while and still be sitting on a stack. I had money but I couldn't take a vacation. I decided to meet with my main niggas for a meeting once a week.

The three people I always wanted to meet with were Big Mel, Lonnie and Fab-Five. But I would include Antoine so he wouldn't feel left out. He had his money in the pot but he had his mind on other shit. He could get annoying because he didn't know how to hibernate. He had just shot a top nigga down with King James but he was still running the streets. I didn't have him doing drop offs anymore. I didn't have him pick up money or anything. A few times he brought a female with him for drop offs and I must had lost my mind. We were supposed to be equals but I was the one making all the decisions. But he was my homeboy that I had much love for. Some people never change though.

This week I met them at the Cajun Garden on Pepper Street. It had just gotten dark when we met up. Everyone ordered his food then we talked. Everyone had changed cars except for Fab-Five and his workers. I had just bought a Range Rover in my sister's name. I had it for a little over a month but I didn't drive that often. She had proof of income through the Pleasure Palace Salon so that was how I was able to get it. It was all white sitting on twenty-four inch rims. I was doing the damn thing. Everyone was admiring my new whip, except for Big Mel who had already seen it, until we got down to business.

"Now that James don't know where we got our spots, it's time we start expanding our operations. I know a few niggas that would love to cop from us wholesale." I started the conversation.

"Yeah, I know some niggas that want to cop our shit up in the Delmont Heights. They say they got to jump through too many holes to fuck with James' shit." Fab-Five commented.

"Well check this out here, we gone go lower than James so we can take some money from him. But don't be dealing with more than one or two niggas. Really only one and watch that nigga. Ask about him first to see if he got any paperwork. If he snitching we need to know not to fuck with him." I explained.

149

"What's up with that spot in Rialto? We can get it buzzing over there. They be searching high and low for some of that raw." Big Mel asked.

"I been thinking about that. You need to find some young niggas that is willing to curb serve on those parts. They got to cop from somebody else besides you because they know where you live. Tell them you have a connection and if they seem like real hustlers we will let them work a half of that raw. But we'll send Lonnie or Chris to deliver the dope but you'll make the money off the package. They don't even have to know you're involved." I explained.

I was saying shit that I didn't have to say to my cousin. He already knew what time it was. But I said it for the sake of the others sitting at the table. I wanted my people to know that we should deal with curb servers as little as possible. I knew they had a few concerns so we got to them so that I could meet with Vanessa. She had been craving my attention. She also wanted to get more involved with the business besides just handling the money. It was always smart not to involve females in certain aspects of the game because they can't do jail time. But Vanessa was different. I was still working out in my head how she could get more involved.

"I seen that nigga Noony coming over there in the Dorjil's the other day. I know he's a snitch so I was thinking about peeling his cap." Fab-Five interrupted my thoughts.

"Naw don't smoke him just yet. You gone make the spot hot if you kill him over there. Feed him some bullshit and see what he does with it." I replied.

"Tell him what? He keeps coming up to me trying to be friendly. It's like someone done told him something I don't know." He said with a perplexed look on his face.

"He sees that nice ass whip you got and he probably see some movement in the Dorjil's. That's cool but I don't know what you can tell him." I replied.

"Tell him you heard some niggas in Delmont Heights might be trying to rob King James since he hadn't done shit about his peoples getting killed in the California Gardens. Tell him you heard they gone meet on Rialto Blvd behind the church." Lonnie interjected.

We all looked at Lonnie with surprise. That was a damn good idea. We would see whom he sent once we scoped out the scene. Either he was working for King James or the police or both. But that would be a clean set up to know what angle he was coming from. Whoever showed up was whom he was working for. I knew word was buzzing on the streets. We had snuck up in California Gardens twice through Rio Vista Park without any retaliation. Now I had been hearing that they had direct-connect phones now to patrol their neighborhood. They probably thought it was the Delmont Heights gangbanging on them. Since King James was supplying dope to both sides now we had to have the Delmont Heights niggas wondering about him. It wasn't too many niggas getting dope from him but there was enough to garner some loyalty. We wanted him to lose his customer base in both hoods as well as the projects. If it were up to me I would try to squeeze him out of the entire West side.

It took a couple of weeks for us to set everything up. I was cool with a lot of Delmont Height niggas so our approach was a little different. Fab-Five had told Noony that the niggas that smoked them niggas in California Gardens was meeting up behind this church all the time. Noony didn't have a clue that Fab-Five was down with the niggas that did the dirt. It was at first suggested by my cousin Big Mel that I didn't go on the ride but I couldn't resist. This time I rented a Lincoln Towncar with tinted windows so that I could be parked for hours before the shit went down. I posted up around seven in the evening right when it had gotten dark. It was cold outside. The valley weather can be really cold. When it is 55 degrees in Los Angeles it is about ten or fifteen even twenty degrees colder in the Inland Empire. I had to keep cutting on the heater while I sat patiently waiting for the shit to go down. I had bought me some binoculars even though it was still difficult to see at night.

Fab-Five was waiting over behind the church. Big Mel was posted in another car across the street from the church. We had Oscar and one of his essay homeboys on the other side of the church. Lonnie, Chris, Antoine and Chucky agreed to be the bait. They had the straps near by but not on them. Just in case Noony sent the police they had to post up without weapons. They had heart for doing this set up. I promised myself that I would give them all a bonus for doing this shit. If the police were to roll up then they would get searched then be let go. They didn't have any contraband and only they knew where the guns were.

A Honda Accord pulled up around eight-thirty cruising by slowly. I noticed Boom-Boom in the driver's seat with a young nigga. He looked like he was from the projects but I wasn't for sure. That was the only place I could picture his face. Boom-Boom went down to the end of the street and made a U-turn. I put in a 911 code to Fab-Five's cell phone telling him we got somebody creeping. He sent the same message to Big Mel. The thing was Boom-Boom didn't stop he cruised the block at least three times then turned the corner. He had to have noticed all four of those niggas outside talking loud. Maybe he thought it was a set up. Maybe them talking loud made it obvious that they were trying to be seen. The thing was that it was in neutral grounds so they didn't have a reason to be cautious. If it was in the Delmont Heights, California Gardens, The Dorjil Apartments or the projects then niggas might be a slight more cautious. I panicked for a moment thinking that he wasn't about to roll up on them. My leg was jumpy as I dialed the number to tell everyone to cancel the plans and head home.

Then three cars suddenly hit the block. They parked far enough where they could walk the rest of the way on foot. They were on the same street as the church with mostly handguns. This Samoan nigga named Gully was leading the pack with another nigga named Turtle. They had three other niggas following them that I didn't know by name. Their faces were familiar but I couldn't put the name to faces. I knew they were down with Boom-Boom but he wasn't with them. My eyes got big as they tried to creep up as silently as possible. I wanted to jump out of my car and start dumping but they wasn't in deep enough to be trapped. I sent a urgent 911 to Fab-Five but him, Mel and Oscar was already in place. The radio was blasting in the same spot but by that time everybody went to their stash for guns. Samoan Gully rolled up on them first but he didn't have time to raise his gun. Lonnie was on him with two quick shots to the neck and chest. He fell to the ground instantly. That startled the other four seeing Gully fall like that. They started blasted everything they had in Lonnie's direction. Lonnie had already dove behind this large trash dumpster. They followed close behind him thinking they had him trapped.

When they got to the side of the trash dumpster fire started coming from behind them. They were trapped. They turned around to face Fab-Five, Oscar, Big Mel and Carlos. The bullets started coming at them in full force. One of them realized he couldn't shoot his way out so he decided to run the other direction. A few shots picked him off in the leg and in the stomach but he kept running. When it became obvious that he could getaway and live Big Mel went after him. Before he made it halfway down the block Big Mel blasted on him with the twelve-gauge shotgun. The force of the shot lifted him in the air and he landed a couple of feet away from where he last stood. A moment later everyone was in their cars and rolling off in different directions. I cruised away in the rented Lincoln having to roll around the corpse lying in the middle of the street.

I decided to spend the night over Vanessa's house that night. I was dealing with attitudes from both Janice and Nakia. I was always welcome as a friend and a lover over Vanessa's house. I felt a little rejected by her not wanting to be my lady so there were times I avoided her. But she had my son and she was teaching him different then how we grew up. But she didn't let him be naïve either. They were the family I really wanted.

She was sleep when I had gotten to her house that night. I had a key but I rung the doorbell this time. I had some things on my mind that I wanted to talk to her about. Her beautiful face was like a breath of fresh air when she opened the door. She gave me a half sleep smile letting me know she was glad to see me.

"Why didn't you use your key?" She softly asked.

"Because I wanted you to greet me at the door." I replied.

She continued to smile and pushed me playfully. I wrapped my arms around her waist then looked into her eyes.

"What?" She exclaimed.

"I can't look at you?" I asked.

"What's up with you Winnie? Is something bothering you? You get like this at times. You being all sentimental and shit." She smiled.

"You know that there is no woman that comes before you?" I seriously replied.

"Except your mama!" She replied.

"Not even my mama comes before you." I firmly replied.

"Whatever Winnie, what is on your mind? We can go on the balcony and talk. You want something to drink?" She dismissed my last statement.

"I'm serious Vanessa, no one comes before you. I know I'm on the grind and in the streets but it would be good to hear that you feel that way too." I complained.

She handed me a beer as we walked on the balcony. The sharp wind was cold but we continued to stand outside. She wrapped herself up tightly in her robe and looked up at me.

"I do feel that way but there is a time and place for everything. You ain't in a position to give me what I want in a relationship. I ain't talking about other bitches either. I know the game goes with that. But I bet you haven't even told your mother you got a son by me." She glared at me knowingly.

154

"I take care of him don't I? I spend time with him and do for him whatever he wants and needs." I said defensively.

"Yeah but you still ain't told yo mama he exists. I believe you are a strong man Winnie. I never looked at you as a punk but when it comes to your mother you are weak as shit. And only reason she doesn't like me is because of my complexion." Vanessa remarked.

"So I'm not ready for a relationship with you because of how I choose to handle my mother?" I asked.

" No it's not just that. You don't have the time to burden yourself with relationship issues. The game needs all yo attention if you really trying to get to where you trying to get to. When the time is right everything gone come into play. You know you always got a home here but you got bigger things to worry about." She touched my face with the palm of her hand.

"Yeah that's true. But who says I'm getting somewhere. Things are good but that can change over night. I don't know what James got under his sleeve." I pondered.

"If anyone can beet this nigga it's you. You can do it baby. That was why he always tried to hold you back. You in a position to take him out of the top spot and he scared. But keep being smart and everything gone work out. Shit, even Antoine is getting smarter about a few things." She laughed.

"I know huh. He still got some issues but he's getting smarter. Yeah maybe you right. Maybe we can do it." I smiled.

The following night on the evening news the dead bodies were reported. The news reported that children walking to school that morning had found the dead bodies. I sort of felt bad about that. They identified two of the victims by name. They even had a victim's mother speak on television. She pled with the television public that they help bring her son's killers to justice. I felt somewhat bad for his mother but understood it was part of the game. If I didn't kill them they were definitely going to kill me. Vanessa was sitting next to me on the couch when they were telling the news story. She didn't even judge me. I loved her for that.

I told everyone to lay low for a while to let things die down. The San Bernardino Sheriffs were getting hot on the West Side. We still had our hustles going on but we were being low key. I wanted to minimize the violence if I could. I knew we had hurt much of King James' muscle. He had money though which meant he could hire new muscle. But when you in a position like him you are insulated. It's hard to trust people and loyalty is but a dream. Niggas is loyal to you a little more when they done came up with you. But that can even be questionable.

To keep things in my favor I had a few of my homeboys patrol by his office to maybe catch him or Boom-Boom slipping. They saw Latrice over there a few times. They called to ask if I wanted them to kidnap or smoke Latrice but I didn't want to involve females. King James' people might be that scandalous but I won't get that low down. He was back peddling right now so he might get desperate. I had to consider all moves he might make. We just had to let King James know that he can't just run up on us and we gone fall down. Now that the message was sent we would lay back. With intentions on still being sharp as a tack.

My cousin Big Mel had made that connect in Rialto. The little curb servers were buying from him now but we were using Chris. Lonnie's little cousin was just as sharp as him. He followed my rules and only dealt with one nigga from over there. I sold a kilo to my cousin for the same amount I was getting my shit from Big Black. I showed him how to stretch that shit with procaine and he was ready. My hoodrat homegirl Tracy worked in a dental office so she was able to get that shit in powder form. I just started bumping into her right before the war. In her conversation she just so happens to mention she was a receptionist at a dental office. We were in contact with each other from then on.

What Vanessa was talking about on her balcony made plenty of sense to me. Now I was supplying my raw to three different sources. If everything went as planned we also could be moving weight in the Delmont Heights. The only open market would be the projects and I hadn't put together how I was going to move in over there. There were always three things that bothered me about crossing King James. One was burning the bridge with him where I wouldn't be able to cop from him. Since Big Black was working out so well I didn't need King James' dope. The second reason I didn't want to cross him was because he had shooters that would be down to put in work. He had killers on his payroll that took orders from Boom-Boom like it wasn't shit. But we had wiped out most of them with that last shootout so he was weak right now. Boom-Boom was still recovering from what Antoine had done to him even though he was out the hospital. I wasn't totally optimistic though. I knew that King James wasn't a nigga that made it to the top without having something up his sleeve. I knew he had a trump card somewhere so I had to brace myself. But I had come a long way from a little over a year ago. I could kick my feet up and hope that King James got the message that I shouldn't be fucked with. It's been a long time coming.

13
PIECES COMING TOGETHER

Them niggas actors they deserve Oscars!
Cam' Ron

Detective Barnes finally exited the freeway into Victorville. He spotted the Carl's Jr. where he had arranged the meeting. He hadn't spoken to him for a while. His informant was in hiding for the last few weeks. He knew that it was serious because he received an urgent 911 page. When he pulled into the parking lot he sat in his car momentarily. He looked in his rearview mirror cursing the traces of gray hair he had begun to notice. He was a tall handsome Black man with a dark brown complexion. He was 6'1 with a healthy crop of hair. He felt old from all of the murder investigations he had worked throughout the years. He had seen young kids grow up to be slaughtered in the streets. Then he would be the one to find them sprawled out in a murder scene that he would have to work. It had become tiring to him throughout the years. It had taken its toll on his fifteen-year marriage as well. Now he was meeting another scumbag that he sacrificed his marriage for. He contemplated these things as he prepared to get out of his car.

He stretched when he stepped out of his brown Crown Victoria. He looked around then wrapped himself up tightly in his trench coat. The wind was sharp and hard and he quickly moved toward the Carl's Jr. entrance. Why in the hell does he want to meet way in Victorville he pondered? But a lead is a lead so he had to accommodate his informant. The arrogant young man smiled haughtily when Detective Barnes walked inside the fast food restaurant. He had the facial expression as though he had it all figured out. How many times he had seen that facial expression wiped off a young hustler's face in San Bernardino. How many times he seen that facial expression changed into a perplexed facial expression while lying in a puddle of blood. They all thought they were special. They all thought they could out game the game. The game never changed just the players. He sat down right across from the well-groomed handsome man. The man was maybe about ten to twelve years younger than him but looked like a millionaire. All Detective Barnes knew was that he probably was a millionaire.

"So Mr. Stuart why did you call me way up to Victorville? Is it relevant to the five dead bodies found recently?" He asked. Detective Barnes gave a sigh of a monotonous disposition.

"First off were you able to catch that shit about Big Melvin Taylor getting out of jail?" King James asked.

"Yeah I was standing by the door when you mentioned him. I saw him right after that hospital visit I had with Mr. Phillips and you. He was over a woman's house that stayed in the Dorjil apartment complex." Detective Barnes replied.

"Yeah, that's the mother of Pooh. Her name is Shirley but I was told she didn't live there anymore." King James said.

"Who is this Pooh? That probably was the young man that looked familiar to me over Ms. Shirley's house. What is his government name?"

"Sherwin something. I want to say Daniels but I'm not for sure. He is the one responsible for those five murders the other night. He's the one you have to investigate if you want to solve those murders. Melvin Taylor is his cousin and he has a lot to do with the violence that has taken place on the West Side." King James explained.

"So you have a rival now. I guess you need me to take down your rivals huh?" Detective Barnes replied with both cynicism and sarcasm in his tone.

"I've been squeaky clean for a few years now. You haven't had any problems from me. I've only minded my own business." King James replied.

"You call supplying the entire West Side of San Bernardino with cocaine being squeaky clean?" Detective Barnes asked incredulously.

"Don't believe everything you hear. I've never been charged with a drug trafficking charge. I am working off the gun charge and that's it. There is no record of me catching a drug case." King James arrogantly replied.

"There isn't any record of Joe Kennedy being charged for bootlegging either. That doesn't mean he didn't do it."

"Joe Kennedy? Who is that?" King James asked.

"Never mind, why did Mr. Uh… Daniels want to kill or have the five young men killed? They were all carrying weapons but were apparently beaten to the punch. Were they friends of yours?" Detective Barnes asked while flipping through his notepad.

"I don't know about why he did it, I just got word from a reliable source that he had them five niggas killed. Pooh is also selling major dope nowadays. You catch up with Melvin Taylor and you might get some leads to where Pooh or Mr. Daniels lives."

"C'mon Mr. Stuart you are giving me very little to work with. You expect me to go after particular people without motives behind the killings." He impatiently replied.

"Well they were associates of mine. More like Boom-Boom, I mean Barry's homies. They were beefing over territory. I don't bother with that small time stuff I just want the violence to stop. This young nigga Pooh, been killing people for years and I'm finally speaking up about it. I heard he killed two niggas at the swap meet not too long ago. They say that was unprovoked too. They just walked up on some niggas they didn't like and started shooting them. I heard it was over a parking spot or some stupid shit like that." King James explained.

"This Mr. Daniels or Pooh as how you call him is responsible for all these murders?" Detective Barnes asked suspiciously.

160

"All of them. Him and his cousin Melvin have been killers from day one." King James continued.

"Why is Mr. Daniels so familiar to me, where do I know him from?" Detective Barnes thought out loud.

"He was the young man I tipped off to you about six and a half years ago. You caught him with a bunch of dope when you were working narcotics." King James admitted.

"Yeah, the quiet young man that was about nineteen years old. He didn't take me as the violent type. I've ran into those types plenty of times to know whose killers and whose not killers. Now he is of course capable of killing but having the appetite is far fetched." Detective Barnes sighed.

"Maybe jail turned him out. Because he's the one that is responsible for all these murders on the West side." King James insisted.

"Why was it necessary to meet in Victorville Mr. Stuart?" Detective Barnes changed the subject. His facial expression was a clear indication to King James that he thought he was full of shit.

"I have a female friend I've met out here. We were spending a little time together that's all. Besides it would be good that no one sees us together." King James retorted.

"Mr. Stuart you are definitely playing with fire. You are married to one of those young girls right? If you are ever discovered everything she knows about you will crumble." Detective Barnes sighed.

"Aren't you divorced? C'mon Detective Barnes stick with what you know. I know what I'm doing, that's the reason I'm way out here in Victorville so I won't fuck up what's at home. I don't shit where I eat." King James laughed arrogantly.

"Oh I forgot that you know everything. Well I will look into the information you gave me and we will move from there."

Detective Barnes got up from the table. He slipped his notepad in his coat pocket. He slightly nodded his head and walked out the door.

161

King James began looking around to see if anyone was looking at him. He would be ruined if anyone suspected he was talking to police. His mind wandered for a moment from his worries to think about Paula. She was so classy. She had cooked him dinner with wine and candlelight. The thought of her made him smile. She had him open. He pondered on his growing feelings for her before he got up to leave. He went outside into the hard wind and clicked the alarm to his Black Cadillac Escalade. He looked around one last time allowing his paranoia to get the best of him.

As he drove down the 15 Freeway back to San Bernardino he pondered on his problems. That young nigga Pooh was a problem. What bothered him was that he never knew where Pooh was getting his dope. He was still hustling because one of the young hustlers spotted Pooh's new dope spot, following up on some information King James got from Karen. It was mostly a Mexican area but some Black hustlers were working the neighborhood pretty good with immunity. Pooh must have had another connect all along he thought. But why did he cop from him in the first place, if he had another connect all along? His thoughts were racing. Before Pooh had gone to prison he had told King James that he wouldn't be working for him anymore. King James figured he hadn't quit hustling but was probably trying to cop some dope on his own. Since the police wanted him to give someone up and Pooh was about to quit working for him, he decided to choose Pooh to get cracked by the police. He had the police raid the stash right when he had given Pooh a new package. King James hated to lose the young hustler because he was always smart on his feet. He was a sound hustler but he never expected him to be a problem for him.

His cell phone rang as he headed into San Bernardino off the freeway. He picked up the cell and seen that it was Boom-Boom on the caller ID.

"What's up nigga?"

"Where you at? I got that nigga you need to talk to."

162

"Meet me at that spot in about fifteen minutes." King James replied.

He quickly hung up the phone not knowing who was listening. He didn't like the way he was feeling as of late. Everything was uncomfortable to him. Now he needed to know what the fuck was going on with Noony. Boom-Boom probably had to have that nigga at gunpoint to get him to meet with him. King James smiled as he pictured Boom-Boom putting the pistol to Noony's head. He had a lot of explaining to do. In times like these misinformation was deadly. Noony was telling the truth about where the niggas was hanging because Boom-Boom seen Antoine with his own eyes. But the ambush was totally unexpected. He lost most of his muscle and he was having a hard time trying to figure out who could be trusted that would be good shooters for him. He couldn't depend on the Delmont Heights niggas because they were down with the niggas that come from the Dorjil Apartments for the most part. He had a few shooters he was considering in the California Gardens that he knew wouldn't have any love for Pooh and his people. He had a lot on his plate.

He jumped out of his Cadillac Escalade right in front of his office with his pistol drawn. Boom-Boom had spotted some niggas cruising by looking at the office waiting for him to get caught slipping. This was the only place he wanted to meet Noony's snitching ass. He couldn't take him to the other spot because only two people knew about that spot. Only Paula and Karen knew about his hideaway spot. He would later tell Karen that it was a friend's place that let him borrow the key when she suggested they meet there again. Boom-Boom didn't even know about this place or Latrice either. He definitely wouldn't let Noony know.

He looked around to see if there were any parked cars with niggas inside the car. Boom-Boom was already outside so he walked upon King James.

"It's straight my nigga, I don't think they coming around here anymore. They haven't seen us in a while so they might think we moved, its all good." Boom-Boom assured him.

"Where is Noony's bitch ass? We need to have a talk with this nigga." King James asked.

"He's inside, scared than a muthafucka. I didn't start questioning the nigga because I didn't know how you wanted me to handle it."

"Yeah well I don't know if I know how to handle it?" King James replied with an unfamiliar insecurity.

They walked inside the office to see Noony shaking in his boots. Boom-Boom made sure he locked the door behind him. He didn't turn on the lights in the front. He left it dark so it would appear as though no one was there. Even though their cars were parked outside there was other offices in the plaza.

"So what's up Noony, talk to me?" King James said in a deceptively jovially tone.

Noony wasn't a fool though, he knew the friendly greeting was a ploy to get him to relax. To get him to make a mistake and say something wrong was why King James was so disarming. But Noony knew he hadn't done anything wrong so he let it come out honestly.

"Them niggas were there like I said but I didn't know they were packing like that King James. Them niggas must have seen someone coming and got prepared." Noony said.

"Did you get my boys set up Noony?" King James asked.

"C'mon King James you know I ain't that damn crazy. I'm only giving information that I receive from the streets. When I hear about it I come straight to you." Noony pleaded.

And to the police King James thought. He leaned back in his chair and smirked at Noony. They both were informants but King James looked at his snitching as being different than Noony's. Noony was snitching out of fear but King James felt like he was snitching out of necessity. He was making chess moves.

"Where did you get your information? If we find that out then we might get a lead to what happened and how it happened." King James replied.

"If you confront this nigga you don't need to mention my name. This little young nigga is a cold piece of work. He will smoke a nigga over fifteen dollars. So don't bring my na…"

"Will you shut yo bitch ass up and name the nigga you talking about?" Boom-Boom retorted.

"His name is Fabian but they call him Fab-Five like the rapper. He told me them niggas be hanging out over there. He's been doing big things right about now too." Noony explained.

"Like what?" King James asked.

"He got some hustling going on right about now with two young workers that he got serving for him up in the Dorjil's. I haven't seen it buzzing up in there like that for a while." Noony continued.

"Fabian, I heard that name before?" King James pondered.

"Ain't that the nigga some was saying Greg owed money to? Word was that if anyone smoked him it was probably him. We had talked about addressing that shit but we got distracted when Pooh got out." Boom-Boom replied.

"Yeah come to think of it, that was his name. Latrice had heard that shit in the streets." King James remembered.

There was a silence for a moment. Everyone in the office was in his own thoughts. King James was thinking of a clever way to recruit the young killer. If he was already moving weight he still might be able to give him a substantial amount of money for freelance work. Noony was pondering on how he could leverage this new information about Fab-Five. He didn't even suspect that Fabian could have killed Greg. He made sure to keep a mental note of this new knowledge. Boom-Boom was a little agitated with himself because he just realized that he had spoke up on a murder in front of a known gossip and snitch. Only reason he hadn't killed him was because King James said he was valuable.

165

"How long have this nigga been hustling in the Dorjil's?" King James broke the silence.

"At least six or seven months. I knew of crack heads that was buying dope in the projects or in Delmont Heights but said that his shit is better. That's what made me start coming around the Dorjil Apartments." Noony explained.

"Alright Noony go wait in Boom-Boom's car and we gone talk to you later. If you hear anything else about Fabian you let us know, alright?" King James smiled.

"For sure!" Noony nodded.

King James handed him two hundred dollars then waived his hand for him to go. Noony hopped up from his seat and had Boom-Boom escort him out the door. After locking the door Boom-Boom came back in and sat in the seat Noony previously sat.

"You think this Fabian nigga might be hustling for Pooh?" Boom-Boom asked.

"Naw, I doubt it. They might know of each other but he wouldn't have told Noony shit about where them niggas was hanging." King James replied.

"I don't know James everybody knows that nigga Noony is a gossip. He is the San Bernardino Times on the streets." Boom-Boom insisted.

"Yeah you got a point there. But Pooh would have a gang of niggas guarding his stash because he done served some of my boys. He is a smart-ass pretty boy nigga, so he gone cover all ends. I think this Fabian nigga is a freelancer but you might be right. We gone have to do some investigating to find out what's going on. If we don't have to kill the young nigga we might be able to use him to help us get rid of Pooh." King James smiled.

"Yeah maybe so, if he ain't working for Pooh." Boom-Boom reiterated.

"Where was you at anyway nigga? I called you for last night and your phone was off. We could have gotten a hold of Noony earlier today." Boom-Boom changed the subject.

166

"Ah nigga you know that middle-aged bitch I told you I met at the Moreno Valley mall, I went to go chill with her in Victorville." King James smiled.

"Victorville? That broad stays way out that way? What was she talking about?" Boom-Boom asked but not really caring.

"She cooked me a candlelight dinner with wine and desert. Then later that night I fucked the shit out of her. She is right. That is the kind of broad I should have married."

"Speaking of your wife, did she have anything to say about you spending the night out?" Boom-Boom asked jokingly.

"Shit, I gave her a few thousand dollars for shopping before I left then her and Karen went shopping." He bragged.

"So what are we gone do about them niggas serving over there at the new spot on the other side of Mt. Vernon?"

"Are you completely healed? You can take two of the young niggas from California Gardens and have them light that spot up. But this time make sure there is some bodies missing." King James sneered.

"Yeah this time we gone pick them off. How did you find out about they knew spot anyway? That apartment is in the cut."

"Antoine's stupid ass was on the phone with Karen and mentioned the other side of Mt. Vernon was the new spot. It was funny as hell because after it slipped out of his mouth he realized that the police could be listening in. He must have some new pussy because he keeps putting her off. But as long as Pooh has his dumb ass around we got a good chance of putting the pieces together and wiping them pretty niggas off the map." King James chuckled.

"Yeah, I can't wait to serve that bitch nigga. He gone shoot me while I'm driving a car. Nine times out of ten Pooh told him to get rid of his old cell phone. He ain't smart enough to do that shit himself."

"I'm knowing. But his pretty ass had to maintain his roster so he called Karen with the new number to flirt with her. He might

167

be living with a broad or something because he keep putting off where he lives."

"Or Pooh told him not to tell anyone. He probably don't see any harm in talking over the phone but Pooh probably told the nigga not to let anyone know where he lived." Boom-Boom considered.

"Yeah that sounds about right. So when you gone handle that shit with that spot?" King James asked.

"Tonight, I won't give you the run down until we meet up tomorrow. But keep ya cell phone on my nigga." Boom-Boom replied.

"Shit I ain't about to be in Victorville, so hit me in the morning around ten or eleven and we'll link up."

They shook hands then walked out the office together with their straps drawn.

After Boom-Boom dropped Noony off he went to the California Gardens. He had already called up Casey and Markell and told them to meet him at the Rio Vista Park in about twenty minutes. He wanted to let the young niggas earn some stripes so they could make some money. They had been trying to be down for some time now. When he got there they were already posted and waiting eagerly for his arrival. They stood up from sitting down to shake his hand and embrace him.

"Ya'll young niggas ready to show if you got heart?" Boom-Boom asked with power resonating in his voice.

They both nodded. Markell was slightly smiling as if he had been waiting for this moment all his life. He was only sixteen while Casey was eighteen. They had put in work against the Delmont Heights when they were feuding. But this wasn't on any gangbanging shit; this was about making some paper.

"It's real simple, ya'll gone roll up on them niggas from both sides and start dumping on them fools." Boom-Boom explained.

"Cool, where's the straps?" Markell eagerly asked.
"In the car. Now let's roll."

Boom-Boom considered what happened last time so he decided against rolling down the street to scope the scene. Instead he parked around the corner and assumed the niggas would be out. If they were lucky he could catch Pooh or Antoine slipping over there and they would be sitting ducks. Boom-Boom stayed in the car because he didn't feel safe doing dirt with the young shooters until he knew what they would do tonight.

Coming from both ends Casey would be the first to approach looking like a crack head trying to cop some dope. Casey had a hood over his head walking up shaking like dope addicts do. Chucky looked at him like he was unfamiliar but took his money anyway. This was a new spot so faces hadn't got that familiar just yet. Chucky pointed towards the back then looked up to see someone else coming up to him with a hood over his head. This one looked younger than the one he just got money from. Then Chucky seen the chrome 357 come out of the pocket of the Hoodie the youngster was wearing. Suddenly he heard two shots go off but the one with 357' hadn't fired anything. Chucky dropped to his knees suddenly feeling the pain of the bullets penetrating his body.

Chris suddenly alerted by the two gunshots grabbed his nine-millimeter to run towards the front. Before he could take five steps he heard the gunshots that pierced through his shoulder blade and the right side of his chest. By that time he could see Chucky on his knees. The man in the Hoodie standing over him fired his gun one last time into Chucky's head and his body slumped to the ground. Chris tried to fire his gun at the two gunmen but they had run off once Chucky's body hit the pavement. Tears ran down Chris's face when he fell on the ground in agonizing pain. He knew Chucky was dead and that was his road dog. He lied in his own blood trying to call either his cousin Lonnie or Pooh to come get them. He dialed Lonnie's number first and his cousin picked up after the second ring.

"What's up Chris?"

"Them niggas got us." He mumbled through the phone then passed out.

14
TWO FAMILIES

Hard and raw no regard for the law!
Eazy E

Lonnie hit me around two in the morning from the hospital. I was so infuriated that I didn't know what to do. He told me Chucky was dead as a doorknob but Chris had a chance. Chucky didn't deserve to go like that. You don't know the pain of knowing you couldn't protect one of your own people. I couldn't think of how King James found out about the spot. I wondered if we had a snitch in our clique. But I had confidence that my boys were on the up and up. When I made it to the hospital Lonnie was in the lobby pacing back and forth. I paused before I went inside. I was bothered about the entire ordeal. But I quickly got my head straight so that I could put on my game face. When I walked into the lobby and went up to Lonnie he embraced me like I was a long lost brother. I felt his pain. It dawned on me suddenly that Lonnie was a young man. He was only nineteen and his cousin Chris had just turned seventeen and had been shot on two different occasions. Chucky died at the tender age of sixteen.

"So how is Chris holding up?" I asked.

"He doing good but he won't never be the same. The doctor came out and talked for a while but he was saying a bunch of shit I didn't understand. I wanted to call my auntie but she was probably running the streets herself. She's on that dope real tough." Lonnie explained.

"What's up with his moms, she be running the streets a lot?"

"Yeah she a crack fiend. She's been hitting the pipe for years now. That's why I've had the little nigga living with me. He ain't like a cousin Pooh, he more like my little brother. This shit is fucking with me." Lonnie vented.

Tears had fallen from his eyes while he was shaking. I knew it was going to be hell to pay for what was done to his cousin. Lonnie was about his hustle but he was a ridah too. That muthafucka King James was relentless. I could only hope he would go away. Now it was obvious that if I don't crush him completely we were going to have more casualties. Just imagine if all of us would have been there. Chucky wouldn't have been the only one to die.

We waited at the hospital until the early morning. I had contacted Big Mel, Antoine and Fabian. They came in one after the other with about an hour between all three. Antoine was the first to walk inside the hospital lobby. He had grown to love Chucky and Chris so his face showed distraught. He actually had his head down when he walked in. He bypassed me and went straight to the front desk.

"Ant, what's up my nigga?" I said.

"Oh snap, I didn't even see you over there. Where Lonnie at, have you seen Chris yet?" Antoine nervously asked.

"Lonnie went to use the restroom and we got to see Chris this morning. He was asleep from the anesthesia so we came back downstairs. Lonnie ain't doing too good. We were about to leave in a little bit. We just want to talk to him while he's awake." I calmly explained.

"Who found out about the spot? If it was King James, I mean James and faggot ass Boom-Boom somebody gave up the spot." Antoine said excitedly.

"I'm knowing. We got a leak somewhere but I haven't figured it out yet. Have you talked to anyone about the new spot?" I had to ask him.

"Hell Naw. I know better than that. Matter of fact I haven't fucked with anybody on the West Side except you, Fabian and Big Mel." He replied.

"Cool, I'll ask Big Mel and Fab-Five when I talk to them."

I was going to ask them as a formality but the only one I was a little worried about was Antoine. He sometimes inadvertently bragged to women without watching what he said. Not anything crazy like murders but he might mention a street or something. Since he said he hadn't talked to anyone on the West Side that worried me more. I also had to worry about finding another spot. We were going to have to shut that spot down for a while. I was trying to figure out every angle but I couldn't figure who could have slipped up. Oscar came to mind when Big Mel walked in.

"What's up Pooh? I got up and shot over here when I checked my messages. I left my cell phone in the living room and Maria told me I had a message." Big Mel explained.

"Don't even trip. We've been waiting here for a while now. We went up to see him but he was asleep. But we all need to talk." I replied.

"Big Mel, did you mention the spot off of Mt. Vernon to anyone on the West Side?" Antoine asked. I was annoyed but tried not to show it.

Big Mel looked at Antoine as if he had crucified Jesus himself. He smacked his lips as if to say 'nigga please' then decided to answer him.

"Why would I do that dumb shit? I live with a bitch and my little senorita don't even know about shit I do." He sharply replied.

"Damn Big Mel, I didn't mean any disrespect we just covering all the bases." Antoine said.

"You think someone leaked where the dope spot is to Barry and James?" Big Mel directed his question to me.

"That's the only way I can think of that they might have found the new spot. But now that I'm thinking about it I don't think it was anyone that is in our clique. It might be someone we fucking with."

Big Mel glanced at Antoine with a vicious look. Then he turned his gaze towards me when it dawned on him who I might be talking about.

"You think Oscar and them said something to them niggas?" Big Mel asked.

"I don't know, but they are the only one I can think of. Boom-Boom was the one that told them we had a spot on Mt. Vernon. That's what Oscar was telling me. Maybe James offered them a better deal for they dope if they gave up our dope spot." I explained.

"Fucking Mexicans done turned on us." Antoine blurted out.

"Hold on nigga, I don't know for sure. Oscar did dirt with us and he always seems to be a stand up Cholo so I ain't for sure. But I got to see. Besides, he could have slipped up on accident just like anyone one of us could have slipped up and told the wrong person." I said glaring at Antoine.

"That don't make much sense for them to be speaking on us and our spot to anyone. They buy they shit from us and besides putting in work they do they thing and we do our thing. If they 'slipped up' and told somebody it was deliberate." Big Mel insisted.

That was when Fab-Five came breezing through the door looking like a million bucks. He was looking so fresh that you would have sworn he had laid his clothes out the night before. He was clean cut with his taper fade and his brown leisure suit. I figured that was some clothing that Shanell had bought for him. He strolled inside the lobby like a lion out of his cage.

"We gone handle these niggas or what?" He viciously whispered.

"Let's step outside and talk about this shit. They got cameras and all kinds of recording devices." I warned.

We all stepped outside into the parking lot. The little white boy security guard looked at us suspiciously. Five niggas walking outside looking paranoid and upset is what probably startled him. I

174

chose to ignore him and get down to business. Before I could get started a familiar face walked up on all five of us. He was a middle-aged Black man but I thought he was still too bold to walk up on us. Then it dawned on me by his walk. He had a military posture as though he had some form of training, he was clean-shaven except for a mustache and he jumped out of a Crown Victoria. I mumbled as calmly as I could without startling anyone.

"One Time!"

The crowd started to disperse when they looked up to see the man. I was calm as I could possibly be. If we had straps they were in our cars. But everyone knew not to carry them into the hospital. But now this muthafucka has seen all of our faces. My entire clique, he now had a mental diary of all our faces.

"You don't have to walk away I just want to talk. How are you Melvin Taylor? I would really like to talk to you, the man with everyone gathering around him, Mr. Sherwin Daniels." He said.

Now he knew my name. He glanced around to make sure everyone stayed in his place. He scanned the faces of all five of us. When he looked at Fabian he gave him a double take. I could instantly tell he didn't like Fabian by the way he looked at him. It was as if he was cringing inside.

"You are welcome to leave after I get the names of you other three. If you don't agree I can just detain you and force you to give me names with the back up here in a heartbeat. Now I know you don't want that. All I'm asking for is your name that's it. If I find out anyone of you lied to me it will be a whole lot worse. Now c'mon let's get this over with."

Lonnie glanced at me as if to ask for permission. I nodded because I knew that all we were required to give him was our name and address. The officer caught the exchange and smiled.

"Got to get permission huh? Well I hope he permits you to do the right thing. By the way, my name is Detective Barnes." He teased.

"Lonnell Jackson!"

"Fabian Gilmore!"

"Antoine Walker!"

"Now that wasn't so hard. Now what's going on? Is the young man in here that was shot last night your friend? What about the teenager that was killed that was with him are either young men any relation to you.

"With all due respect Detective Barnes, we are required to give you our name and address by law. Now if you want our address so be it, but if not can we leave now?" I said.

"You're right, you have a nice day Mr. Daniels. And Melvin, be careful out in these streets because anything can happen. I might be talking to all of you soon enough." He spoke loudly as we all walked to our perspective cars.

I had just got sick in the stomach from seeing the detective. He had to know we were coming up there or was it just plain coincidence. I've never believed in coincidence. I wanted to see Vanessa so I drove towards Cal State when my cell phone started ringing. When Janice called the first time I chose to ignore it. When she called the second time I considered that it might be important.

"What's up baby?" I asked.

"This is Janice baby." She said.

"I know who this is. What's going on baby?"

"Could you come home so we can talk? This is something I want to talk to you about in person."

"Okay, I'm on my way home now."

I turned around and headed towards Colton. She had been preoccupied with the Pleasure Palace so our time was valuable together. I didn't mind her being so busy and since she had her own business she didn't mind that I was so busy. Lately we would probably spend the day together on Sunday. This was the middle of the week so I figured it had to be important.

When I walked inside she had the stereo playing Mary J. Blige. I could tell from the climate in the atmosphere that she was in a good mood. The stereo in the living room was up loud but she

176

was in the bedroom. When I walked inside she was making up the bed. It then dawned on me that she hadn't gone to work yet. That was strange.

"Winnie, baby I'm glad you are here. Sit down on the bed so we can talk." She jovially suggested.

"What's going on?" I asked after kissing her.

She was too happy for my taste. One of my boys got killed and another got shot. Now I know that a homicide detective knows my first and last name as well as my entire clique. So her good spirit, no care in the world disposition was unsettling. I tried to relax but a blind man could tell I was tense. I guess she was beyond blind.

"Winnie I'm pregnant. I'm a little over ten weeks. I just got off the phone with your mother about ten minutes after I called and she was so happy." She said with exhilaration.

I was stressed out so the news was lukewarm to me. Besides, I already had a son that my mother didn't know about. So having a baby wasn't something I was hoping for with Janice. Don't get me wrong I was cool with it but I wasn't as excited as she was.

"Baby that's beautiful, you and I are about to be a mama and a daddy." I falsely celebrated.

Whoop-de-doo I was thinking inside. My eyes watched her get up from the bed and begin tucking in the sheets. She was so happy that she couldn't sit still.

"Everything has to be right. We gone have to step it up with the family thing. It's about time we take this living in together to a whole new level Winnie." She commented.

I knew what she was hinting towards because she wouldn't give me eye contact. This bitch is crazy if she thinks I'm ready to get married. A baby don't make people stay together. If a nigga were looking at 25 to Life would she be hinting towards that marriage shit? With Detective Barnes lurking around like he's doing I just might be looking at life in prison. Now she wants me to step up and get married. I'll tell you what bitch; I'll take care of my baby as long as I'm free to do so.

"Yo mama was talking about us having a big wedding and everything. She was calling me daughter in law. I love yo mama. And I love you even more Winnie." She smiled.

"I love you too."

I wanted to leave so bad. I didn't want to be around this shit right now. It's crazy because my mother was so eager for me to marry Janice because she fits her complexion criteria. I guess since Janice passed the paper bag test then she was okay to marry. I walked into the bathroom and shut the door behind me. Damn I craved to see Vanessa right now. After about ten minutes in the bathroom Janice finally knocked on the door.

"Winnie I just got off the phone with your mother and her and Sharon are stopping by. They are both excited about the news." She said through the closed bathroom door.

"Okay baby, I'll be out in a minute." I replied.

I threw some water on my face then took a deep breath. Well at least I would get to see Sharon for a change. Marcus was probably available but he couldn't tolerate being around my mother and she couldn't tolerate to be around him. It would have been good to see him and have some testosterone in the room beside myself. I knew Sharon would have my back but she couldn't help but sympathize with the women because she was one.

About fifteen minutes later my mother and Sharon walked in the door. Janice hugged the both of them like they were having the wedding today.

"Winnie I'm so proud of you and Janice. Come give me a hug." My mother said.

"Congratulations Winnie!" Sharon smiled.

I could tell she was irritated about something. I chose to ignore it for the time being. Everyone settled into the living room after grabbing refreshments Janice had set out. Once they were in the groove of things I excused myself to step outside. I needed to smoke some Cush. I already had one rolled up in the Range Rover so I grabbed it and leaned on the car to puff. Shortly after I stepped outside Sharon came outside looking for me.

"Damn Winnie I can smell that strong shit way over here. What's that some Cush?" She rhetorically asked.

"Please believe me." I replied.

"Yeah well they in there having a war party concerning you. They so wrapped up in that shit that I was able to sneak outside to look for you." Sharon laughed.

"What was you irritated about when you came inside?" I asked.

"Yo mama, she keeps telling me that I shouldn't have a baby by that dark ass nigga. Yet she overjoyed that you got a baby on the way. She berated me the entire ride over here." She sneered.

"Yeah so what! What difference does it make you ain't pregnant and even if you were that's between you and Marcus." I commented.

"I am pregnant but I haven't told mama yet. I'm about six weeks pregnant." She replied

"Congratulations Sharon! See you and Marcus were trying to have a baby but Janice and I wasn't trying. She was supposed to be on birth control pills but she said they were making her sick so she stopped taking them."

"So you don't want this baby by Janice?" Sharon asked.

"It ain't that, it's just not a big deal to me like it is to her and mama. Plus I got other shit on my mind. My little homie Chucky got killed and Chris, Lonnie's cousin got shot again. He's gone live but the whole thing is fucking with me."

"King James and his peoples is catching up to ya'll like that? Damn Winnie you need to be careful. I want my baby to know his or her uncle." Sharon said sympathetically.

"I'm knowing, but I should have expected some type of retaliation. And now I got the police knowing my name as well as everybody in my clique. It's just this baby shit was just bad timing."

"Speaking of King James, I seen Latrice out in L.A. this weekend at the Beverly Center." Sharon commented.

"Oh for real? What her fine ass talking about? She was always cool even though I want to smoke her husband right about now."

"Shit! She was up there shopping with all kinds of bags and shit. That bitch being doing the damn thing. But she was with her nasty ass cousin. Some little fast tale bitch named Karen. She was all up in Marcus' face like I wasn't even standing there. Latrice seen me getting heated so she walked off with her before I went off." Sharon said.

I laughed aloud. I tried to picture a young girl flirting with Marcus in front of my sister.

"What did Marcus do?" I asked but still laughing.

"He knew better. He pretended like the bitch wasn't even there. I gave his ass a sharp look and he knew not to even look her way." She rolled her eyes.

Her and I started laughing aloud. That was good for me at the time. My sister always could make me laugh or feel better when I was feeling down. Her and I laughed outside for another thirty minutes before my mother came outside.

"C'mon Sharon let's go." She walked up on us laughing.

"What's so funny?" Mama asked.

"Nothing, you would have had to be here from the beginning." I replied.

"Well come give me a hug."

I walked over to hug and kiss her on the cheek. She grabbed me tightly around the neck and whispered in my ear.

"You make a honest woman out of Janice, ya hear?"

I didn't respond I just loosened my embrace then hugged Sharon. Sharon smirked as if she knew what mama had said. I smiled confirming my mother's comment.

"We got to get together and do the double date thing some time Sis. Ay mama how is your girlfriend Paula doing, I haven't seen her in awhile?" I asked while they were walking away.

"She got her a new man so she ain't been having time for her girl. But I talked to her yesterday on the phone and she might come down here for the weekend." Mama said while opening her car door.

"Well ya'll be safe."

"We love you!!!" They both said simultaneously.

It felt so good to hear them say that my spirit was rejuvenated. I walked towards the apartment and waived.

"I love both of ya'll too."

When I made it upstairs to the apartment Janice was watching television in the living room. I sat next to her on the couch and we cuddled. We watched television until we both fell asleep on the couch. Some time in the middle of the night Janice woke up and tapped me so that we could go to bed.

The next morning I got up early to holla at Lonnie. When we talked on the phone he sounded a little upbeat. He told me that things were looking better for Chris. I was happy to hear that. I told him that I would take him to breakfast. We sat up in IHOP and talked about future plans. I was thinking about having him serve some homies Fabian was talking about in the Delmont Heights. I didn't want him going back to the spot off of Mt. Vernon until I figured some things out. I would have him make the drop off to this nigga named Turtle. His real name was Travon. I went to Cajon High School with him. Fabian was real cool with him from back in the day. We would start him out with half a bird and see what he does with that. Only Lonnie would deal with him and I would split the profit with him. He figured Chris would be getting out of the hospital real soon so that was his number one concern for the moment.

"Another one of my concerns is when do we plan on riding on them niggas that killed Chucky and shot Chris? I'm ready to peel they caps backwards." He said with venom in his voice.

It was a lot of weight in his words. He had faith in me to know when we would take care of the people that did this to our people. Then he was also testing to see if I was up to the challenge. I knew I had to pacify him for a while but honestly I didn't know whom we were gone ride on or where to find them.

"Yeah we looking into who did the shooting but I also want to find out who told King James and them where the spot was." I replied.

"Why don't we just go after King James and Boom-Boom straight up? If we find out where them niggas is hanging it will be all over." He said.

"Yeah but finding them is the hard part. If I knew where they were hanging do you think we would be eating breakfast? King James don't roll like that so I got some people looking into where I can catch up with this nigga so we can serve him." I replied.

I was telling the truth about not being able to find King James. But I lied to him about having someone look into his whereabouts. The streets have a code with ranks. So when a nigga holds you in a position of a higher rank than him you won't survive too long by admitting you don't have things under control. When a crisis happens it has to appear like you expected it and had a plan prepared. You always got everything figured out. He nodded his head as if he was waiting on me to make the move.

The game makes you old quick. I had to be the guardian to too many people. If I failed then everyone was affected if I succeeded then everyone was ungrateful. I had two families that I had to protect. One was my biological and the other was my street family. It was much easier when I was a curb server trying to stack my bread so I could live well. When I felt like my back was against the wall then self-preservation was what drove my hustle. Now it falls on my shoulders if either family is sustained or is crushed. The talk with Lonnie had me thinking about the trials to come and to anticipate future problems. I had to play chess.

15
THE STREET TALKS

More money, more problems!
Notorious B.I.G

Vanessa had just gotten back from taking my son to school. I startled her when she walked in to see me sitting on the couch watching television. I knew she would be right back so I patiently waited. She smiled after recovering from being startled. I turned the television off so that we could talk.

"I know this is a little sudden but I was wondering if you wanted to go to a funeral with me today?"

"A funeral?" She asked. She almost choked on the orange juice she was drinking.

"Yeah, my little homie Chucky got killed the other night. That's why I haven't been by for the last few days. I've been dealing with that shit lately. He was only seventeen I think. My little homie Chris had gotten shot also but he doing better. I think he was dysfunctional for a few days from the shock of being shot." I explained.

"What time is the funeral?"

"At noon. Go in there and put on a good-looking funeral dress. I got my black suit in the car."

"Okay." She replied. She had the facial expression as if she was deciding what to wear.

"You knew we were in a war with King James so you should have bought a few dresses for that. You should buy a dress just in case you have to attend my funeral." I commented.

"Don't say that!" She snapped.

I had touched a nerve. She walked into the bedroom after rolling her eyes at me. Man I loved that woman. Vanessa was like a man in a lot of ways. She didn't bitch at you and she didn't nag. When she was pissed at you she would check you then give you the silent treatment. Besides the silent treatment there was nothing else she did with an attitude.

I walked out to the car to get my suit from out the back seat. I had my suit in plastic on a hanger with my black gators in my other hand. I had taken care of the entire funeral. I gave Chucky's mother some cash so that she could at least be okay for a little while. Chucky had two little sisters and he was the only man in the house. I promised myself that I would look after them as long as I was able.

It was about eleven by the time we had finished getting dressed. She was wearing black so good that I wanted to make her take the clothes off for a quickie. But I didn't want to be late. We decided to roll in my Range Rover.

"I heard about a young nigga getting smoked near Mt. Vernon the other day. I was talking to Sandra at the hair salon and she was talking about it. You know she be fucking with Boom-Boom?" She asked as if I already knew.

"Naw I didn't know that. But it ain't gone do me any good unless she gone set him up for me." I replied.

"Yeah, you get rid of Boom-Boom then King James is gone fall. He got the connect but Boom-Boom got the muscle. Boom-Boom got the respect in the street where niggas would be down to rally behind him. Especially those California Garden niggas."

"Yeah Chris told me that it was some young niggas he hadn't seen before. It wasn't Boom-Boom because his presence is too intimidating for someone not to notice him walk up. He said they had to be about his age." I explained.

"Yeah, probably so. He can always get some young fools trying to come up in the game to do his dirt. Get rid of him and James will be weak." She insisted.

"What else are the streets saying? I know Sandra wasn't the only one running off at the mouth." I grinned.

"Word on the street is that some young up and coming from the Dorjil's is giving King James a hard time. This was said after Sandra had left. People are also saying that since Big Mel done got out of jail niggas coming up missing." She commented without looking my way.

We rolled up into the church and the sermon had just begun when we sat down. Chris was in a cast sitting up front with the family. Lonnie sat in the row behind him. I began looking around while the preacher started screaming and hollering. I wasn't in the mood to feel guilty but what did I expect I was at a funeral. I was at a funeral for a young man that worked for me and hadn't even become a legal adult. The preacher explained how us young people today got chips on our shoulders. In fact, he reiterated his statement by saying that many of us have boulders on our shoulders. They had a closed casket funeral with a picture of Chucky someone must have found somewhere.

Chucky's mother was crying while what appeared to be his little sister sat with a stone face. No tears fell down her face. I wondered what her state of mind was while Vanessa sat next to me. I saw Big Mel straggle in almost towards the end. He was walking in with Maria, Fabian and Shanell. They sat right behind me as the preacher closed out his sermon.

"How long have you been here?" Big Mel whispered.

"About thirty minutes ago. You and Fab-Five gone probably be late for ya'll own funerals." I commented.

"I hope so." Big Mel chuckled

"You know how it is with females, they want to take forever and a day." Big Mel whispered then glanced back at Maria.

I don't even think he noticed Vanessa sitting next to me. She didn't turn around but kept her eyes focused on the preacher. Antoine never made it to the funeral. I was a little disappointed but I also knew how Antoine could be. He had been missing after we all had met up at the hospital.

It actually bothered me when I seen them lower him into the ground. It was the finality of his death that really sunk in. I thought I actually seen a tear come down Vanessa's face. She was so beautiful standing in her black dress. If I had told her I was going to a slaughterhouse she would have rode with me. I had a lot on my mind and Vanessa standing next to me settled it for the time.

After the funeral I spoke to the family and gave my condolences. I spoke to Chris but he seemed despondent. In fact I got the impression that he was resentful. I chose to ignore it because we were at a funeral. That was his road dog since they were little boys so I knew he took it hard.

"Where is Antoine? He was pretty hurt about that shit I'm surprised he didn't come." Lonnie asked.

"Yeah that was a trip to me too. I don't know where he could be. I talked to him yesterday over the phone and he was buying a suit for Chucky's funeral." I replied.

Vanessa glanced at me. I could tell she figured I was lying to Lonnie. She knew that Antoine would miss his own funeral to chase after some pussy.

"Ay Lonnie, I want you to meet a dear friend of mine. This is Vanessa." I said.

"Nice to meet you Vanessa." He replied. I could tell that he was a little stunned from her beauty. He tried to play it off as best he could. I knew that it was only out of respect for me.

"Nice to meet you too. Was he your family, the deceased?" Vanessa asked.

"Naw, but he was like family. He was my cousin's best friend. Only other nigga Chris hung out with besides me was Chucky. He will be missed by everybody." Lonnie explained.

Chucky's birth name was Lorenzo Charles Atkins. We stood around momentarily until Fab-Five and Big Mel came over with their women. Chucky's family had gotten in the limousine. When Big Mel finally got a chance to see who was standing with me he grinned from ear to ear.

"How have you been Vanessa? I see you still hanging around my cousin Pooh like back in the day. Girl come over here and give me a hug." Big Mel embraced her.

Maria looked a little jealous for a moment but she must have suddenly remembered Vanessa was with me. Gradually a smile appeared when she realized it was strictly platonic. Vanessa had that effect on women. They usually thought their man wanted her. They were usually right.

"Ay Vanessa I was real hurt when I heard about your brother when I was in the pen. He was a real nigga down and dirty." Big Mel said.

"Yeah he was set up by some punk bitch. But I take it in stride now. Did Winnie tell you I have a son now?" She glanced at me.

"Yeah he sure did. I've been meaning to meet him some time soon. But you know my cousin he likes to keep things secret. Even from his big cousin." Big Mel lied.

I hadn't told him shit. But he was covering for me and nine times out of ten Vanessa knew he was covering for me too. She glanced at me again as if she wanted to talk later. I perfectly understood her look. That was when I thought it was best to introduce all the women to each other. This way my clique and I could talk alone without any disturbances for five or ten minutes. I told Fabian to make sure Shanell didn't mention anything to Janice. Fabian told me that they were mad at each other so he doubted that she would say anything anyhow. But he assured me he would talk to her anyway. We walked a little ways from the women to be closer to the cars.

"So have you heard anything about who shot Chris and killed Chucky?" I asked everybody.

"I haven't heard anything about what happened to Chucky and Chris but would you believe that them niggas came to me offering me a job?" Fab-Five sneered.

"You bullshitting me? When and how did they do this?" I asked.

"Yesterday Noony came by talking his shit like he do. I thought about peeling his cap right then but I thought about how you said we could use him for our benefit. He told me that he had a hook up where he could get me a brick for seventeen even and I won't have to pay upfront. I asked him where he got that kind of hook up and he smiled. I knew where he had got the hook up at but I wasn't sure if he was setting me up with the police or he was serious…" Fab-Five briefly paused.

"When did you know he was for real?" Big Mel asked.

"When that nigga handed me a nine millimeter fresh out the box. It didn't have any bodies on it or anything. Talking about *'a nigga like you can be used in a lot of ways if you down'.*" Fab-Five teased then continued. "I wanted to shoot him in his face right then and there. I told him to give me a couple of days to think about it. I wanted tell you about it and figure out a plan since I knew I would see you at the funeral."

"The way I see it he is trying to recruit some niggas to be shooters for King James. He won't deal with you direct so he will probably send Boom-Boom to meet with you. This is good because if we can get Boom-Boom out the way then King James won't have any muscle. So we got to think long and hard about this shit." I explained.

"How about we do him the same way like last time? We make sure we kill the nigga this time though." Lonnie commented.

"Naw, because if Boom-Boom is meeting with a shooter he won't be dumb enough to meet him at night. Boom-Boom is a seasoned nigga of the streets he wants to read the nigga first so he would meet him somewhere in the open. It would be in a public place like a shopping center." I explained.

"Besides, we don't know if Boom-Boom not setting him up. Noony scary ass probably told them where he got the information when they tried to set us up. Barry might be pondering on killing Fab-Five anyhow. We got to watch out for that too. He might have made Noony think he wants to hire him when in fact he might be trying to kill him." Big Mel interjected.

189

"Barry?" Lonnie asked.

"That's his government name." I nonchalantly explained.

"Why don't we let the streets talk? Now that I think about it even if he thinks Fab-Five is down with you he gone try to offer him a sweeter deal to get him to turn instead of outright trying to kill him when he don't know for sure if he down with us. What if we told niggas and bitches on the West Side that Pooh done taken over the West Side and niggas is fucking with him now if they want the raw." Big Mel said.

"Why in the fuck would I want to do that? That's gone bring on the police to be searching to crack my ass. It's already bad enough we got Detective Barnes sniffing around." I said incredulously.

"That's the beauty of it. We spread the word where you gone be at and that you running shit nowadays, them niggas is gone get desperate. They gone have to react. You be the bait in a trap. It's always good to use females for that kind of gossip. Let Noony overhear that shit and when they come after you have the police waiting to crack they ass." Big Mel explained.

"But ain't that low key snitching? If we sick the police on him then we doing what a snitch would do." I protested.

Everyone glanced at Big Mel. His plan sounded good except for the police part.

"That's the thing, we won't be snitching someone else will be snitching. You best believe that nigga James is putting the police on us. Why do you think we had a visit from the detective at the hospital? But instead we reverse the shit. Let Fab-Five meet with the nigga in a public place. Then Fab-Five you go to the bathroom or some shit. Then Pooh, you pop up out of nowhere and make sure he sees you. He ain't gone pass up that opportunity to try and smoke you even if its daylight. His ego will get the best of him. The whole time the police is watching you they gone catch up with him. We just spread the word through a few females that know Noony that you got a major deal going down in whatever place Barry chooses to meet Fabian." Big Mel explained.

"That just might work. With him locked up we could really wipe out James for good. We still gone have a problem catching up to where he is but he won't be a threat anymore." I agreed.

"We have to spread the word to loud mouth Tracy and her homegirls that Pooh be copping at whatever place you and Barry meet." Big Mel directed his statement to Fab-Five.

"Just so Noony could know in enough time to call the police, huh? I think Fab-Five should be the one to suggest they meet in a public place. That way Boom-Boom will respect his precautions and believe he's on the up and up. And Noony knows Tracy and I used to fuck around. He knows me and Fab-Five is cool too but he don't know if we working together. I think that's a bomb idea, what ya'll niggas think?"

"I think the shit can work, but you better make sure you not in close enough range for Boom-Boom to blast on you." Lonnie warned.

"A million things can go wrong. So if that nigga get too close then we gone have to put him down, police or not." Big Mel replied.

"Yeah, it will look like I'm pillow talking with Tracy. That bitch runs her mouth a mile a minute. And we will tell a few more people like Noony's cousin that stays up in the Dorjil's. That way its damn near impossible for him not to hear about it." I pondered.

We set up the date for Fab-Five to meet up with Boom-Boom one week after the funeral. He suggested that they meet in a public place and Fabian said he felt like he could see Boom-Boom smiling through the phone. Tracy and her girls were like the West Side newspaper. When they talked about shit they were loud and boisterous. I wanted to get the word spread fast and they had shit spreading around like wildflower in less than a week.

I rented a car around twelve-thirty that afternoon. I decided to choose a bright red car that was more flamboyant and easy to spot on a sunny day. We had it planned in a shopping center on Highland and Mt. Vernon. It was perfect because I was in the mood for some Louisiana Chicken so I drove up and I noticed the

191

police instantly. Once again they were stupid enough to be staked out in a Crown Victoria. I hadn't seen Boom-Boom but I had a good idea where he might be. I got out the car and leaned on the car as if I was waiting for someone. I put a jolly rancher in my mouth and waited for about ten minutes without making a move. I would glance over at the police through my peripheral and they were on me like a hawk. I glanced in another direction opposite of the blue Crown Victoria and seen a more inconspicuous car. There were two men sitting in that car as well and they also looked like cops. I wasn't really nervous about them but I was concerned about Boom-Boom because I knew on sight he might start dumping.

Then suddenly I saw someone creeping up from the side of a car. He was squatting a good distance away from me but he was trying to creep. Boom-Boom was a big man so he couldn't hide that good. I went to the passenger side of the car walking fast in front of the rental. He seen my movements and reacted quickly. He started shooting from a distance away without a care to who was watching. Damn I didn't think this was going to be this easy. He must have really wanted me bad. He busted out the window in the driver's side of the rental and kept blasting. I had ducked under the car upset with myself that I didn't carry a strap. But the only way this could work was if I wasn't carrying a weapon. That way he would be the only one going to jail. Big Mel and Fabian were close by but he was trying to take my head off. Then my thoughts went to the dumb ass cops sitting on the stake out for me, when were they going to move?

"Freeze!!!" A plain clothed officer yelled.

"Drop the fucking gun." His partner insisted.

Boom-Boom sat his gun on the pavement and slowly lifted his hands in the air. I was peaking up by then looking at them arresting him through the passenger side window.

"Mr. Daniels will you stand up and allow us to search your person?" An officer spoke to me.

I slowly rose up from the side of the car from off the pavement. A crowd began to gather around the scene when they noticed the police. They handcuffed me as well while they were reading Boom-Boom his rights. He didn't know if I was strapped that was the reason he tried to shoot from a distance. He looked at me with so much venom when we first made eye contact. I smiled in a narcissistic way. That shook him to the core. I could see in his eyes that he couldn't figure why I was smiling when we both were going to jail. Then a light went off in his head, they hadn't read me my Miranda rights yet.

"Mr. Daniels, can we search your car for any contraband?" The first one to approach me asked.

He had a crew cut like he had once been in the marines. I continued my staring match with Boom-Boom and simply replied.

"Do you have a warrant?"

They already searched my body and hadn't found anything. So I knew they would ask me for permission to search my car. It was only right that I gave them a hard time to play along. I knew what his response was before he even spoke again.

"No we do not. But we can hold you here until we can attain a warrant." The same officer replied.

"Go right ahead, the keys are right here on the hood of the car." I commented nonchalantly.

They searched the rental car from top to bottom. It took them twenty-five to thirty minutes to go through every inch of the car. I was so relaxed but I feigned nervousness. When they were finished they looked over to the officers who had Boom-Boom in custody and shook their head. The crew cut officer twirled his hand around indicating to the other police that they can take Boom-Boom to jail. I knew he would catch all kinds of charges. He drove off in the back seat mean mugging me and I stared back with a smirk on my face. One of these days he would understand what happened to him.

"Mr. Daniels why were you up here sitting by your car? Were you waiting for someone to appear? Were you expecting someone to meet you here?" Officer Crew Cut asked.

"No, actually I was basking in the sun before I went inside Louisiana chicken. I was hungry but the heat felt good since I had been in the car with the air conditioner." I replied.

"So you were in this shopping center to buy something to eat?" Officer Crew Cut asked sarcastically.

"What is your name detective?" I asked.

"Were you here to buy food only Mr. Daniels or were you here to meet someone?" He asked again. The impatience was evident in his voice.

"If you are not arresting me then I shouldn't have to answer any more questions, isn't that right?" I asked.

"I am Officer Yates and this is my partner Officer Hudson. We are in the narcotics division for the San Bernardino County Sheriffs." He surrendered.

"Well like I said Officer Yates, I only came to buy some food and then head home. Am I free to go or do you have any more questions for me."

"No Mr. Daniels but we would like your address?"

I gave them my mother's new address then opened the car door to the rental. I grabbed a towel so that I could wipe off the broken glass that had fallen in the driver's seat. They walked away without saying a word. They were pissed off and I knew it. That made me a little uneasy because angry police make it a vendetta to go after you when you are in the game. I considered having Noony smoked but I was trying to end the violence. If things could calm down a little on the West Side then we could hustle well. I watched them get in the black jaguar and then I thought about Latrice's pretty black jaguar. She had a pretty ass jaguar that looked just like the car the police were driving but a later year no doubt. Then a thought came to mind suddenly.

194

The phone rang three times before she picked up her cell phone. I thought it was about to go to her voice mail. Pick up, pick up I kept saying as though she could hear me.

"Hello! Winnie what's up?"

"What's up Sharon? Ay real quick, what was the name of that girl that was with Latrice? The one you were saying was her cousin or something?" I quickly asked.

"I think her name was Karen. Yeah her name was Karen, why?" She replied.

"How did she look?"

"She had braids when I seen her. But she was like caramel complexion with a pretty face. She had a cute little shape to her but that little bitch ain't got anything on me." Sharon sassily replied.

"How tall was she?"

"About 5'2, she was maybe about an inch shorter than me. Why are you asking me all these questions about that little hootchie? I know you ain't trying to hook up with her and she is Latrice's cousin. Besides, you too scared of your mother to date a girl with that complexion." She teased.

"You tripping, did she have a small tattoo on her left shoulder of a rose?" I pressed forward with questions.

"I don't know because she was wearing something that was covering her shoulders. Winnie, why you keep asking me about this girl? What's up with her?"

"I think that's the same girl that's been fucking with Antoine. I haven't heard from Antoine since before the funeral and I think he was with her."

"Aw shit!!!" Sharon finally understood.

16

ANTOINE

I stop breathing damn I see demons!
Snoop Dogg

He decided to wear a leisure suit today. He was supposed to go to a funeral the following day. So he had promised himself that he would have some fun today. It had been a long time since he had hooked up with Karen. It was something about the way she fucked him that made him yearn for her. She didn't have any inhibitions about her sexuality. She did everything he desired to please him. He was planning to hook up with her later on that night and he was a little excited.

Pooh was right when he said she wasn't as fine as he was used to. But sometimes sexiness overwhelmed looks. Karen had that special sexuality that made him tingle all over. She was able to make his toes curl. But Antoine wasn't concerned too much about Pooh's opinion because he knew that Pooh just didn't like the girl. He would never explain why or would he even admit the truth. What made Antoine stay away for so long was because Pooh had premonitions sometimes that was scary. He could feel the vibe of someone and know they were up to something. The nigga wasn't a prophet or anything though, Antoine considered. Besides, Pooh had taken over the entire organization that started from a spot that he started. It sometimes bothered him how Pooh just put himself in charge. For once he was stepping out against Pooh's suggestions and do what he felt like doing. He had it in his mind that he wasn't going to bring her to his house though. He would rent a room and they would kick it there.

He stepped off his apartment porch holding his hand over his face to protect it from the sun. He walked down the stairs then

196

glanced back at the San Bernardino Mountains. Today was going to be a special day. The first thing he wanted to do was buy a black suit for Chucky's funeral. He hopped into his brand new dark blue BMW after clicking the alarm. He just had the car detailed the day before but decided to spray more of the peach scent around the car. He turned on the radio and blasted his Beanie Siegal 'The Truth' CD. He was feeling good and enjoying the spring day. After he picked out a suit he would then go by the barbershop. He headed out to the Riverside Galleria so that he could get away from the scene of San Bernardino. It was about a twenty-five minute drive but that gave him time to think. Then he would head right back in the city to get his haircut. He hopped on the 215 Freeway towards the 91 Freeway engulfed in the music. It was very pretty outside.

"I should have gone to six flags Magic Mountain or some shit." He commented to himself.

He pulled into the mall parking lot and searched for a convenient parking space. It wasn't that crowded since it was only eleven in the morning on a weekday. He strolled through the mall not having a destination just yet. He wanted to buy a suit but he didn't exactly know where. Besides, he wanted to window shop and look for what else he might want to buy.

His sweat suit was all white with a blue stripe going down the sides of the arms and legs. He only wore a tank top under the jacket and a gold chain with a cross emblem hanging from it. He had just got his taper fade haircut just three days ago but he felt he was in need of another. His tennis shoes were some fresh white Jordan's with blue to match the blue in his sweat suit. It wasn't a doubt in his mind that he was looking fresh and clean. He passed by several shops then heard his phone ring. It was Pooh calling. He debated on picking it up because he was in his own world. He decided to go ahead and see what's going on.

"Hello?"

"Hello? What's cracking Ant, this Pooh?"

"I know who this is nigga? You act like I ain't got caller ID. What's up my nigga?"

"What are you about to get into?"

"Just running a couple of errands. I'm in Riverside buying a suit for Chucky's funeral." Antoine replied.

"Ah snap, you way out in Riverside? What, you went up to the galleria?" Pooh asked.

"Yeah, I just wanted to get everything ready for tomorrow. That's fucked up how they did that young nigga. I swear someone needs to handle that nigga James."

"Let's talk about that shit later. I was gone try to hang out with you a little later on. We ain't hung out in a while." Pooh replied.

"Yeah, I know huh? We should hook up or some shit. I'll be back out that way in about an hour. I wanted to get my haircut."

"Cool my nigga, we can get something to eat or something." Pooh said.

"Alright then, I'll hit you in about two hours. Is that good?"

"That's cool! One!"

"One!"

Antoine smiled when he got off the phone with Pooh. That's his nigga if he don't get any bigga. Antoine admitted to himself at that moment he had really been a little salty with Pooh because Pooh never told him about his connect. He didn't have to introduce him to the nigga but at least let him know he had another connect besides King James. But truthfully there wasn't anyone in the world he had more love for. He briefly reminisced when they were younger chasing after pussy together. Niggas and bitches used to call them the down ass pretty boys. Antoine smiled after that thought. And Pooh was trying to hang out without it being about business. This was guaranteed to be a good day.

At that moment he passed by a suit shop. He walked inside the store with a grin on his face. An Middle Eastern man came from behind the counter.

"How can I help you?" He asked with a thick accent.

"I need to buy a black suit for a funeral. You got any single breasted four buttons? I'm a size thirty-eight."

"Right this way sir. I have just the right suit your looking for."

Antoine glanced at his tag and seen the name Ahmed. He followed Ahmed towards the back of the store. On the top rack was a nice black wool suit. It was exactly what Antoine was looking for.

It took him about an hour to try the suit on then get the pants altered to fit his height. He decided to buy a pair of black gators to match his suit. After buying a shirt and tie to match he spent about eleven hundred dollars. Ahmed smiled the entire time he was shopping.

"Before you go sir, here is my business card if you need anything else. I have business suits, leisure suits, mock necks, and sweaters, dress socks, and you name it."

"That's cool, but can I keep this here until I'm done shopping because I don't want to carry it around the mall?"

"Sure you can." Ahmed smiled.

Antoine walked out of the shop laughing to himself about how friendly Ahmed was. Most of the Middle Eastern men he had ran into were rigid. But he didn't want to think like a racist. He walked down the walkway then decided to take the escalator all the way up to the top floor. He hadn't even made five steps on the third level when he spotted the dime piece walking in front of him. She had her hair in a shoulder length wrap with auburn streaks going through it. She had on some white booty shorts with some cute matching Air force Ones. She was petite with a nice bubble butt that stuck out like a sore thumb. She wore a spaghetti strap tank top with a butterfly tattoo right across her chest.

"Damn she bad." Antoine said aloud.

She glanced back to see who was behind her and she smiled. That was his cue to move in. He began walking a little faster to catch up with her. He decided to slow down and follow her into one of the department stores. She paused and went towards the shoe department. He followed close behind her, hoping she would stay put.

"Those shoes would look cute on you." Antoine commented. He had gotten directly behind her.

"You think so? What about these?" She picked up another shoe.

"I like the ones you had at first. They look like they go with your style and your flavor." Antoine smiled when she turned around.

"Is that so? What is my style and my flavor since you know me so well?" She said sarcastically.

"I'm talking about the way you look. You got that nice little petite frame and that pretty ass face. I think these heals with the open toes would go good with your shape and accentuate that body you got." Antoine explained.

"Check you out. Are you a fashion connoisseur? How do you know what gone look good on me?" She openly flirted.

A conn-what, Antoine thought. He didn't know what she was talking about. But he didn't want to look stupid so he kept talking like he understood her.

"I just know that's all. What is your name sweetheart?"

"My name BeBe."

"Well my name is Antoine but they call me Ant."

"Ant huh? Where is your girlfriend at Ant?" She looked him up and down.

"I don't know where she's at right now. I was hoping you could tell me." Antoine smiled.

"How am I supposed to know?" She giggled.

Antoine knew at this point he had her. She was the type that didn't care if he had a girlfriend or not. He talked to her long enough for her to give him her phone number. He entered it into his phone and told her he would call real soon. He would have called her to hook up that night if he hadn't had plans with Karen. That made him reminisce on Karen. Karen had a way of giving head that would make any man scream. He was hurting to get next to her again. Yeah BeBe would have to wait. Closing his eyes he dreamt of how he was gone wear her out. Today was definitely going to be a good day. After getting BeBe's number he decided to go pick up his suit and head back to San Bernardino. Ahmed had his suit hanging behind the counter. He snatched it up and headed out the door. Once he had gotten his haircut he could hang with his road dog until it was time to be with Karen.

"Bitch no you didn't just tell me you been fucking my husband? I got to be hearing things." Latrice lashed.

She just caught King James pulling off from in front of their grandmother's house. He didn't see Latrice but Latrice saw him. She supposedly went to get her hair done but decided to go visit her grandmother forgetting that she had went out of town for the week.

"Bitch you tripping. You don't even want to be with the nigga. You complain about leaving him everyday. Then you say you getting tired of all his shit. Now you hating on us fucking around?" Karen despondently replied.

"You my cousin and that's my husband, you janky bitch. I should beat yo muthafuckin ass. That's what I should do." Latrice screamed.

"But you can't, so you need to stop tripping. I ain't trying to take him from you, we just fucking. You want to dump this balling ass nigga but you won't let yo cousin get something out of it?" Karen waived her hand to dismiss Latrice.

"Damn Karen, I thought it was a code among family. We blood and you gone do me like this?" Latrice lamented. She couldn't grasp Karen's logic.

"Miss me with that shit. Yeah bitch we blood, so you shouldn't let a nigga come between us. I've been trying to get you to hook me up with one of his homeboys like Boom-Boom and you kept putting me off. We still blood, I'm just fucking a nigga you used to fuck and is still married to." Karen snapped.

"You ain't shit! You don't ever say we family." Latrice snarled.

Latrice walked out the door grabbing her Louis Vutton purse. Her high heels were stomping away towards the door on her grandmother's tile walkway.

"You need to get over that punk shit Latrice. You and me supposed to be better than that." Karen yelled behind Latrice.

She jumped up from the couch and ran towards the door. When she reached the screen door she could tell that Latrice had started crying.

"You are a weak bitch for crying over a nigga you don't even want. That's all I'm saying Latrice." Karen yelled through the screen.

"I ain't crying over James, I'm crying over how my own flesh and blood did me dirty. I don't know how you don't see that." Latrice yelled back.

"Whatever! I got tired of hiding it from you. I try to be real with you and you can't even handle the shit. That nigga the biggest baller on the West Side so you had to know he was fucking other bitches besides you. Especially if you been holding out on him. C'mon Latrice grow the fuck up."

Latrice hopped in her jaguar and slammed the door. As she rolled down the street Karen came outside in the yard barefoot looking at her car speed away. Latrice was truly heartbroken. Her eyes were hurting from the tears flowing down her face. She knew he was fucking other women but her own cousin. Latrice didn't really mind his infidelities but she expected better from Karen. She pondered on her expectations and realized suddenly that she was being naïve. Karen had always been a skank ho. She decided to go to the Pleasure Palace to get the works. She needed to release some tension.

Karen was at home laughing to herself. That little miss too good needed to hear some real shit. It served her right to have access to a nigga like James and not give him the pussy.

"Latrice is always on her high horse." Karen retorted.

She felt like it was better now that she didn't have to hide. Now when she met with King James she would be able to be open about it. She hated being so secretive. Now she could share him with that bitch that's fucking him that lives up in Victorville. Latrice had complained that he was spending days in Victorville. It had to be a woman out there he was seeing. But Karen knew in her heart that she was his San Bernardino pussy and that was fine with her. King James took care of her. Especially when she did shit for him. That reminded her of something she was supposed to do today. She picked up her phone and started dialing the familiar digits.

"Hello?"

"What's up Antoine? How you doing baby?" Karen purred.

"I'm doing real good now that I'm hearing your voice." He replied.

"What are you doing right now?"

"I'm getting my haircut right now."

"Oh for real, we still on for tonight?" Karen asked.

"No doubt. I was gone hang with Pooh for a little while then pick you up after me and him kick it."

"Oooh you want me to bring Stacy? I can call her up right when I get off the phone with you." Karen eagerly asked.

"Naw, it's just gone be you and me. Pooh can holla at Stacy some other time." Antoine replied.

"What are ya'll getting into?"

"I don't know! Ain't no telling with Pooh. He so paranoid nowadays that he won't say where we going until we face to face."

The telephone was quiet for a moment. Karen knew that if she could get Pooh and Antoine, King James would take care of her for life. She was desperately trying to think of a way she could hang out with Antoine and Pooh. Antoine on the other hand didn't want to hurt her feelings by telling her that Pooh didn't like her.

"I want to see what you guys are doing. Can't all three of us hang together then baby." She playfully pouted.

203

"You know I would Karen but I think Pooh wants to talk some business with me so he would be pissed if you were there." Antoine lied.

"Okay baby, so what time are we going to hook up?" She surrendered.

"Oh I'm saying around seven depending on how long Pooh wants to kick it." He replied.

That made her think about his homeboy Pooh. She always wanted to fuck him. She couldn't understand how her girl Stacy didn't whip it on that nigga.

"I would have had that nigga sprung if it was me." She whispered to herself.

"What did you say?" Antoine brought her back to reality.

"Never mind, just be sure to call me later so we can hook up."

"You spending the night with me right? I have to go to a funeral tomorrow so it would be best I drop you off in the morning."

"Yeah that's cool, I'll bring a change of clothes." Karen replied.

Once she was off the phone she began sorting out her clothes for later. She was gone fuck him one last time before James and his boys took care of him. She always thought Antoine was cute as hell but he didn't have money like James. She had her heart broken by a pretty nigga like Antoine when she went to Lynwood High. She wasn't bitter behind it, but it taught her a lesson to never fuck with a low-ball nigga no matter how fine he was. Unless you were getting something out of it.

She pondered on her days growing up in Lynwood. She had grown up around the Palm & Oak Gangster Crips and the Peck Street Crips in Lynwood when her mother was alive. She didn't move in with her grandmother until she was nineteen years old. Latrice had been living with their grandmother most of her life. Karen considered that was why she was so naïve to things.

"These Valley niggas don't know anything about that real L.A. shit." Karen commented to herself.

Lynwood was a city right next to Compton in Los Angeles County. So San Bernardino people were like country bumpkins to her. She dug into her closet trying to pick out the most seductive clothing she could find. She wanted Antoine to want to fuck her the moment he seen her. He had to miss it because it had been some time now since they hooked up. Once the war started he had cleaned his slate with everybody so she was put on the back burner. But he kept her phone number in his cell phone and decided to give her a call. After months of not seeing each other now they were about to hook up.

After she packed everything for her one night out, she decided to take a nap. He wouldn't be coming through for another four or five hours. It would have been easier for him to just spend the night at her grandmother's house. That was the way King James wanted her to do it. But she didn't want anything going down at her grandmother's house. The neighbors were so nosy that they were probably going to report the argument she had with Latrice earlier today. She didn't need to hear her grandmother's mouth.

She had slept a good three hours when the phone woke her up. She stumbled around trying to grab the cordless.

"Hello?" She said

"What, you asleep?" Antoine asked.

"I had dozed off for a minute. What time is it?"

"It's a little bit after five. That nigga Pooh got tied up so I decided to come get you a little early. Is that cool?"

"Yeah that's cool. Let me jump in the shower and you can come through in about thirty minutes." She replied.

"Ah baby what you gone have me doing for thirty minutes?" Antoine teased.

"You want me to be my best for you right baby? You can think of something for thirty minutes." She replied.

He had been over her grandmother's house only once before but he remembered how to get there. He decided to get him something to eat while he waited for her to get ready. He was really disappointed that he didn't get to hang with Pooh. He knew that he would probably see him at the funeral though. But it would be with everyone else. He wanted some man-to-man alone time with his road dog.

After he sat down to eat a hamburger he decided to call Karen. She had just gotten out the shower and told him to come through. He didn't want to eat too much because he was taking her out to eat then to a hotel. He drove over there with a big smile on his face. He had missed Karen so much that he felt ashamed to admit it.

When he pulled up in his blue BMW her knees actually went weak. He had come a long way from being a curb server on Mt. Vernon. The car was so pretty to her that she could taste it. She locked the front door then ran outside to greet him with her bag in hand. The car looked so good that she considered not going through with everything. Her second thought was that it was just a car and King James had a lot more to offer than a car.

"Damn baby come give me a hug. I missed you so much Antoine."

She sat her bag down to wrap her arms around his neck. They began French kissing right on the walkway. When they finished she realized that her neighbors could be looking. She looked around then rushed towards his car.

"When did you get this beautiful car?"

"You like?"

"I like!"

"I've had it for a few months now. Get in."

She sunk right into the leather seats. Before he could get in on the driver's seat she was already adjusting his five-disc CD changer.

"Where we going?" She asked.

"This new Mariah Carey CD is banging." He replied.

206

"You not gone answer me?"

"Oh, my bad. We going to get something to eat then I was going to rent a hotel suite. Is that cool?" He replied.

"I thought we was going to your new spot?"

"I'm living with some people right now." Antoine lied.

He didn't know if he was ready for her to know where he lived. She turned her head with disgust. Just like a trifling nigga to have a bomb ass car but no bomb ass place, she thought. There wasn't much to say while the Mariah Carey CD hypnotized their thoughts.

"I don't want to go get something to eat. Let's get the room right now and if we get hungry then we will order something later." Karen suggested.

"You sure? Because we already out right now."

"I'm sure." She replied.

He rented a suite with a Jacuzzi inside. They didn't waste any time with small talk. Right when she sat her bags down they were all over each other. She gave him head for about ten minutes then he bent her over doggy style until he had cum. It was more an angry sex act between the two. She wanted him to give it to her that way. Antoine passed out on the bed panting heavily. She lied next to him gently rubbing his chest.

"Baby I don't want you to get mad at me." She said.

"Mad about what?" Antoine was still panting.

"After that crazy episode I'm a little hungry can you go get us something to eat?" She asked.

"Oh that's it, let me catch my breath and we can roll."

"Do you mind going by yourself? I wanted to freshen up a little bit." She said.

"Okay!"

He quickly threw his clothes back on and walked out the door. Karen walked to the window to see him get in his car. Right when he started the car she turned on her cell phone.

"Hello?"

"Hello? What's up Karen?"

"I got that nigga Antoine out getting me some food right now. We over here in downtown by the mall at this big white hotel, I think it's the Renaissance, right off the 215 Freeway." She blurted out.

"I know which hotel you talking about. Ya'll staying the night?"

"Yeah!"

"Cool, get that nigga to come outside to the car in about an hour." King James replied.

"Okay. I'm gone cut my phone off so you can't call me anymore tonight." She explained.

"That's cool we gone be there."

Antoine came back with Popeye's Chicken in hand. They ate then watched television. Suddenly she looked at her watch realizing that the hour was about up.

"Baby, go get my slippers from out the back seat of your car. I must have forgotten to bring them up to the room." She said.

"Damn, I wasn't expecting to go out anymore tonight. But it's cool."

He threw on his pants and shoes then went to his car. Once he reached his car he started turning the car upside down looking for her slippers. It was frustrating to him because he couldn't find them anywhere. He decided after awhile that she must have brought them upstairs but forgot she did. He closed the backdoor of his beamer. As he stood up to close the front door he noticed a large figure right in front of him. He looked up at the masked man and stood there in shock. The man's face was covered but Antoine knew who it was. Standing behind him were two other men with masks on. They were all armed. Antoine didn't know what to do. He glanced in every direction out of panic. He noticed a big grin through the mask. He didn't say a word. He was trapped. His last thought was 'that bitch set me up'.

The first bullet pierced through Antoine's chest. The second bullet pierced his skull. Then an array of bullets began to riddle his body. He slumped to the ground whining softly. Tears welled up in his eyes as the pain of the fire began to wear away. He leaned backwards, coughed up blood and died.

17
DEDICATED

I tell you life ain't shit to fool with!
Ice Cube

It had been more than a week since I last spoke to Antoine and I was scared. I knew Karen probably had something to do with his disappearance. I was hitting up every female that Antoine might have been affiliated with. I even tried to call Stacy but she wasn't picking up the phone. Every time I called her phone it went straight to voice mail. I suddenly remembered that my mother had a spare key to Antoine's apartment.

"Hello Mama?"

"What's going on Winnie baby? You gone have to excuse me because I've been drinking some Christian Brothers. So what's up?" She replied.

"You still got a spare key to Antoine's apartment?"

"I sure do but you can't have it. What you want with it anyhow, don't you have your own place. I can't wait until my grand baby is born." Her inebriated voice echoed through the phone.

"Mama this is serious. Antoine has been missing for over a week so I need to come pick up that key." I yelled through the phone.

"What do you mean he's been missing?" She snapped into reality.

"He's been missing mama. I talked to him the day before little Chucky's funeral and haven't heard from him since." I replied.

"Well I'm coming with you boy."

I didn't want to tell her that I was 90% sure he was dead. I didn't want her to panic while she was drunk. I had a lot on my mind. I was feeling guilty because I was supposed to hang with him the day I spoke to him. Janice had me tied up on some baby shit. She wanted me to help her pick out some outfits for the baby. I tried to get out of it but she started laying this guilt trip on me about not being involved. I had to swallow that shit and roll with her. All of that was on my mind as I rolled over to my mother's house. When I pulled up to my mother's apartment she was already waiting outside. She jumped in the car appearing to be a little more sober than she sounded over the phone.

"Mama you getting drunk in the middle of the afternoon?" I asked once she had gotten comfortable.

"I'm a grown ass woman boy. Mind ya business and let's go find Antoine." She sharply replied.

I could tell at that moment that she was still drunk. We quietly drove over to Antoine's house. When we pulled up to his apartment complex the first thing I did was look for his new BMW. It wasn't in his parking space, which indicated he hadn't made it home. Moms and I quickly walked up the stairs. While she was unlocking the door I glanced out at the mountains. The sky was clear and the sun was out. I had always thought this was a nice view of the San Bernardino Mountains.

When we walked inside there was no indication that someone had been there in days. Just as I had expected he just disappeared. I tried to look for anything that might tell me who he was last with. I had told him not to invite Karen or any crazy females he doesn't know down and dirty. It appeared as though he had followed my instructions. I went through his drawers but nothing was there that I could go on. Finally I told my mama after the umpteenth time we had searched the place that it was time to go. Then my cell phone rang as we walked out the front door. I looked at my phone and noticed that it was my sister Sharon.

"What's up Sharon?"

"What's up Winnie, did ya'll find out where Antoine was? Mama called me when you were on your way to get her." Sharon said with strain in her voice.

"Naw, I was hoping he was laid up but that ain't the case." I replied.

"I also was calling to tell you that Latrice is up in here. She's been coming up in here for the last five or six days straight for the massages. She looked stressed out." Sharon whispered.

"Damn, okay I'm gone drop mama off and then I'm gone shoot down there to holla at her." I replied.

"Why would you do that?" Sharon asked.

"Because she might know the whereabouts of either Karen or Antoine. And if…"

"You ain't taking me home, I want to find out where Antoine is, just as bad as you do." Mama snapped.

"Okay, Okay."

"That's yo mama!" Sharon laughed.

It took us about fifteen minutes to drive down to the Pleasure Palace. Sharon had been running it mostly since Janice had been pregnant. Janice found herself sleepy all the time. I walked in and went straight towards the back to interrupt the masseuse. Latrice was lying on her stomach with her shirt off when I walked in.

"Excuse me sir, but you can't walk in." The masseuse blurted out.

Latrice patted her on her arm indicating that it was okay. Latrice covered herself and sat up. She had an 'I've been expecting you' look on her face.

"What's Up Sherwin? How have you been?" She calmly replied.

"Fuck all that, yo cousin Karen set my homeboy up." I lashed out.

"Probably so." She calmly replied.

"You admitting that shit. I need to smoke yo ass right now. Bitch that was my muthafuckin road dog and you saying it like he was a piece of meat." I snapped.

I was up in her face by then. She didn't lose her cool for nothing. She knew that I was capable of killing her ass. I was on fire. I could have ripped her head off her neck at that point.

"Yeah, that bitch Karen is scandalous. She ain't any damn good and she never meant Antoine any good." She said.

"Oh so now you gone pretend you didn't know shit about it? I'm telling you Latrice we go way back to jr. high school but if you don't get to clearing some shit up for me you gone have problems."

"The truth is, that bitch is doing everybody scandalous. But she lives with my grandmother. But listen Sherwin, don't bother my grandmother because she ain't got anything to do with this." She rolled her eyes.

This threw me for a loop. It sounded like she wanted to let me know where I could find Karen. I wasn't for sure so I had to ask for sure.

"What are you saying? You know where she's at?"

"Yeah I know where she's at. Better yet you can find her at my grandmother's house here let me give you the address."

She stood up and walked over to her purse and grabbed a sheet of paper. She began writing down the address. She handed me the sheet of paper like it was a piece of gum. I was skeptical. But she knew that I was skeptical.

"That bitch has been scandalous from day one and I could give two fucks about her. Now you gone do what you want to do and I'm telling you I'm out of it. And no, I'm not trying to set you up…I can see that question in your eyes. I'm through with James' trifling ass too. But I don't know where he's at anyway." She waived her hand like she was through with it all.

"What about Antoine? Where is my homeboy? Is he alive or are they trying to use him against me or hold him for ransom, what?" I said. I was borderline hysterical and extremely hopeful.

213

She had sympathy in her eyes. I thought it was sincere. Then she dropped her head. She felt bad but I needed to know.

"If you expect to find Antoine you best go down to the Simpson Mortuary." She somberly replied.

"No!!!" I screamed through my teeth.

I didn't want to believe it. I couldn't believe it. I glanced down at my watch to maybe catch them before they closed. My heart was broken into a thousand pieces. As many times I had complaints about Antoine I couldn't picture him dead. I would have swallowed his annoyances in abundance if he could only be alive. That shit was so hurtful that I kept banging my fists against my head. Latrice started crying.

"Hey Winnie is everything okay in there?" Sharon asked through the door.

I swung the door open and barged out of the shop. My mother didn't say anything to me because the look on my face was vicious. She had never seen her son with that much anger written on his face. I hopped in the Range Rover and drove over to Simpson Mortuary. I knew I was pressing my time because I was supposed to hook up with Oscar to read into if he set Chucky and Chris up on the dope spot. I wanted to read into his disposition and feel him out. I wasn't in the right emotional state to read someone though. I considered canceling the meet but I knew I couldn't do that. Big Mel, Fabian and Lonnie were meeting me in an hour and a half.

When I reached the Simpson Mortuary they were about to close in ten minutes. I walked up to the desk with an urgency a mother would have for her dead child.

"Do you have a Antoine Walker hear at your mortuary?" I asked. I was panting when I asked the front desk clerk.

"Let me check and see."

She went towards the back and came back out in a matter of seconds. She had paperwork in her hand when she came back up to the desk.

"Yes we do have Antoine Walker. Are you a relative?" She asked.

"Yes I am. Can I see the body?" I asked.

"Let me make sure."

She went towards the back and took a little longer than before. When she came back out she nodded then led me towards the back. She decided to explain the circumstances on the way back.

"The police have been here on numerous occasion concerning the autopsy. They are investigating the homicide of your family member. I didn't want to disrupt anything involving the case." She said.

"Is that so?"

I was at a loss for words. When we went to the body I could tell that it was Antoine. I stared at the body and tears fell down my face. I've known the nigga all my life. Since we were kids I knew him. He was pale and his skin looked dry and his lips were white. He looked cold and stiff like it was a waxed version of him. My tears fell like never before. I didn't really know how to handle myself. The clerk stood behind me as she watched a grown man break down and cry. My macho side first thought was that she probably thinks that I'm a bitch ass nigga. My realistic side had me come to understand that she probably saw this all the time.

After dropping to my knees and burying my face in my fist, I shook uncontrollably. I'm not exactly sure the different stages of people when they have lost a loved one. My stages went from denial, to hurt and deep sadness then to bitter anger. I knew that my mother would be hurt as well. We were his only family. My mother practically raised him since we were like seven or eight. He had another house to live but he usually ate with us. He usually shared things with me. He never knew his father and his negligent mother moved away once he turned eighteen.

When I stood up to face the desk clerk there was a scowl on my face that was deadly. The look in my eyes made her eyes

215

widen. My stone face walked out the back room with hate in my heart. So much I have lost trying to survive in this game. I began with the plan of taking care of myself without slaving a few bucks an hour. I began with the plan of being able to have not only the basic necessities but also a nest egg for future plans. I had gotten greedy and what started out as self-preservation resulted in tragedy. But now I was about to inflict my own tragedy. From that day forward I was dedicated to serving King James his balls on a platter.

"I will pay for all the arrangements. I want him to have a nice oak casket and I will be by to deal with all the details a little later. Here is five thousand dollars to start you off. I can trust you with this right?" I asked.

There was no doubt that she understood what I was implying. At this point if anyone sought to harm or mishandle something involving Antoine there would be some consequences. She got the message loud and clear. Slowly nodding her head she never broke eye contact.

"Good. I'll be back tomorrow to sort out anything else that may be needed." I replied.

"What is your name sir? I need that information to prepare everything."

"Sherwin Daniels. Be sure to prepare everything in the best of manner because money is not an issue."

I stormed out the door. I had about twenty minutes to meet up with Lonnie, Fabian, Big Mel and Oscar. I was about five or ten minutes late when I arrived. Everyone was waiting on me. It was a look of surprise because I was usually punctual about everything. I was already having second thoughts about Oscar's suspicion on the way over there. My boy was dead and I loved him but I seen it as very likely that he slipped up and mentioned it to Karen. I had to still go through with it. My face had tragedy written all over it. I walked up on everybody with the most earnest look I could muster.

"What's up Pooh? Are you good?" Lonnie chose to break the ice.

"Not really. I just found out that my best friend just got smoked. Antoine is dead than a muthafucka." I blurted out.

My eyes were baggy and my lips were chapped. I knew that traces of tears were still evident on my face.

"You seen him and everything?" Big Mel asked.

"Yeah Big cousin, he dead for sure and it's fucking me up."

"Ah naw!" Fabian lamented.

"We gone handle this shit though. Let's keep our composure with Oscar." I said.

When we met up with Oscar he seemed normal as possible. He wasn't jumpy or suspicious.

"So how is everything with your supply? You liking the prices that you getting everything for?" I asked.

"Nothing could be better homes. I should be buying three of them things from you real soon." He replied.

"You hear about my little homeboy Chucky getting killed the other night?" I asked.

"Naw, but is that why you shut down your spot over there? That's that little young guy huh? If you need something from me we can take care of that shit right now. I liked that fucking young guy. He had a lot of heart." He said.

"Yeah, I just lost Antoine a couple of days ago as well." I sighed.

"Fuck no, I've known you two together since we were in high school. They killed him? No way homes, we got to handle this essay." He replied.

I felt the sincere anger in his voice. I patted him on his shoulder and shook his hand. I explained briefly that I should be getting up with him in a few days.

"What are we going to do about what they did to Antoine?" He asked.

"We still need to find some answers to how he got caught up. When we find out I will let you know." I lied.

217

Maybe he knew and maybe he didn't but it was a test for him. I had to check all my options. My gut was telling me that he was sincere. I left it at that. I walked away from him with a clear thought about him.

"Ay Sherwin, homes I'm loyal to those that are loyal to me. I'll live and die by that code essay." Oscar said.

I nodded my head letting him know that I believed him. I stopped short of walking up on my clique then looked at him.

"I know Oscar. I know."

He gestured with his head that we understood one another. Oscar wasn't a dumb man and he had to know that I considered him a suspect. But it is one thing to consider then it is to believe. I didn't believe him to be a traitor. But he understood why I had to make sure.

Lonnie, Fabian, Big Mel and myself had a small talk about what happened. With respect to the dead we knew that if Antoine would get caught up it would be over a woman. I told them to prepare to go all out because from this day forward we were gone ride on anyone affiliated with King James. I knew he had money but his connection to the street was mostly severed. Getting rid of Boom-Boom was the plan to shut him down. But now I wanted to crush him.

My thoughts and my plotting was in full swing when I drove over Nakia's house. I hadn't been staying there that much for various reasons. Janice was pregnant which made her demand more time. Vanessa was suggesting that I spend more time with her in subtle ways. Then Chucky died and Chris had gotten shot. So her place was last on the agenda except when I was cooking up my dope. She hadn't really been calling me that much complaining or anything so I knew she wasn't tripping. But I knew that I had to make a house call soon. Besides I didn't know just yet how I would tell Janice and Vanessa that Antoine was dead. They would both be devastated. I was avoiding that awkward moment by going to Nakia's house because she didn't really know him.

218

I pulled up in the apartment complex and realized her car wasn't there. I figured that she would be home shortly because it was Sunday and she didn't work on Sundays. I walked upstairs to the apartment with my head down. I was stressed and could use some serious aggressive freaky sex to calm my nerves. That at least was what I was feeling at the time.

When I unlocked the door and walked in the apartment it looked completely different. When I walked down the end of the hallway I realized there wasn't any pictures on the wall. When I went into the living room all the furniture was gone. There was nothing left inside the house. She had moved out without telling me anything. She didn't even leave me a voice message. I looked in my closet and noticed that my clothes were still in the closet.

Then I panicked. I ran into the kitchen to look under the sink and my shit was gone. I had three kilos stashed under the sink in this hole I had put down there. I loudly cursed. That bitch took my dope. I had to figure things out because I wasn't due to cop anything from Big Black until Wednesday. He was really particular about changing the days of our meetings. Plus he knew my homeboy Chucky had gotten killed. The first thing he was gone think was that I was up to something. Then he knew that I would buy only a certain amount so he would only bring a certain amount. I would have enough for my clique once I recopped on Wednesday but not enough for Oscar. And more than likely he would run dry no later than Tuesday. I had to catch up with Nakia. If I was lucky she might have took it with her so it wouldn't be in the house. I made up my mind at that moment that I would drive down to L.A. and visit her job. I didn't want to have to kill this bitch.

I went home to Janice that night. But I knew that Monday night I would be driving down to L.A. to see if I could catch up with Nakia. I knew she was somewhat of a star up at her strip club. So certain days of the week she was sure to be there. Her days off were Tuesday, Wednesday and Sunday. Her regulars came in on Monday so I was expecting her to show up that night.

The hour drive had me thinking about everything in my life. My homies dying, the women in my life and my family were heavy on my mind. I was beginning to hate being the only one having to hold this shit together. I wondered if niggas got caught doing dumb shit so they wouldn't have to deal with the stress of the game. Then I always had to worry about shisty muthafuckas all around me.

By the time I got to the strip club it was around eleven. More than likely she had been on stage at least once. She usually would show up around nine-thirty at night, which was kind of early. But she was all about her money.

I paid the ten-dollar cover charge and began searching in the dark. They had Lil Wayne playing when I walked in. I sat down away from the stage so I wouldn't be so noticeable. A cute little waitress walked up to me asking me did I want a drink. I ordered a Long Island Ice Tea and watched the performance on stage. The girl on stage was new but she was working hard for those tips. She was petite and top heavy. She didn't have much in the ass department but she was sexy enough to pull it off. She had to be about twenty-one or twenty two years old. Finally after a few performances on stage I saw a familiar face. She was this dancer named Paradise that came to Big Mel's party. She didn't notice me at first. I sort of flagged her down and her first thought was that I wanted a table dance. As she drew closer she began to realize who I was.

"Wait a minute, you Princess's dude Pooh, right?" She asked.

"Yeah, how have you been baby?" I asked.

She plopped down in my lap like she knew me all my life. She lifted my glass to see what I was drinking then wrapped her arms around me.

"I'm doing good now that I'm seeing you?" She flirted.

I chuckled to myself. She was so used to treating everyone like a trick that she must have forgotten who she was dealing with.

"Baby I'm here to see Princess." I calmly replied.

"Oh shit, Princess ain't been working here for at least three weeks. Shit, I would go as far to say a month. That bitch came into some money or something. She packed up like her shit didn't stink and was like fuck all us bitches." She laughed reminiscing on the incident.

"What did she say she was going?" I asked.

"She didn't say. It seemed like to me she was going out of town or something. Like leaving the state. She had got her a new whip and everything." She replied as though envy had suddenly sunk in.

She must have found a way to get off that dope. These stripper girls come in contact with all kind of niggas so she could have had a connect for some time. I kicked myself for the stupidity. I would have to wait for Big Black on Wednesday.

I drove back to San Bernardino infuriated. At this point I probably would have killed Nakia if I would have seen her. Big Mel hit me on the phone in his own way letting me know he was going to need to recop. I had Lonnie opening up the spot on Mt. Vernon again once Boom-Boom was arrested so I knew he'd be calling soon. This time they were prepared for anything though. Fabian had found some young niggas out of Rialto that were shooters. He had told me about them after we had met with Oscar. I had another mission I had for him to do as well but I didn't know how long that would take. When I made it over the hill on the 10 Freeway near the Mortuary I thought about stopping by to holla at Ace in Montclair. He was nearby. He was a night owl so I knew he wouldn't mind. His counsel would have done me some good. Right when I got off the freeway my cell phone rang again. At first I thought it was my cousin reiterating that he needed more dope. But when I looked at my caller ID I realized it was Fabian. I answered the phone wondering if he needed some more product as well.

"What's Up Pooh?" He said before I spoke.

"What's happening Fab-Five?"

"Ain't shit, but I got what you talking about."

I didn't understand what he was talking about. I racked my brain and only one thing came to mind.

"You ain't got that already?" I asked.

"Yep my nigga, right now."

Fabian wasn't bullshitting. I thought I was dedicated but he was just as devoted as I was. The phone was silent for a few moments as I tried to choose my words wisely.

"Information is key. We want to learn all we can." I replied.

That was my way of telling him not to kill her.

18
THE WORLD IS MINE

But it wouldn't be a damn thing without a woman's touch!
Yo-Yo

Janice was closer to the Freeway so I spent the night at our spot again. But that following day I linked up with Vanessa. It was Tuesday and I wanted her to handle some business with me. She was already dressed when I got there. I called her on the way telling her we needed to roll somewhere. This time she didn't even give me a chance to come up. She ran out the house and jumped into the car. I smiled when I seen her. That was my first true love sitting right next to me. She smiled looking as pretty as she wanted to be.

"Vanessa it is always good to see you. I wanted to talk to you on the way to where we headed." I began.

"Where are we headed?"

"I'll have to show you when we get there." I replied.

"What's going on with you? You look like you done been through a lot lately. You still fucked up over what happened to Chucky?" She asked.

"Naw, but I got to tell you something that is going to fuck with you. Before I say what I'm about to say, are you ready?"

Her eyes tightened up and I seen a flash of fear go across her face. I was skeptical about telling her but I knew I had to. Vanessa was good at reading me but she didn't have a clue. I could tell from the puzzled look on her face. But she braced herself for the worse.

"I'm ready!" She sighed.

"Antoine got killed the night before Chucky's funeral. He got shot up pretty bad." I said as calmly as possible. My voice was shaking when I spoke.

"Oh no!" She cried out.

She kept shaking her head in horror. I seen a tear fall from her face. She was genuinely hurt as I knew she would be. I hadn't seen Vanessa cry too many times. I knew she cried when her brother was killed but I was locked up when that happened. I think only once she cried in my presence besides now. That was when she knew I was about to go to jail for my dope charge. She was sitting in my car when the police rolled on me and found my stash. Honestly I think she knew she was pregnant. That probably had hurt her more knowing she was having my baby while I was doing time. All these thoughts ran through my head while we sat quietly mourning the death of our friend.

"When is the funeral? I got to call Shawna because she gone want to come to the funeral too." She said.

She was emotional at that point. She was referring to Antoine's ex-girlfriend and first love. I could only imagine what she was feeling. I decided to drive off so we could quickly get to our destination.

"How did he get killed?" She asked when we were halfway there.

"He was set up by this punk bitch named Karen. She's related to Latrice." I replied.

"Latrice that went to school with us. King James' wife. Did she have anything to do with it?" I felt the venom in her tone.

"She probably knew something about it but she's good with me. I'm going to give her a pass." I replied.

Vanessa didn't ask why. I left it at that until we cruised up into an empty warehouse. She didn't know where I was leading her but she followed nevertheless. I unlocked one metal door then walked down a hall to unlock a second wooden door. Vanessa didn't ask any questions but followed my lead. When I opened the door Fabian and Cornell were sitting on some picnic chairs. In the middle of the floor a few yards from them was a woman tied to a chair. There was plastic laid out under her in a square about five yards wide and long. Her hair appeared as though it was freshly done and fingernails and toenails were manicured. She had a cute little beige and brown one piece dress that matched her Louis Vutton platform shoes. Fab-Five jumped when he heard us walk in the door.

"Oh shit what's up Pooh? I knew you were on your way but me and the homie been relaxing."

I didn't reply. I nodded towards her to see if she was alright. He nodded to indicate that she hadn't been touched. I walked over to her and seen that she was sound asleep. Fab-Five and Cornell had McDonald's food spread out around them.

"You got anything in that cup?" I asked.

"Nothing but melted ice!" Fabian replied.

I held out my hand for him to give me the cup. I took the plastic top off the McDonald's cup and threw the water in her face. She jerked in shock from the cold water hitting her face. She was still half sleep so her vision was somewhat blurry. She tried to focus in on who I was. When her eyes became clear I could see the terror. She began looking around for some form of aid but there wasn't any to be offered. I smiled in a conniving manner that unnerved her more. A lone tear fell from her eye as though she was staring at her executioner.

"We just want some questions answered. That's all." I said.

"You gone kill me anyway. What do you want?" She asked. Tears fell from her eyes but I didn't feel any pity for her. No one in the room felt pity for her.

"Where is James at? You tell us where he's at and we will only hold you long enough for you not to warn him. You lie to us then we are going to have fun making you starve to death." I replied.

"I don't know where King James is at? He lives in Rialto with Latrice but that is all I know. You gone still kill me?" She panicked.

"I told you I don't kill female bitches. I kill niggas that act like bitches or niggas trying to kill me. You don't have to worry about me killing you so stop tripping. It ain't in me to kill a female even if she is a scandalous low down dirty bitch. If I didn't have compassion I would show you the same mercy you had shown Antoine." I explained.

"I didn't have anything to do with that. Them niggas followed him and me when he came to pick me up. They followed us around for the whole fucking day. Then that night they came over there and killed him, I swear it wasn't my fault." She cried hysterically.

I had a hunch she was lying but I wasn't for sure. I backed away from her and remained silent for a moment. She was growing impatient but I could tell that she had a glimmer of hope that I believed her. I had to see somehow if she was more involved than she let on.

"You know I talked to James over the phone. He threw it up in my face that I had a leak in my clique. He said that you led them niggas over there at the new spot because Antoine took you over there. He said that he could live without you so he didn't have any problem letting me know the source of my leak. Matter of fact he is the one that told us where you lived." I explained.

She was furious. I thought she might break the ropes we had around her. I guess she never fathomed betrayal from the king of betrayal, James.

"That muthafucka is lying I never been over there on the new spot on the other side of Mt. Vernon. Don't believe that lying muthafucka." She growled.

"How did you know the spot was on the other side of Mt. Vernon? Who told you where it was?"

She looked up in horror realizing her mistake. Now she knew she was doomed. I smiled as if to let her know that I had set

226

her up for the slip up all along. She began crying again. There was a cold chill that went down my spine when I looked at her tears. She didn't deserve any mercy but I was still going to grant her mercy.

"I'll tell you everything." She surrendered.

"That's all I'm asking." I replied.

She paused a minute to catch her breath. She glanced around looking at Vanessa, Fabian and Cornell. She was desperate and would have said anything to escape her situation.

"From day one King James wanted me to watch over Antoine and his hustles. I thought he was cute but James told me he was a pussy hound nigga that was only good for curb serving. But he had a friend that might be getting out real soon that was a snake so I should watch both of them. I didn't know who he was talking about until you got home from the pen. He made sure I reported everything I heard from Antoine. Then when you got home he started being more quiet about what he was doing. So then he asked me to do other things to get shit from ya'll so that was when I hooked you up with my homegirl Stacy. But you wasn't feeling her for some reason. So eventually me and him started fucking around and he would give me money so that I could keep watching over Antoine." She paused for a moment.

That moment I understood why Latrice was so willing to give up her cousin. She knew that we would serve her ass for killing Antoine. She must have found out they were fucking.

"So everything was going good with me and James but for some reason I couldn't get close to Antoine. So James threatened to cut me off if I didn't connect with him. But then that punk muthafucka started fucking this bitch up in Victorville named Carla or Paula, some shit like that. I overheard him say her name once. He was so into that bitch that he didn't need me for shit so I started calling Antoine more and more until he finally hooked up with me. He told me I would be set for life if I can get a hold of Antoine for him. I did that shit and he gave me up anyway. So fuck him and everything he stands for. I'm telling ya'll I liked

Antoine I just was trying to be loyal to that shady muthafucka James." She sobbed.

"You only know about his house? Where is that?" I asked. I had totally shut off any compassion at this point. Especially after hearing her admit that she set up Antoine for King James.

"It's in Fontana, you can write down the address but I doubt if you see him there. You might see Latrice but that is about it. He haven't been home to that house in months." She continued to sob.

"You know you are a low down dirty bitch. How are you gone give us an address to where yo cousin live and you know we know that he's married to her. You just gave up yo own cousin like it wasn't shit." I replied.

"How did you know that she was my cousin?" She looked puzzled.

"I've known for more than a week now. You bumped into my sister at the Beverly Center. You was flirting with her man while you were with Latrice."

Suddenly a light flashed in her head. She realized instantly that King James might not have told me where she was living. What benefit would it do him to turn on her that easily? Her head slumped when she realized her blunder. She knew she had crossed Latrice but she couldn't think of anything she did to cross King James. I seen every expression on her face that indicated her thoughts. At this point she was that easy to read. But she had confessed everything.

"You know of anything else?"

I knew she had said enough but pushed her anyway. She shook her head while still allowing it to slump.

"Latrice found out you were fucking James huh?" I asked.

She looked up at me with fierce hatred. She knew she had blundered now. She felt betrayal in a different way.

"What are ya'll about to do to me? Because I ain't saying another muthafuckin word." She snarled.

"We don't need shit from you bitch. Like I said I ain't going to kill you because I don't kill women. That ain't my style."

I untied the rope around her arms and told her she was free to go. She was a little reluctant to trust me. I figured she would be so I backed away from her and she turned around to look and see what I might do. When she seen I was a safe distance away she turned in the direction of the door.

Before she could take one step in the direction of the door, the blade of a knife was on her neck. She gasped for breath seeing the blade at her throat. Then suddenly the edge of the blade slid across her neck quickly. The cut was deep and blood began to splash on her attacker and on the plastic underneath her.

Vanessa backed away from her with the blade still gripped tightly in her hand. Karen dropped to her knees still somewhat in shock. She grabbed her neck as if to stop the bleeding.

"Did you think you can kill one of our own and we would let you live? Bitch you gone die slow today." Vanessa whispered in her ear.

She made sure she was loud enough for us to hear. Karen began gagging as the blood poured from her neck. She collapsed on top of the plastic and began having seizures. Her body shook uncontrollably while she still held on to her neck. Then suddenly she passed out with her mouth wide open dead as a doorknob.

Vanessa went to the nearby sink and washed off her hands from the blood. She was my Bonnie and I was her Clyde through and through. She had a stone look on her face that I understood. You are never the same when you kill someone. It changes you one way or another.

We left the warehouse and Fabian promised me that he would clean up the body. On our way back to her house we didn't say a word to one another. We were both lost in our own thoughts. She had her burden to bear and I had mine. But we were connected until we died. She was my wifey through and through. Not because she was willing to kill for me. But because she knew when to kill for me. She knew when to step in and make the decision. Niggas in my line of business pray for a woman like that. With her on my side I felt like the world was mine. It belonged to me. Hustlers in the game have to stress everyday in the world of cutthroats then got to come home to a bitch that want to stress him out more. I swallowed the loss that Nakia gave me because the woman I had sitting next to me in the passenger seat was worth more than her weight in gold.

She got out the car when I pulled up to her apartment complex. She still hadn't said anything. She began walking up the stairs as I watched her. Then she turned around.

"Be sure to tell me when is Antoine's funeral." She said.

I nodded then watched her walk up the stairs. I decided to pay the remaining balance on Antoine's plot before I went home to Janice. I knew when Vanessa needed time alone. This was definitely one of those times. I was in need of a nap myself so I had plans to run that errand then go to sleep. I kept rubbing my eyes.

On my way home Sharon hit me on my cell phone. She was hysterical for a moment then it dawned on me that I hadn't told her yet. I barged out of the Pleasure Palace without informing them that Antoine was dead.

"Is it true Winnie that Antoine is dead? He got killed, please tell me that it ain't true Winnie. That's just a rumor huh?" She asked while on the verge of exploding.

"Yeah it's true." I calmly replied.

"Oh no mama it's true." Sharon screamed.

I heard my mama scream in the background. I knew they would be devastated as much as I would. We had lost one of our family members. I heard the phone fumble around before someone got on the phone.

"Hello Winnie, how in the fuck did this happen? Who would kill Antoine like that? That boy ain't ever meant any harm." My mama cried.

"I know mama, I just wasn't able to protect him."

"Why the fuck not. You so busy trying to be rich that you can't even protect your best friend in the world. Damn Winnie, we ain't ever gone see him again." She screamed.

I didn't take her words personal because I did feel somewhat responsible. If I would have realized earlier that Karen was related to Latrice I could have saved him.

"When Ace and your father would talk about the first law of nature they wasn't only talking about themselves. They were talking about each other. How the fuck you gone preserve yo life but don't preserve the life of yo peoples?" She screamed.

"I'm knowing mama, I'm knowing." That was all I could say.

Tears welled up in my eyes when mama reminded me that I would never see Antoine again. All over again I felt bad every time I knocked his decisions. I felt bad every time I thought he was being stupid. All of the unpleasant moments was because of me.

"Winnie you there?" Sharon had grabbed the phone.

"Yeah I'm here."

"We are here to help in any way you hear? Have you viewed the body yet?" She asked much calmer than before.

"Yeah I seen the body. He down at Simpson Mortuary right now. I'm going to go pay the difference right now on his funeral expenses. It's still fucking with me Sharon." I admitted.

"Yeah I know Winnie. You have to excuse our mother for her harsh words. She is just really upset like we all are. We all loved that nigga. You tell Melvin yet?"

"Yeah I told him the other day. It was harder to tell you and mama for some reason. I was dreading the day I had to tell ya'll."

"Because you were afraid we would act the way we were acting right now." Sharon replied.

"Who told ya'll anyway?" I asked out of curiosity.

"Fabian's girl Shanell came in and told us. Apparently she knew for a couple of days now." Sharon said with sarcasm.

I ignored her comment and dwelled on the fact that Fab-Five was pillow talking. That girl Shanell must really got him open I thought. Sharon was rambling on about a few things concerning the funeral but I paid her little attention. I would allow them to sort out all the details once the money was paid.

Once I got home from the mortuary I fell into a deep sleep. The stress had burnt me out for the day. Janice was already asleep when I walked in the door. She slept a lot since she was pregnant. I worried about my meeting with Big Black the next night. I was somewhat skeptical about cooking up the dope in Nakia's empty apartment. I didn't know if she told the police or what. I had to question everything at this point. I couldn't do it where Janice stayed because the cocaine smoke would have been bad for the baby. Plus I never really brought that shit around her. She was my squeaky clean girl. I didn't want to take it over Vanessa's house because of my son. Besides she was dealing with a lot right now and I knew it was best to give her space. I didn't want to think about it.

The next day I woke up a little past twelve in the afternoon. It wasn't because I was sleepy but because I was stressed out. I staggered when I got out of bed to take a piss. My eyes were blurry and muscles were weak. Janice must have heard me stumbling around. She yelled into the bedroom asking me if I wanted some breakfast. I grunted in a way where she knew to start cooking. Since she was pregnant I chose not to tell her about the funeral. She hardly seen him anyway so why stress her out while she carried the baby.

Later that night I met up with Big Black at the appointed time. He didn't do the search like he usually does. He was more relaxed than usual. I was relieved to see him that way because he was easier to talk to.

"I heard you got rid of one of your problems. Some nigga named Boom-Boom or something like that got locked up?" He asked.

He said it as if he already knew but wanted me to confirm it. I nodded my head telling him it was true.

"That's good then, young nigga." He replied.

"Not all the way. I just got rid of the muscle the top nigga that got the connect is still around. As long as he around he can hire some shooters to do his dirt. All he has to do is get Boom-Boom to get on the phone with a couple of niggas and he on the move again. Which he's probably already doing." I explained.

"Why can't you catch up with him?" Big Black was being unexpectedly inquisitive.

"That nigga hiding so that he could regroup." I replied.

"Shit, sometimes niggas can be found where you least expect."

From that point on he got straight to business. I told him that I needed ten bricks before but now I explained to him I would actually need fifteen. I thought that he was going to have to link up with me later but to my surprise he had the dope on hand just in case I wanted more. As much precautions as he took I was damn near in shock.

I decided to take my chances over Nakia's apartment since the final month wasn't up. I knew that I wasn't going to cook everything that night so I picked up a lock and put it in the storage place, which she never used. I had to prepare myself for a long day of cooking up that raw. By the time I was done I was going to be high as a kite. But at least I had the supply that was needed to get everything back in order. I still went to sleep feeling guilty about Antoine's death.

The funeral was scheduled a week from the day I met up with Big Black. We were the family in the front row of the church. Everyone that knew of Antoine showed up to pay their respects. It was mostly women. A few of them claimed to have had children by him. At least two of them looked just like Antoine. I made a mental note to take care of his children. At least the ones that resembled him.

Vanessa showed up with Shawna sitting right next to her. Even though it was a sad occasion I was happy to see both of them. When I first started dating Vanessa, Shawna started dating Antoine. I hadn't seen Shawna in years so it was good to see her. After the church services was over we gathered towards the back before we went to the gravesite. My mama noticed Vanessa and Shawna so she curled her lips up at me. She then spoke through her teeth just in case someone could read her lips.

"What is that heifer doing here Sherwin?"

"Because I asked her to come. She had love for Antoine as much as anyone of us sitting in the front row." I replied.

"You don't have any respect for the woman that is carrying your child at home. You don't got enough respect to not invite your ex when you didn't invite your current girlfriend. What the fuck is wrong with you Sherwin." She snarled.

I could tell a nerve had been touched because of her calling me Sherwin instead of Winnie. But I was tired of running from my relationship with Vanessa. She meant a lot to me.

"Look mama, I love her and have always loved her so it ain't shit you or no one else is going to do about it. In fact, she gave birth to your first grandson while I was in prison." I replied.

Even Sharon had to look at me in awe. Not because of the new revelation of her nephew but she had never seen me stand up to mama. But mama wasn't going to allow shock to alter her course.

"That little bitch ain't got any grandchild of mine. So if you don't have a paternity test to prove it you need to get that little bitch out of my face." She fired back.

"No mama! She's staying and she is following us to the gravesite. Now if you don't like those conditions that too bad. But you the only one around here dwelling on some complexion complex. Sharon can't admit she's pregnant because she believes you are going to reject your own grandchild. I've been afraid to tell you about my child because of this reaction. I'm tired of tiptoeing around you mama. You the one with the problem and you have always been one with the problem. Black people are Black people in all our different shades and I ain't hiding Vanessa anymore." I firmly replied.

She suddenly broke down and cried in her best friends arms. Paula held her tightly but the look in Paula's eyes indicated that what I said was long overdue. Paula walked my mother out to the limo with Sharon on their heels.

When I walked up to Vanessa she gave me a kiss that could last a lifetime. I was tired of her being down for my dirty drawers and me not being down for hers.

"Go catch up with your mama Winnie. I love you."

Those were the best words I could hear from Vanessa. I hugged her one last time then hopped into the limo with the rest of my family.

19

KILL AT WILL

Headed for the nigga he was after!
Scarface

My mother didn't look at me the entire time we stood near the gravesite. She kept her head down while Paula kept one arm around her. Sharon was sad but she was proud of me for standing up to mama. We made eye contact and she slightly smiled. I watched them lower my best friend into the grave and the reality of the situation sunk in.

After the funeral I stayed a little while longer at the cemetery. Everyone jumped into the car while my mother and sister hopped into the limousine. I was standing around waiting patiently for everyone to leave. I wanted some weed at this point. As I stared at Antoine's tombstone she walked up on me. The smell of her perfume was intoxicating. I couldn't believe she wrapped her arm around my neck and gently kissed me on the cheek.

"This was the kiss your mother intended to give you. I will give it to you in her place." She said.

"Why Thank You!"

"What I can't figure out for the life of me is, how did you know that he would come up and talk to me?"

"It is always good to know what kind of woman a man is into if he might become your enemy."

"How do you know what kind of woman he wants? He's married a young woman." She replied.

"Yeah but that was for show, and once he realized she wasn't going to have his baby he grew tired of her. You play chess in the game or you get wiped out Paula." I calmly replied.

236

"Well here is the key to where he is hiding momentarily. He gave me the key about a week ago. Your mother was having a hard time getting in touch with you. But I couldn't see him anymore knowing that he killed Antoine. I seen that little boy grow into a man and now I'm at his grave. He usually stays in the back of the office space. He has furniture all in the front even though he hardly ever brings over company if ever. At least that is what he tells me." She explained.

"How much does he trust you? Do you think he might consider you someone that will give him problems?" I asked.

"He trusts me because he knows that I'm not involved in that life. I have invited him to my house and everything. I'm his legitimate chick that stays in Victorville."

"I heard!" I chuckled.

"What's that supposed to mean?"

"Let's just say he has mentioned your name a few times." I smiled.

"Well I'm in my forties and I still know how to make a man weak for me." Paula blushed.

"Yeah, I must admit you still got it going on." I eyed her sexually.

"Boy you crazy." She giggled.

"Paula you gone keep talking to my disrespectful son or are you riding with us?" Mama yelled out the limousine window.

"Girl here I come." She yelled back.

We hugged one last time and she gently touched my face. She smiled at me while walking away.

"You take care Winnie and I will talk to you soon."

I had whispered to Vanessa to stay over so that I could talk to Paula. I had paid cash for a Mercedes Benz CL class for her a few days before Antoine's funeral. Shawna was already sitting in the back seat when I jumped in on the passenger side. We drove off the cemetery grounds in a hurry. We were done with mourning.

237

I wanted to make my move on King James about two days after Antoine's funeral. I had to make sure he was there and he was comfortable. It was a nice set up from the outside so I could imagine how he had it on the inside. It was still in the cut away from everything. It was a real good hide out. We watched him for two days to see his schedule and if he had any visitors. He stayed pretty much to himself. His wife Latrice didn't even come to this spot. But it was obvious after awhile that he was laying his head at this office space.

I made sure to tell Paula to always act as if she wasn't interested in his lifestyle. Always standing firm to her independence would keep King James interested. Plus she didn't have anything to do with the game; so he thought. I remember how he admired women his age or older but messed with young girls because he could. He would always call young girls stupid. So I knew it would be wise to give him what he wanted. I had to be wise in dealing with him because he was so calculating.

The day we decided to move in on him was on the weekend. We knew that no one would be in the offices around the area. He had posted up for some time and his black Bentley was parked outside in the back for several hours. I was hoping he was asleep when we crept in on him. Big Mel and Fabian followed behind me as I unlocked the door. They told me to stay back and let them handle this but I wanted in on the kill too bad. Him and I needed to talk.

Once inside, all of us were in awe as we seen how decked the office was. He must have had interior decorators come in to fix the place up. He had the large flat screen television on the wall. It was laid out in Burgundy carpet and drapes with matching leather couches. He had a bar at the other end of the room. We had to pause to take in all of the art and style. Artifacts that were probably worth hundreds of thousands of dollars were in the room. I thought that he might have heard us come in because the door squeaked slightly but he had music playing softly in the back room. I still signaled to everyone to be cautious.

It sounded like he was on the telephone. I relaxed a little bit and leaned on the wall to listen in on his conversation.

"Yeah man, I always wondered about recruiting that Fabian nigga because he stayed up in the Dorjil apartments. He probably knew Pooh all his life. So more than likely he had something to do with the set up." King James spoke on the phone.

For a moment he paused listening to the person on the phone. It was a crack in his voice that signaled that King James was stressing.

"Well we will call them niggas on the three-way and hook this thing up. But yo books is okay right?"

"That little young nigga Pooh probably thinks I'm finished because you got a little stretch. If he only knew."

"Naw, but that Delmont Height thing can be okay again once Pooh is out the picture...I don't know them niggas well enough to dump that on them for the California Gardens. But lets first connect with them on that hit and run shit. We know where one of his spots is. Over the phone you know how it is Barry. You call me collect tomorrow and I will call those young niggas so we can make it happen."

"Yeah, but your baby mama told me she was going down there Friday so I just gave it to her. Was that cool?"

"Ah nigga you crazy. So they done brought it down to eight years huh? I told you my lawyers ain't a muthafuckin joke."

"I haven't seen Latrice since I last seen Karen. Now that's the bitch I'm looking for is Karen. That little young broad told me she would get pregnant for me. I gave her some money and she just disappeared. As for Latrice I was tired of her ass anyway. Her young ass ain't shit compared to my Victorville broad. And she doesn't do all that whining like young bitches do."

"Yeah I can't wait until you get out either. But we gone wait until the D.A. drop it down to five years then we gone be talking. Trust me, my lawyers can do it.

"Alright, for sure my nigga! Stay up and holla at me tomorrow about the same time on this phone."

When he hung up the phone I tensed up. Now was the time to move in on him and I froze for a moment. I took a deep breath then walked through the back hall right into his office.

He was sipping on a drink that appeared to be Courvoisier. I smiled when I walked into his office with my nine-millimeter drawn. He actually jumped when he seen me, slightly spilling his drink. We stared at each other for a moment without one of us speaking. He decided to speak first.

"Damn Pooh, you got it all figured out. I didn't think you would be this cold but you proved to be colder than I thought." He admitted.

"Yeah well I learn fast. If you watch and observe then you start to understand how the game is played."

"It's been a while since we have seen each other face to face. Moving in on Boom-Boom was pretty clever." He continued.

"Yeah that move on Mt. Vernon hurt me pretty bad. I was hurting a little bit when ya'll got me with that. I'm suspecting Boom-Boom put together that little squad huh? Probably some niggas out the California Gardens." I replied.

"Yeah but you killed four of my shooters in one swoop. That damn near dropped me to my knees. I didn't know you had it in you. Your big cousin Mel set that one up huh?" He replied. He had a condescending tone when he made that statement.

"Yeah, but who would have thought that the mighty King James was a snitch." I sharply stated.

He didn't respond to my statement. He didn't appear guilty or innocent so I decided to drive my point home further.

"Yeah I wasn't for sure until Detective Barnes showed up at the hospital. Me getting locked up right after I hand you your money six and a half years ago made me consider it. Detective Barnes knocking on my mother's door and asking about my cousin and I, made me suspect it. But I wasn't for sure until he came up knowing our names at the hospital. I don't believe in coincidences James." I smiled wickedly.

"Yeah well you use what you can when an enemy is going against you. I saw an opportunity to rid myself of a foe so I took the chance. It was business and don't act like you wouldn't have done the same." He snarled.

"I wouldn't have done the same. I believe in the code. But C'mon Mr. King James you didn't only do it for business. You got caught on a charge and couldn't handle the time. You a bitch-made nigga." I snapped back at him.

All of the diplomacy and etiquette went out the window at that point. I didn't respect him as a man any longer. If I would have beat him in the streets but he kept his code then he would have at least had my respect.

"But maybe you never lived by the code. Maybe you one of those niggas that know the code but never lived by it." I continued.

"Fuck you little young nigga. You ain't in my shoes to judge me. I did what I had to do, so fuck the code." He fired back.

"Now the real you is coming out. What questions you have to ask me before you leave up out this bitch. I'll be sure to make it quick." I replied.

"First off how did you find me and how did you get inside." He asked.

I looked at him like he already knew the answer. I seen the wind leave his body. He was crushed in a manner of microseconds. His head dropped as he shook it in disappointment.

"I remembered how you would visit your sister in Moreno Valley then go shopping afterwards every weekend. I remember when I was a teenager you would school me about the differences between older women and younger women. Remember, younger women to bare children and older women to be with. You remember those words." I smiled.

"When did you decide that you could go up against me?" He asked. I could feel his defeat in the tone of his voice.

241

"When you gave Antoine those two kilos on consignment. At first it was all about staying alive and preserving self. Then you backed me into a corner that made me come out swinging."

"The first law of nature huh? So that is your excuse. That's bullshit and we both know it. You go in the game thinking that's what it is about but greed sinks in once you taste that money. Every nigga screams out the first law of nature when they get into the dope game. But you can get a job and still be able to preserve self. I'm a man that is about to die Pooh, at least tell me the truth, it is always about the money and the power."

"Okay you right. Maybe it ain't truly about that. But this conversation has went on long enough so I will grant you one more question then I'm going to end this." I replied.

"You know what, let me reach for my bible and pray one last time before you handle yo business."

I nodded. He reached for the large Bible and said a few words over it. He recited that verse from Psalms about the Lord being his shepherd. Then he slowly opened it up and pulled out a small snub nose thirty-eight revolver. He aimed straight for my head with his hand on the trigger. He was less than two yards away so it would damn near been impossible for him to miss. I tried to duck before he could squeeze the trigger. But I didn't have enough time. So I squeezed the trigger of my nine and plugged him three times in the abdomen.

The Holy Bible fell to the ground from the impact of him hitting the wall. He belted out an agonizing moan then slowly slumped to the ground. When I looked down at the Holy Bible that landed on the floor it was wide open. A bulk of the pages were cut out of it so that the gun would fit inside. I never once considered he had that trick up his sleeve. As many times as he had that Holy Bible sitting on his desk I never thought to look inside. After hearing the gunshots Big Mel and Fabian walked in the back office.

"Took you long enough." Big Mel said.

"Hell yeah, I thought ya'll was about to have coffee and a Danish." Fabian remarked.

Fabian checked his pulse to make sure he was dead. We walked out of his office and into the dark San Bernardino night. I made it a point to leave the door unlocked so the police won't have to pry the door open to find the body. My nemesis was dead and I felt like a monkey was off my back. I threw the key away in a trashcan bin miles away from the office.

The next day I contemplated what had taken place between King James and I. Any one of us could have ended up as the winner. We both were manipulative and we both schemed. I wasn't a snitch but in many ways we were alike. I figured after so many years some young hustler was going to come after me. It was a thought that haunted me the entire day. The game is an insecure game and I knew that better than most. You don't know who might turn on you at any given time. But that was the life we chose.

Later that night Big Mel called me up and told me to watch the ten o'clock news. I turned on the television to see a white woman news reporter directly in front of King James' office. Down at the bottom of the screen it said that it was live. I turned up the television to hear what the news reporter had to say.

"The victim was a Black male thirty-eight years of age. The police released the victim's name and that is James Stuart. He was known as a notorious drug dealer in the city of San Bernardino. He leaves behind a grieving wife and mother."

Later that night I fell asleep like a baby. I think the news confirming that he wasn't a worry to me anymore settled my nerves. I didn't have much to worry about coming from him. And Boom-Boom would at least get five years. I figured I would cross that bridge when I got to it.

Two months later Janice went into labor. She remained in labor for almost sixteen hours. She screamed at me the entire time trying to push the baby out. My mother and Sharon came up to the hospital and gave their support. Sharon was beginning to show in her pregnancy.

At some point I stood outside in the hallway with Marcus who was in full swing of our businesses. He had opened three more businesses for me in the last six months after helping me open the Pleasure Palace. When I wanted to hang with someone outside of the game he was the man I went to.

When my mother yelled into the hallway the baby was coming Marcus and I rushed inside. I seen the head of my daughter come out of the womb and I was excited. She came out screaming and hollering as the doctor cut off the umbilical cord. I smiled, as my daughter was slowly calmed so that she could go to sleep in Janice's arms. Both Sharon and my mother asked to hold the baby then told me to come over to hold my daughter. I silently promised my daughter that I would kill anyone that came even close to harming her.

My mother tapped me on my shoulder and motioned for me to follow her into the hallway. I handed Janice back our daughter who she named Shanee Lakisha Daniels. We walked out into the hallway to talk. Once we got out there no one spoke for several seconds. We were trying to establish eye contact between us two.

"Look Winnie, you have always been a good son. I know that you love that girl...Vanessa. And you are a grown man able to decide whom you want to be with. Maybe I do have a problem when it comes to complexion with black people. That's something that I'm working on. Your sister has been helping me with that when I deal with Marcus. But know that I will love you no matter what. And I would love to meet my oldest grandson if that is alright with you?" Mama said.

I was honestly shocked. I knew how much it took for her to say those few words so I hugged her. She held me tightly for a moment as though she might lose me at any second. When we finally let go of each other I put my hands on both of her shoulders.

"Mama you can meet him as early as this weekend."

She smiled and went back into the hospital room. That had made my day. Now both of my children would be fully accepted into my family. I was on top of the world at this point. It was definitely a new day and age for my family and me.

I no longer had to kill to survive. If someone needed to go it was because they were violating our business or the code. I could now kill at my own will but not out of necessity. But even in that case I had a five-year plan to eventually get out the game before the game got me. I knew in my heart and mind that at some point if the police don't get me someone else will. An up and coming hustler was sure to try and take me out the top spot eventually. I had cleared one obstacle but the game offered many more to come.

20

A BIGGER THREAT

Better a thousand enemies outside the house than one inside!

Arabic Proverb

The bright sunny day made Pooh lazy even though he had to run a few errands. He was going to all his spots to collect his cash. It was like payday for him and he wanted to get it done before the rush hour traffic. He left his house a little after one in the afternoon. His mother had just met his son and she fell in love with her oldest grandchild. He looked just like Pooh had spitted him out. She made sure that he called her big mama instead of grandma.

"I'm not that old to be called someone's grandma!" She said.

Pooh chuckled to himself thinking about how his mother wanted to stay forever young. She was still considered a beautiful woman, especially to be middle-aged.

He decided to go over to the Dorjil Apartments first to pick up his money from Fabian. Fabian had it buzzing over in the apartments for some time now. He wanted to go by there early so that he could shoot the shit with Fab-Five.

When he pulled into the apartments he noticed that the police were over there deep. About four or five police cars were parked inside the parking lot. Pooh thought about turning around but one of the police spotted him and it would have made him look suspicious. He thought for a moment that the police had found the stash. But seeing that there was too many police for a drug charge he dismissed the idea. He drew closer to see Tracy standing outside watching the spectacle. As subtle as possible he walked up next to her.

"Ay Tracy what's going on?"

"Oh snap, what's up Pooh?" She smiled.

"What happened over here? Why are all the police over here?" Pooh asked.

"Ain't he yo boy, I thought you knew? The police are charging him with murdering Gregg. You remember fat Gregg that got killed more than two years ago? They are saying that Fabian did that shit." Tracy replied.

"Fab-Five is the one they got in that police car?" Pooh asked but tried not to get too close.

"Yeah, I don't know but they got the gun somehow, that's what I heard. They brought a whole army around to catch his ass. You know that nigga got a reputation. They came with a warrant and everything." Tracy gossiped.

"But he doesn't live over here in the apartments anymore. How did they get a warrant for his mother's crib?" Pooh asked.

"I don't know but I think they were staked out waiting for him to come to his mama's house." She replied.

Pooh swallowed his fears and decided to walk over to the police car where they were holding Fabian. He looked inside the backseat of the police car and tried to speak to Fabian.

"Tell Shanell where I'm at, she's pregnant so she will get all emotional but tell her for me Pooh." He yelled out the police window.

"Shut the fuck up!" A uniformed cop yelled at Fabian.

"I got you, my nigga, I got you!" Pooh replied.

Pooh decided to back away from the police car when the same officer from before started mean mugging him. After backing up a certain amount he bumped into someone that made him suddenly turnaround.

"So Mr. Daniels I haven't had the pleasure of bumping into you as of lately. No pun intended." Detective Barnes said.

"I'm hoping we don't bump into each other ever again."

"C'mon Mr. Daniels, why the hostility? You and I both know that you might see me sooner than you like." Detective Barnes teased.

"I can still have wishful thinking can't I? You have a good day Detective Barnes isn't it?"

"We should talk some time." He handed Pooh a business card.

"Not really, no thank you. It's against my religion to talk to police." Pooh denied the card.

"Oh yeah, the code. Everybody doesn't live by that and it will probably be your downfall. You never know how I can help you."

"Tupac said it best, I rather die as a man than live as a coward. So let us both walk away believing in what we believe." Pooh replied.

He rushed back to his car and hopped inside. As he was pulling off Cornell came from the other side and startled him. He gently tapped on Pooh's window.

"What's up Pooh?" Cornell said while panting.

"Ain't shit going on. What's up with you little Nelly."

"I got that count you wanted. Fab-Five told me to make sure you get it before you leave. And we still gone need that brick tomorrow." Cornell said.

"You little young niggas think you gone be able to hold it down while Fab-Five is locked up?"

"For sure! That's the way he taught us how to do it anyway." Cornell replied like Pooh should have known better.

"Cool, well I will drop the package off tomorrow and we'll go from there. You know how we do it, so keep it trump tight, ya feel me?"

"I'm knowing!"

Cornell slid him the bag of money and he drove off trying to be as discreet as possible. Now he had to go over on Mt. Vernon so that he could pick up the cash from Lonnie and his crew. They had it back buzzing again with Chris being Lonnie's right hand man.

On the other side of town Lonnie and Chris were talking. Chris had been a little uncomfortable about how things had went in retaliation against the niggas that shot him and Chucky.

"So is he ever gone ride on the California Garden niggas that did what they did to Chucky and me?" Chris asked.

"I told you before that them niggas were the shooters but the niggas responsible for sending them is taken care of. Quit tripping about that petty shit Chris." Lonnie replied with irritation in his tone.

"Yeah but when his homeboy Antoine got smoked they went into full action like me and Chucky wasn't shit. Then the cold thing about that, it was probably Ant that leaked where the fuck we was slanging." Chris complained.

"Shit it was Ant that leaked it through this bitch named Karen. But that's beside the point. That bitch gave the spot up and her ass got served so nigga everything is good." Lonnie replied.

"Whatever nigga! I heard only reason those California Garden niggas ain't got served because Pooh giving them weight. The same niggas that blasted on us is getting dope from that nigga." Chris said in disgust.

"That's bullshit! Where you here that from?"

"I got my ways of finding out shit."

"Don't believe everything you hear. Can't any nigga say he got dope from Pooh up in the California Gardens. If someone did say that shit he's probably lying. Unless you see a nigga doing that shit it would be smart not to repeat it." Lonnie warned.

"Whatever nigga."

As their conversation ended Pooh came driving up. He remained in his Range Rover when Lonnie brought him the money. Pooh rolled down the passenger window and they shook hands. Pooh gestured for him to get inside. Lonnie hopped in then he rolled the window up. Pooh glanced at Chris and told him what's up and Chris lifted his head in response.

"You and Chris doing good?"

"Yeah my nigga, we doing real good. Here is that dough." Lonnie replied.

"That's straight, throw it in the back seat. I'm thinking about having you make my runs for me. I'm going to deal directly with you and that's it. You gone start collecting from Cornell now over in the Dorjil Apartments. Fab-Five just got locked up on a murder charge. I rolled up over there and the police was everywhere." Pooh explained.

"You bullshitting? You think they got a case?"

"I'm not knowing. Tracy was outside when he was being arrested and she said that they found the gun. So I have to get him a lawyer and make sure his girl is straight. We gone have to make some changes on some things." Pooh continued.

"I feel you! So when is this gone start... these changes?"

"I'm going to have some fresh raw tomorrow so we can start then? Is that cool?"

"Yeah that's cool."

"You gone get a bonus for this shit too, my nigga. Then little Chris can handle the spot. I know he's capable of running this shit by himself. So he's getting promoted too." Pooh smiled.

"Yeah that nigga gone be happy to hear that." Lonnie replied.

They shook hands then Pooh drove off. Lonnie hadn't even been on the concrete for ten seconds before Chris came over.

"That nigga came over to get his money huh?" Chris asked

"Yeah but he also came by to tell us some good news. You and I are getting promoted. But the bad news is that Fab-Five just caught a murder charge." Lonnie explained.

"A murder charge? How the hell that happen? Now that's a nigga that will ride for you. Only reason he didn't go after those California Garden niggas was because Pooh probably told him not to." Chris retorted.

250

"Damn Chris you act like you don't want to like that nigga Pooh. He promoting you to running this here spot and all you got is bad words for the man." Lonnie grew tired of the conversation.

"Naw it ain't like that. I just think he should handle all the business that go down with niggas that's hustling for him, that's all. I got love for Pooh it's just shit I don't understand."

"You understand making more money?" Lonnie snapped back.

"Hell yeah I understand more money." Chris laughed.

"Well let's stop talking about Pooh and what we don't think he done right. Let's worry about getting the cheddar. That way we can be pushing a pretty ass Range Rover like that nigga. You see that Mercedes he bought one of his bitches? I heard that series he bought her cost close to a hundred grand. That's the kind of paper I'm trying to get." Lonnie smiled.

"Real talk. But I wouldn't buy one of my bitches one. I would buy me one and she can ride with me." Chris replied.

They both started laughing. Lonnie sometimes worried about Chris's attitude about things. But he loved his cousin to death.

Pooh had two more stops before he could post up at the house for the rest of the day. He had to stop at Big Mel's house so that he could get the money from him to recop. Then he had to drop the money off to Vanessa so that she could go to different banks and exchange the money. She would always get hundred dollars bills while dressed up in her business suit. Pooh stayed careful about marked money by undercover narcotics police. He would play with his son while she was gone. Big Black always complimented him on his organized money.

When he made it to Big Mel's house, Big Mel was still in his boxers. He had been in the house all day watching ESPN. Pooh banged on the door the second time after not being heard the first time. He heard Big Mel's heavy feet walking towards the door.

"Damn Pooh, why you knocking on the door like you the Po-Po?" Big Mel said while opening the door.

"I knocked the first time and you didn't hear me. What you expect me to do, keep knocking soft?" Pooh laughed.

"You came by to pick that up that bread?" Big Mel rhetorically asked.

"You got it ready?"

"Yeah nigga, I've been here all day. That shit was ready about an hour before I went to sleep last night."

"Where is Maria?" Pooh asked out of curiosity.

"She went shopping with Sharon, Janice and Auntie Shirley. The doctor says she needs to walk in these last weeks of her pregnancy."

"Oh yeah, that's right Janice was telling me about that shit. They went up to Ontario Mills. She is going to get plenty of exercise walking around that big muthafucka."

Big Mel led them to the back bedroom where the television was blasting through the room. Pooh could instantly tell that Big Mel hadn't left the room for most of the day. There were plates piled up next to the bed on the dresser. He had potato chip bags laying on the ground. He also had a big two liter bottle of soda halfway empty sitting on the dresser next to the dirty dishes.

"You better clean that shit up before Maria get home and cuss yo ass out." Pooh commented.

"I don't feel like hearing her mouth. But I'll get around to it." Big Mel swatted his hand down as if to dismiss the idea.

"Well hand me the money so I can raise up out of here nigga."

"Oh I'm tripping."

Big Mel reached under the bed then tossed Pooh a paper bag. Pooh was about to walk out the bedroom.

"Oh yeah, from now on Lonnie will be doing the drop. He will pick up the money and give you the dope. Then I will tell him how much to give to who. You know Fabian got locked up today for a murder charge?" Pooh suddenly remembered.

"Are you fucking serious?" Big Mel instantly gave his undivided attention.

"Yeah, I pulled up over in the Dorjil's and they already had him in the car. Damn that just reminded me I have to stop by Shanell's house to tell her the bad news. I'll take care of all her expenses so they will be straight because she's about to have a baby too."

"Aw that's fucked up. He gone be locked down while his baby mama is pregnant. Give that nigga my number so that he could hit me collect. I know how it is when you locked down and you want to make a phone call." Big Mel replied.

"For sure. But don't forget Lonnie will be doing the drop off from now on. So you gone have to get yo lazy ass out of bed to meet him somewhere." Pooh teased.

"Fuck you! You making the change because Fab-Five got locked up?"

"Naw, but it made me put it into effect a lot sooner. It had been on my mind for some time now. You should only be dealing with two niggas at a time in my position, you feel me."

"Yeah, but you can have me do all that. What made you choose Lonnie?" Big Mel looked confused.

"First of all, it would be hard getting yo fat ass up and about to make the drops and pick up the money."

Big Mel gave him the middle finger.

"Then I'm giving you the raw for the same price I'm getting it for; you may pay me a few thousand for the stretch when I cook the shit for you, but you basically are getting what I'm getting. So it's time for Lonnie to get a promotion anyway. Plus if some shit goes down I can trace it back to one nigga."

"Yeah that makes sense. Is Marcus still washing that money good for you through those businesses?"

"Yeah, all that shit is running smooth. That was the best thing for me to do was hire that nigga." Pooh replied.

"I'm probably gone need him to get something like that for me started. So we should link up soon."

"Yeah we need to hang out anyway. You don't know what tomorrow might bring. So it's good to chill with your peoples when times are good."

"That's real talk. Let's link up this weekend some time." Big Mel offered.

"That's good for me. How about Saturday? Janice is going to be busy with the shop for most of the day. Mama and Sharon will watch Shanee. So let's do that."

Big Mel nodded his head. Pooh walked out the room then made sure he locked the bottom lock before he walked out the door. He had to go by Vanessa's house and then Fabian's apartment to holla at Shanell. It took him about twenty minutes before he pulled up at Vanessa's. She was already in her business suit when he walked in the door. He kissed her and picked up his son who was getting too big to pick up. Vanessa snatched up the money that she put in her briefcase.

"I'll be back in an hour."

Maria wanted to sit down in the food court the moment they got there. She was walking around with her stomach out like a giant tumor. Sharon went to order some California Pizza for her. Sharon just had a little boy a couple of months back who she named Marcus Jr. Marcus was at home watching his son while the girls hung out.

"Chile, I tell you, Melvin big ass got you carrying a big baby. I can't see how yo stomach could get any bigger." Shirley commented.

"I know, and Melvin still wants to have sex. I told him to carry this heavy load in his stomach then want to have sex with me." Maria replied with her thick accent.

"That boy has always been big. He was even big as a little boy. He was bigger than most kids his age. If you have a boy he is probably going to be just as huge as him." Shirley explained.

"Yeah, I'm glad my Winnie didn't have me walking around with a belly that big girl. But don't worry about it Maria it will be over sooner than you think."

"I can't wait." Maria replied.

Everyone started laughing simultaneously. Everyone's company was enjoyable and they were really having a good time. Then Janice decided to ask some questions she had to get off her chest.

"So Winnie got this girl Vanessa pregnant before he went to prison? Are they still seeing each other? You know that homie, lover, friend thing is something I'm not too cool about."

"I know Janice how you feel. I love both of my grandchildren but if it were up to me I would hope he has enough sense to marry you. That girl Vanessa was a childhood thing, that's all." Shirley replied.

"I'm just saying Ms. Shirley, if I can't have him all then I might have to go my separate way." Janice insisted.

It got quiet for a moment when Sharon walked up. Shirley had no doubt in her mind that Sharon would go back and report what she heard to her brother. Shirley decided to pacify her by gently touching her on the arm.

"Baby, don't talk like that girl. He knows who is best for him." Shirley attempted to quell the conversation.

Janice not catching the hint wanted to discuss it further.

"To be honest with you he should have told me a long time ago that he had a son in the first place. All of this secrecy is what got me asking all these questions."

"Yeah, but what you got to understand is that Winnie just got bold enough to tell his mama. I think the things he went through in recent times made him change in a lot of ways. Like when he lost his best friend Antoine." Sharon cut in.

"That's the other thing, how is he going to have his best friend's funeral and not invite me. I'm supposed to be his girl and everything." Janice retorted.

"But you didn't know him like everyone else. Winnie told me you might have talked to him over the phone at best. He didn't want to have you being all sad and shit when you were pregnant." Sharon defended her brother.

Shirley didn't say a word at this point because she agreed with Janice. He invited Vanessa as though she was his main girl instead of Janice and Shirley thought that was dead wrong.

"If Melvin have a girl like you say with a baby by him without me knowing, I'll cut his dick off." Maria cut in.

Everyone started laughing. But Janice deep down didn't see it as a joke she looked at her situation as pathetic. She was just like every other female that messes with a cat in the dope game. She has to tolerate him having other bitches on the side. She wasn't even for sure if she was on the wifey status with him even though he lived with her.

"I'm just saying, I don't even know if I'm his main girl or if Vanessa is his main girl. What kind of shit is that?" Janice continued.

"You don't have to worry about that shit Janice, you are his only girl. He just has a child by that girl. That's all." Shirley lied.

Sharon just looked at both of them knowing that her mother was in denial. She was going to have to talk to Winnie about this she pondered. Shirley on one hand felt that lying was the best thing to keep the girl's day out a pleasant event. Janice on the other hand decided to keep her mouth shut at this point. She thought about what Ms. Shirley said and knew that she had just told a bold face lie. Maybe they weren't the ones to talk to about this? Maybe they will side with Winnie no matter what? If it turns out he is playing me then I'm going to make sure he gets played, she thought.

He decided to order some food since he was about fifteen minutes early. He looked around to make sure no one was familiar. The last thing he wanted to do was be seen by someone

256

he knew. But this was a good place to meet up with him if any. He was out of San Bernardino and in Riverside waiting to talk. That was all he was going to do was talk. He had enough of some of the shit that went down in the past. After he sat down with his tray of food he didn't hesitate. He dug into his El Pollo Loco burrito and that's when the person he was expecting walked in. He was walking as if he had just gotten out of the military. That long trench coat hung off of him like it was always a part of him.

"I don't like the smell of El Pollo Loco whenever I walk into a restaurant. I live nearby one in San Bernardino and I never have the desire to eat here." Detective Barnes commented.

"We not gone talk too long."

"C'mon young man let's just settle in for a short spell and see how things go." He replied.

"All I know, if my cousin was to find out I'm talking to you he would want to smoke me himself." He said with fear in his eyes.

"Why do your cousin have to know anyhow? All you and I are doing is talking every now and then. Nothing more, nothing less." Detective Barnes tried to relax him.

"I ain't saying shit about my cousin. So don't expect me to give him up for nothing in the world. I got too much love for him."

"Well what about everybody else. You were right about that gun though. It was a match. The same gun was used in the murder of Gregory Adams. We found the gun over there just like you said but we still only got circumstantial evidence. He probably has posted bail by now."

"But that nigga done that shit. You best believe that." He said with certainty.

"What about Mr. Sherwin Daniels? Can you tell me anything about what's going on with him?" Detective Barnes got to his main target.

"Naw he stays pretty trump tight. I got promoted recently so that might bring me closer to things."

"Oh is that so? Congratulations, but like I told you in the hospital he doesn't care one way about you. He only cares about that money. The minute you aren't able to bring that money home you will start having problems. He doesn't love you he loves that money." Detective Barnes explained.

"Like a pimp does a ho. I ain't no ho to anyone. I'm my own man." He snarled.

"Yeah but if you help me bring him down you can really be your own man. You can start over both you and your cousin."

"Like I said he only deals with one nigga and that ain't me. He doesn't even make the runs anymore. But you best believe once I got something on that nigga I'll shoot that shit straight to you. But you got to take care of me." Chris smiled wickedly.

Pooh met up with Big Black once again asking for more than before. They had developed a bit of a rapport in recent times so they were able to talk openly. In many cases Pooh looked forward to his meetings with Big Black. He didn't care that he couldn't tell you his government name.

"So you want even more than before? You are a young hustler that is dear to my heart. You don't see young niggas come up so fast like you did. You kept your eyes on the prize and got there." Big Black firmly stated.

"Yeah, but Biggie wasn't lying when he said more money, more problems." Pooh replied with a chuckle.

"Yeah that goes with the territory baby. Success breeds envy and hatred. You just got to let that shit go and watch who you dealing with. Learn what makes a muthafucka tick and you can last longer than the average." Big Black explained.

"But sometimes betrayal is lurking around the corner and you don't have any way of scoping that shit out before it comes." Pooh sighed.

"Betrayal is the game's middle name. But check this out here young comrade. These niggas and these bitches is always gone be loyal to they self first. If you know who is around you,

you can peep out what is they breaking point to make them turn on you. Everybody got a breaking point. Some might break when it comes to money. Some might break when it comes to the law. Snitching and whatnot. Some females might break when they find out you fucking other bitches besides them. Some bitch made niggas might break because of all the bitches you got. Some people break because they don't like a decision you made. You never know. Yo job is to find out what will make them break and at what point will they break. This game we fucking with is cutthroat anyway but self preservation makes a nigga watch the people around him the closest."

"I'll keep that in mind!"

"You better!"